LOYALTY

KATHLEEN HELMS

Loyalty / Kathleen Helms - 1st ed.

Library of Congress Control Number: 2020908765

Ebook 978-0-9600923-3-8

Paperback ISBN 978-0-9600923-2-1

For my Mother, Marta Palmerton
A true example of love and loyalty

PROLOGUE

The five senses can be deceiving. Situations occur where one sense is more amplified than the other. Alone in bed on a pitch black night? The ears perk up, magnifying ordinary sounds, speeding up the heartbeat. Driving in a deafening thunderstorm? The eyes desperately seek familiar landmarks, the ears useless against the roar. A Santana in Southern California? The nostrils flare as they seek the scent of smoke in the dry blasts of wind. Fog is an outlier. It deadens the senses. Sight diminished, sounds muffled, scents faded; ghosts floating just beyond reach.

Lacey's senses were straining against the thick enveloping fog as she walked briskly down the deserted trail. She knew she was safe here on the lagoon trail, but at the same time wondered if she should be out here alone. The fog was so dense. She reached her arm out straight in front of her and watched as her hand disappeared into the gray. She knew it was still attached, but had lost sight of it. Her footsteps were the only sound she heard. Lacey was aware that a decision needed to be made. The responsibility of that decision weighed heavily on her. Someone would be devastated. She wished she could go back in time and start over, but life had no rewind button. Past decisions had led to the present situation. She desperately needed this time to think.

The thump of footsteps behind her startled her. Pounding feet, heavy, approaching fast. Lacey stepped to the side of the trail, turning sideways and peering into the deep gray. A man morphed out of the fog. Tall, strong, moving fast. He raised his hand, she saw a flash of white teeth as he smiled and said "Ma'am," then he was gone. Swallowed. Invisible. Lacey took a shaky breath, tried to calm her pounding heart. She leaned forward, placing her hands on her thighs, and breathed in slowly and deeply.

"You are fine," she told herself. "You are safe, it was just a jogger." She stayed in this hunched position for a moment. Just as she began to straighten the first blow landed. It came from below, landing squarely beneath her chin. Her head blew back, her neck cracked, consciousness deserted her.

1

LOYAL TRUESDALE

Loyal Truesdale, towel wrapped around his midsection, stood in front of his bathroom sink and mirror. His reflection shimmered in the steam covered glass. Leaning forward, he used his palm to wipe clear a face sized circle. Shaving cream was applied, then removed, with steady strokes of the blade. Shaving complete, Loyal leaned in again and studied himself. Shaggy light brown hair, still wet from the shower, was combed and behaving itself for the moment. Clear brown eyes, wrinkles forming at the edges, cheeks starting to sag a bit, large nose. He smiled at himself. His lips were thin, but his smile was wide and bright. Good teeth, white and straight. He straightened, rinsed the blade and washed out the sink.

His mind wandered back to the previous evening. His

daughter, Stella, and her long time live-in boyfriend, Mitch, had taken him to Las Olas in Cardiff for a birthday dinner. Loyal still had a hard time believing he was 57. Dinner had been delicious, conversation animated, the company fun. Just as dinner was winding down Stella had slid an envelope across the table. Loyal opened the birthday card, he couldn't remember the sentiment now, something silly about getting older. It was Stella's message, printed in her familiar blocky way, that he saw again in his minds eye. *Happy Birthday Grandpa.* He had looked up at her. She looked at him with expectant brown eyes, his wide smile duplicated on her face, and he had said, "are you getting married?"

Stella's smile had blinked off, her bright eyes dulled. The words had dropped out of Loyal's mouth before he could bite down on them.

"I'm sorry," he had said immediately. But his words hung in the air, an echo of disappointment ringing in their ears.

Loyal brought himself back to the present with a sigh. He dressed in baggy shorts with an elastic waistband and a loose T-shirt. A far cry from his customary slacks and Tommy Bahamas. He decided he would call Angela, second ex-wife, dear friend, sometimes lover. Perhaps she could help him find the right words. He wasn't sure why he had asked about marriage. Both of his had failed, as had his parent's before him. Stella and Mitch had been together for years. Their relationship was solid. Maybe them having a baby and him being a grandpa would be a good thing. Just because his child was having a child of her own didn't mean he was old. Did it?

Loyal exited his apartment, slid in his Altima, and drove toward Interstate 5. The fog was dense, visibility just a few feet. He heard sirens in the distance, muffled by the fog. He crept along at half speed, deciding on surface streets rather than the freeway. The fog was so thick he nearly missed the driveway leading to the small gym's parking lot. Loyal had been coming to exercise with his personal trainer three times a week since his heart attack six months ago. His doctor had prescribed the exercise, along with a heart healthy diet and less stress. The less stress part of the equation had him on disability. He had been on suspension from the Carlsbad Sheriff's Department at the time of the heart attack, and had yet to return to his position of Homicide Detective. An exploding house the previous August had led to a series of decisions on Loyal's part that his Captain had taken issue with. Not to mention the scrutiny of the FBI that had followed Loyal for months.

Loyal parked the Altima, grabbed his towel and water bottle, and walked to the gym door. JK Gym was an old school facility. Owned by a man in his 70's named Joe Kagen, hence the name JK, the establishment lacked all the bells and whistles many of the newer gyms featured. The gym was small, with a reception desk, a small room with a padded floor, and a slightly larger area with machines and free weights. It was busy despite its small size. Millennials searching for something retro swelling the ranks of the gym members.

Loyal entered the gym and saw Adelle behind the reception desk. She was in her mid forties, but looked late thirties. She was tan and lean, all muscle.

"Hey Loyal," she said. "Lacey didn't show up today. I have a call out to a substitute. Her name is Sunshine and she's very good."

"Lacey didn't call?" Loyal asked.

"Nope, and she's not answering her phone," Adelle said.

"I know my circuit," Loyal said. "I'll go through it on my own."

Loyal walked past reception thinking about the sirens he had heard, and hoping they weren't for Lacey.

An hour and a half later, sweaty and stretched, Loyal exited JK and found the fog had been burned away by the springtime sun. He was concerned about Lacey. She had been his personal trainer since he had the heart attack. He couldn't remember her ever missing a session. Lacey was in her early thirties and married to an incredibly wealthy, and much older, man. She and Loyal had become friends over the past months as she had gently but firmly directed his workout regimen. Loyal knew that he was lucky to be alive and was trying his best to live a healthy lifestyle. He began each morning with a green smoothie; two chunks of pineapple, three strawberries, half an avocado, a mint sprig, juice from half a lemon, three cups of greens, ice and water. He exercised with Lacey three days a week, and walked two miles on the other three days. Sunday was his day of rest. Loyal's problem was that despite his good intentions each morning, by the time the sun went down he felt the pull of alcohol and fatty food. Strongly.

He sat down in his Altima, picked up his cell phone, and dialed Angela.

"Hey there baby," Angela said.

"Hi Angela," Loyal said. "How are you?"

"Today is a good day so far. How are you?"

"Stella's pregnant." Loyal blurted the news out.

"Oh my God!" Angela squealed. "How exciting! How far along is she? When is her due date? Does she know the gender yet?"

"That's what I should have said," Loyal said. "Instead I asked them if they were getting married."

"Oh Loyal, baby, why? Now Stella's upset and you want me to help you fix it."

"That's pretty much it. Any suggestions?"

"I'm at home," Angela said. "Come on over. I'll help you make it right."

Two hours later, and with a wallet several hundred

dollars lighter, Loyal left Angela's condo. She had helped him select numerous baby gifts online to be delivered to Stella and Mitch. She had also helped him compose a heartfelt apology.

2

LOYAL TRUESDALE

Loyal was not an introspective man. Ironically, he was aware of this fact. The role of Homicide Detective had fit him well, like a favorite jacket. Solving other people's problems was his strength. He missed the intellectual stimulation and routine the Sheriff's Department had provided. Each day, after his walk or workout with Lacey, he dreaded the return to his one bedroom apartment on Roosevelt Street. He felt boxed in, the living room and bedroom somehow smaller, the walls closing in on him. He had moved all the alcoholic beverages into the one car garage below his apartment and stopped meeting his group of friends on Tuesdays for beer and pizza. He shopped at Sprouts, buying only items approved by his doctor. And yet, temptation was everywhere. He heard the siren song of Pizza Port, only a block from his apartment, singing to him of garlic cheesy goodness and cold pale ale. Hennessey's Tavern's onion rings, burgers, and steak and garlic shrimp called to him, seducing him with memories of tastes and smells.

To escape the magnetic pull of booze and fatty food Loyal had taken to driving. He went wherever the mood struck. Sometimes South on the Coast Highway, traveling through Encinitas, Solana Beach, and Del Mar. He had taken Interstate 5 South and crossed the span of the Coronado Bridge. He had traveled East to Ramona, driven through the Julian Mountains, and explored the metal sculptures of Borrego Springs. As he drove he listened to books on CD.

Stella had been the one to suggest audio books to Loyal. She had given him The Black Echo, a novel by Micheal Connelly and the first in the Harry Bosch series. In the six months since his heart attack Loyal had listened to all the Harry Bosch novels, as well as the Mickey Haller series, and most recently the Renee Ballard series. The most recent offering from Connelly, Dark Sacred Night, had paired Bosch, the character Loyal most identified with, with Renee Ballard. Loyal dreaded hearing the last sentence. He couldn't imagine finding any author that he enjoyed as much as Connelly. He had mentioned this to the librarian at The Georgina Cole Library where he checked out the audio books, and she had promised to create a list of authors he might enjoy.

. . .

Loyal inserted disc 5 into his car stereo as he drove away
from Angela's condo. He decided he would take the 76 East
and drive up Palomar Mountain to the observatory. He had
made this drive once before and found it to be quite
relaxing once he crossed over Interstate 15. His route
towards Interstate 5 North took him past JK Gym. He
glanced in the parking lot and saw an older unmarked
Crown Vic that he recognized as a Carlsbad Sheriff's
Department vehicle. Loyal turned right at the stop sign
and went back around the block. He pulled into JK's
parking lot, parked, and entered the gym. His well trained
eyes took in the scene. Adelle was crying quietly at the
reception desk. Gym members were huddled in small
groups whispering softly. The owner, Joe Kagen, was
standing in a corner talking with another man who's back
was toward Loyal. It took Loyal a moment, then he recognized the second man as Detective Hammond, previously
of Vice. Hammond had been moved to the Homicide division when Loyal was placed on a thirty day suspension the
previous August. It had been a temporary move, but had
been extended following Loyal's heart attack and placement on disability. Loyal and Hammond had a history; it
wasn't pretty.

Loyal approached Adelle at reception.

"What's going on?" he asked.

"Loyal, it's Lacey. She's dead." A fresh round of sobs
escaped Adelle's lips. "He hasn't told us anything." She
pointed at Hammond. "Only that she died under suspi-

cious circumstances. He's been with Joe for about fifteen minutes."

Loyal stood near Adelle and watched Joe Kagen and Hammond talk. Their body language didn't suggest animosity or anger. Kagen had a stricken look on his face, seemed older, diminished somehow. Loyal was familiar with this look; grief. Hammond and Kagen shook hands. Hammond gave over his business card, then turned and strode quickly out of the gym. Loyal followed him.

"Hammond," he called.

Hammond turned at the sound of his name and saw Loyal.

"Truesdale," he said.

"What's the story?" Loyal asked as he approached Hammond.

"Nothing that concerns you, Truesdale. Police business."

"I knew Lacey, Hammond," said Loyal. "What happened?"

"You aren't working this one Truesdale. Back off."

As Hammond turned towards his Crown Vic Loyal reached out and grabbed his arm. Hammond turned, anger flashing in his dark eyes.

"Hands off Truesdale," he barked. "You have no right to information."

Loyal saw something in Hammonds eyes, something dark and dangerous. He slowly released the Detective's upper arm and dropped his hand to his side.

"Hands off me, and hands off this case, Truesdale," Hammond hissed. He turned and opened the door to his ride, looked over his shoulder and said quietly, "She's mine."

Loyal stood and watched Hammond execute an illegal left turn out of the gym's parking lot, gun the engine, and disappear down the block. He wondered about Hammond's last statement. Was the "she" Hammond referred to the case or Lacey herself?

Trinity Glass gazed out the window of the Lear 35. The sky was blue at this altitude. Glancing down, she could see the thick fog into which the captain had just announced they would soon be descending. Trinity felt the familiar tug in her stomach as the plane dipped gently toward Earth. She watched as the long tendrils of fog slowly wrapped around the fuselage and windows, obscuring any view. With vision suspended, she sat waiting for the sound of wheels on the runway. When it came, accompanied with a slight jolt and the pressure as the plane decelerated, she let out the breath she had not realized she had been holding.

The wind blew Trinity's unfastened jacket out to her sides, revealing the outline of the Sig Sauer Compact 45, as she strode away from the chartered airplane that had just landed at Western Flight Jet Center at Palomar Airport in

Carlsbad. Her phone pinged as she passed through the security fencing and peered through the fog looking in the parking lot for the Mercedes e class she had requested. She glanced down at the message.

Roberts' wife deceased. Check secure email.

"What the hell?" Trinity said out loud. This was an unexpected twist. A press of the key fob in her hand not only unlocked the elegant Mercedes, but also led her through the thick fog to its location. She tossed her carry-on bag and her purse onto the passenger seat and slid into the driver's seat. Trinity sat for a moment, re-read the short text, and rolled her shoulders forward and back a few times. She used her long fingers to gently pull her long cinnamon-ginger hair into a bun at the top of her head. In that brief moment she felt every one of her forty-four years. She was tired. The flight had been long and she was coming off a particularly difficult assignment. Now this disturbing news. With a slow sigh, she entered the Airbnb's address into the navigation system and began the short drive to her new temporary home.

Forty five minutes later Trinity could be found sitting at the table in her private condo inside the La Costa Resort and Spa. Her employer had seen to it that the condo was set up to her exact specifications. The kitchen was well stocked with the foods she had requested, and there was a computer and printer set up and ready to use. Both plain white and photographic paper were provided. Trinity had brewed a cup of Earl Gray, then settled at the dining room table. She opened her briefcase and removed a wallet sized photo. A man in military dress blues looked out at her. His expression was serious. Trinity looked for the laughter that once danced in his eyes, at the corners of his mouth that had always hinted at a smile. Not there. She placed the photo beside her Earl Gray, paused a moment, picked it up and returned it to her briefcase, then turned to her computer.

She checked her email and read the few details available about Lacey Roberts. She spread documents and photos relating to her research on Bertrand Roberts out on the dining room table. Trinity sipped her tea and carefully reviewed everything. The answer had to be somewhere in this jumble of paper. The problem she was working on was not assigned by her employer. This case was personal.

LACEY-MARCH 2010

"Eighty-six, eighty-eight, ninety." Lacey said under her breath as she counted the pills by two's, tipped the tray, and let the ninety pills fall gently into the prescription bottle. She checked the label again for accuracy, then handed it off to John. The elderly pharmacist checked the original bottle the pills came in, compared it to the information on the prescription bottle label, then added his initials at the bottom right.

"Good," he said as he handed it back to her. Lacey read the name on the label; Coraline Roberts. Coraline was Lacey's favorite customer at the small pharmacy in Carlsbad. She was in her late forties, so sweet and kind, and dying of uterine cancer. Coraline rarely picked up her own medication anymore. Lately her husband, Bertrand, came in for it. The bell on the front door tinkled and Lacey looked up to see both Coraline and Bertrand walking down the center aisle toward the pharmacy register. She stepped down from behind the pharmacy counter to greet them. Their progress was slow, Coraline's pain evident in her drawn face and uncertain steps. Bertrand held her arm gently, guiding her towards the pharmacy counter and Lacey.

"Coraline," Lacey said, reaching her hands out to gently clasp Coraline's fragile hands, "it is so good to see you."

"Lacey, my dear," Coraline's voice was a mere whisper, "it is good to see you too."

Lacey felt her eyes fill up with tears. Coraline's hands were cold, the dark circles beneath her eyes pronounced, her frame skeletal.

"Lacey, sweet girl, don't be sad." Coraline's face was close to Lacey's, she could smell the impending death on her breath.

"I've had a beautiful life Lacey. I wouldn't trade anything." Coraline's eyes were looking deeply into Lacey's. "And you have been my angel these last seven months."

A tear dropped out of Coraline's eye. Lacey felt her own tears threaten, then spill slowly down her cheeks.

"You have been mine Coraline."

Lacey bagged up Coraline's medications and passed the bag to Bertrand. "Thank you for everything Lacey," he said. She watched their slow progress back towards the front door. The bell tinkled as they exited.

· · ·

Lacey stepped back behind the pharmacy counter and returned to filling prescriptions. She and John worked in companionable silence. He had seen her tears after the Roberts left and knew better than to ask about it. Coraline was dying, he knew, and Lacey was devastated. What could be said? The phone rang and the front door bell tinkled. John answered and Lacey moved to the front register. When she spotted the customer she cringed and looked back at John. Seeing that he was still on the phone, she took a breath and prepared herself. The man approaching the counter was slender and about 5'10". He walked like a predator, balled up energy, shifty eyes, closed mouth, tight jawline.

"Mr. Hammond," Lacey said as he approached the counter. A smile slowly appeared on his face.

"Come on Lacey," he said, "call me Len."

"I prefer Mr. Hammond," Lacey said cooly. "How can I help you?"

The man's smile widened, looking wolfish and hungry now.

"I can only count the ways," he said.

Lacey felt the heat rising in her fair cheeks. She hated this about herself, the red cheeks revealing her embarrassment and discomfort. She forced herself to meet his dark eyes. He held out a pack of gum.

"I'd like to buy this."

"Fifty-nine cents."

He handed her a dollar, brushing his fingertips along hers. She shivered involuntarily. As she handed him the forty-one cents change he said, "Just got accepted into the Police Academy. Going to try to get hired on by Carlsbad Sheriff Department." The wolfish grin again. "I'll be protecting and serving you Lacey.

L oyal opened the car door and sat down heavily in his Altima. He ran his left hand across his forehead and through his shaggy hair. A deep sigh escaped him. Lacey, dead. He closed his eyes and pictured her. Long black hair pulled up in a bun, green eyes bright and sparkling, white toothed smile; vibrant. Hammond had warned him off, but Loyal knew that he wouldn't be able to let her death go. He leaned to his right, opened his car's glove compartment, and pulled out his notepad. Even in this age of computers, Loyal was a pencil and paper guy at heart. He flipped the pad open, pausing on the last page with writing on it. The notes were from last August. The names Maggie Macphearson and Elsie Davenport caught his eye. He ran his finger lightly over their names, still unsure what the hell had actually happened last Summer.

Loyal brought himself back to the present, flipped to a new

page, and wrote her name at the top. Lacey Barnett-Roberts. He considered what he actually knew about her and concluded that it was very little. She is, or was he thought with a small sigh, in her early to mid-thirties, married, no children. He thought about Adelle at reception, started his car, and exited the parking lot to the right. He drove to Baba Coffee on State Street and by some miracle found parking in front of the busy shop. He purchased a decaf coffee for himself and a lemon ginger tea for Adelle. On the way back to JK's, Loyal stopped at a liquor store and bought a few small plastic single serve bottles of Jim Beam, the size a person might get on an airline. He returned to JK's, parked, considered the alcohol, then tossed the unopened bottles into the glove compartment. Exiting the car, he stuffed his notepad and a pen in his shorts pocket, leaned in and grabbed the hot drinks, and returned to the gym.

The scene inside the gym hadn't changed much in the last half hour. Adelle still sat at reception, no longer crying, just staring into space. He approached her and handed her the tea. She accepted it with a small, sad smile and sipped.

"Thanks Loyal."

"Wish I could do more, Adelle."

"I can't believe this. Who would want to hurt Lacey?" Adelle asked.

"I don't know, Adelle. But I'm going to find out," Loyal said. "Tell me what you know about Lacey."

"Not a lot, now that I'm thinking about it," Adelle said.

"She was a pretty private person." Adelle looked around the gym then leaned in toward Loyal and whispered, "Do you want a copy of her employee file?"

"That would be helpful," Loyal said.

"Be right back," Adelle said. "I'm glad to know you are looking into this, Loyal."

"Let's keep that between you and me for now," Loyal said, thinking about Hammond and his warning not to get involved.

Adelle returned with a copy of Lacey's file. Loyal took it with a whispered "Thanks" and returned to his Altima. The file was thin, listing Lacey's date of birth, address, phone number, next of kin, and previous employers.

Loyal took out his phone and sent a text message to Detective O'Keefe.

Lunch? Usual spot?

The reply came less than a minute later. *Yes. 1:00.*

O'Keefe had been a patrol cop prior to Loyal being suspended and his subsequent heart attack. When Hammond had been moved from Vice to Homicide, O'Keefe had been tapped to fill the empty spot on Vice. The transition had been difficult for O'Keefe. He and Loyal frequently met for lunch at a vegan restaurant in Encinitas, a place where they were sure they wouldn't see anyone they knew. Loyal started his car and glanced at the dashboard clock. 11:50. He looked again at Lacey's file, noted her home address, and exited the parking lot.

· · ·

Lacey's address was on Shorebird Lane in Carlsbad. Loyal took I 5 South to Poinsettia Lane and headed East. Google maps directed him to turn right on Batiquitos Drive, which he did. Shorebird Lane was on his right about half a mile after the right turn. Like most of the cul de sacs in the community, there was a gate barring his entry. He drove slowly past the street and saw police tape covering the entry into what appeared to be public parking for the lagoon trails. As he drove slowly past the parking lot he spotted a few uniformed guys he recognized but didn't know well. Loyal assumed this was the scene of Lacey's death. He saw a man about his own age walking two large black dogs, each sporting a white patch on its chest. Their heads were huge and square, their eyes dark. Loyal pulled his Altima to the side of the road and lowered the passenger window. The man walking the dogs made a small jerking motion on the leashes and the dogs immediately stopped their forward progress.

"Sit," the man said as he leaned down and looked in the lowered window. "You need directions?" he asked Loyal.

"Just wondering what kind of dogs those are," Loyal said. "They are impressive."

The man smiled widely. "Thanks. The breed is called Cane Corso. These guys are a little over three years old. Full size."

"Cane Corso?" Loyal said. "I've never heard of them."

"If you are thinking about a dog, and have time and space, you should look in to them," the man said. "They run anywhere from $1200 to $4000 depending on their lineage."

"Thanks," said Loyal, "I'll keep them in mind."

As the man leaned away Loyal asked, "What happened back there?" and pointed up the street to the police tape.

"Not sure," said the man. "They are being pretty tight-lipped. I know it was a death because I saw the coroner's van this morning."

"Sad," said Loyal. He gave a small wave, said, "Enjoy those dogs," and drove away.

Loyal pulled a u-turn a bit farther down the street and drove slowly past the cordoned off parking lot and the closed gate on Shorebird Lane. If he had his badge he would have been investigating Lacey's death. He realized as he thought this, that if he had his badge he never would have met her. Glancing at his dashboard clock, he saw that it was almost 12:30. With a parting look at Shorebird Lane's closed gates, Loyal headed toward Encinitas and his meeting with O'Keefe.

6

I t took Loyal about fifteen minutes to navigate the 4.4 miles from Lacey's home to Plant Power on Santa Fe Drive in Encinitas. As always, Loyal was surprised by the amount of traffic on El Camino Real and supposed the freeway would have been a better choice. The previous August Loyal had had the opportunity to drive a Meyers Manx dune buggy deep into Baja. He felt a longing now for the profound sense of solitude he had experienced on that long drive. Driving in coastal Southern California was a battle, everyone jockeying for position and racing each other from stoplight to stoplight.

Loyal found a parking spot in Plant Power's small parking lot, ordered two meatless hamburgers and two meatless chicken sandwiches, French fries, lemonade for himself, and root beer for O'Keefe. He sat down at a small table and waited for O'Keefe, who arrived several minutes later.

"Hey Loyal," O'Keefe said as he sat, "thanks for ordering."

"Hi Pat," Loyal said. "Thanks for coming."

Patrick O'Keefe was an Irish stereotype come to life. Bright red hair, close cropped so that it looked as if his head was glowing, bright blue eyes, pale skin, and freckles scattered across his face. He was one of the most optimistic people Loyal had ever met. O'Keefe took a large bite, chewed, swallowed, then said, "I don't think I told you yet. Captain Williams finally received the grant to start a computer forensics division. He moved me out of Vice two weeks ago."

Loyal smiled, genuinely pleased to hear this. "That's great Pat."

"Yeah," O'Keefe said. "So, what's up?"

"What can you tell me about the homicide this morning at Batiquitos Lagoon?" Loyal asked.

O'Keefe turned and gave Loyal an appraising look. "You missing work? Hope that means you are coming back soon."

"This is between you and me Pat," Loyal said. "She was my personal trainer, and friend."

"Oh shit, Loyal, man I'm sorry." O'Keefe looked genuinely pained. "Potter was the uniform on that call. He's pretty shook up. Someone beat her, badly. I don't think they found the weapon yet, might be something like a baseball bat. Hammond is all over this case. I don't think I've ever seen him so worked up before."

Loyal set his food down and silently stared off into space. He saw Lacey clearly in his minds eye; green eyes, bright smile. He knew he was going to work this case on his own, despite Hammond's warning this morning.

"Get me as much as you can on this Pat," Loyal said. "And keep it between us."

Thirty minutes later Loyal was back in the Altima and driving north on Coast Highway 101. He passed through Encinitas and Leucadia then, on impulse, pulled into parking for Ponto Beach. He reached in his glove compartment and grabbed the tiny bourbon bottles he had purchased that morning. Stuffing them in his shorts pocket, he walked down to the sand. It was 2:00 in early April, a Monday, and there were only a handful of people on the sand. A few wet-suited surfers braved the cold water. The breeze coming off the water was cool, the sun a watery pale yellow in the sky. Loyal sat in the sand and gazed out at the expanse of blue. His thoughts were dark, images of Lacey's battered body flashing every time he closed his eyes. He was grateful he had not seen her in death, although he had seen enough during his years on the force that he had no problem imagining her broken, battered corpse. Uncapping the first bourbon bottle, Loyal downed it in two large swallows. He repeated the process with the second bottle. His head swam as his first alcohol in months hit like a hammer. Loyal lay back on the sand and closed his eyes. He fought past the grue-some images and finally landed on happier ones. The sun and the sand warmed his body, and before he knew it, he was asleep.

Loyal was awakened by a gentle tap on his shoulder. He opened his eyes, focused, and saw first an older woman's face, then a man's.

"Are you ok, sweetie?" the woman asked. "The sun is about to go down." Loyal struggled to sit up, blinking his way back to consciousness.

"Oh, yeah, I guess I drifted off," Loyal said, aware of the bourbon on his breath and feeling embarrassed by it. These people probably thought he was an old drunk sleeping it off on the beach.

"Thanks for waking me," he said as he stood.

"Sure honey," the woman said. "You take care now." Loyal brushed the sand off his shorts and legs as the couple moved slowly away. His mind was foggy. He made his way to his Altima, started it up, and drove home.

Loyal parked in front of his apartment, exited his car, and unlocked the garage. He grabbed a bottle of Jim Beam from the box of booze he had removed from his apartment after the heart attack. He closed and re-locked the garage, walked slowly up the stairs, and entered the apartment. He took an extra long shower, but knew he was only delaying the inevitable. Once he was dried and dressed, he poured a large glass of the amber liquid, sat in his recliner, and drank.

L acey climbed the stairs to her apartment slowly. She rarely wore heels and her feet ached with each step. She paused at the landing, taking a moment to still her troubled thoughts. Coraline's funeral had been lavish. John had given her the day off so that she could attend. It was held at a giant church in Carlsbad and well attended. Lacey guessed several hundred people had been there to pay their respects. Bertrand had looked sleek and polished as always, but the dark smudges beneath his eyes, the slump in his shoulders, and the way the suit hung on his too thin frame betrayed his grief. He and Coraline had been married twenty-four years and had two adult children. The son was tall and trim like his father, but his features resembled Coraline. The daughter looked more like Bertrand, dark eyes and tan skin, but with a slight build more like her mother. Lacey supposed both of them were close to her twenty three years.

.   .   .

After the service Bertrand and his children had greeted the receiving line. Their grief was buried deep, barely visible save for the red rimmed eyes. Lacey wondered about the dynamics of the family, what their relationships would be like without Coraline to light the dark corners of their lives. She tried to remember what Bertrand did for a living and realized she had no idea. They were fabulously wealthy, that was obvious. She found herself wondering how far money could go in the soothing of pain. While she waited in the receiving line she watched Bertrand greet each mourner personally, say something, then listen with genuine attention to their response. When she reached him he clasped her small hands in his large ones.

"Lacey, thank you for coming," he said. "Coraline would be so happy to know that you were here."

"I'm so sorry for your loss Mr. Roberts," Lacey said. "I loved Coraline."

"And she loved you Lacey," he replied, before sending her on down the line as he turned to the next guest.

Standing on the landing of her apartment now, Lacey let out a sad sigh. She had loved Coraline. As Lacey opened the door to the apartment a swirl of smoke poured out and engulfed her. She ran into the apartment. In the kitchen she found a smoking pan on a still lit burner. She grabbed the kitchen towel, pulled the pan off the burner, turned the heat to off, and ran cold water on the smoking pan. She turned her face quickly, barely escaping the rush of steam created by cold water hitting heat. Leaving the pan in the sink, Lacey turned to open the kitchen window and tripped over something on the floor. Bending down, she saw the smoke alarm, smashed into pieces, dented battery on the floor beside it. Lacey entered the first bedroom and found her mother huddled in the corner, arms wrapped around the thin legs drawn up to her chest.

"Mom," Lacey said as she ran to her. Linda was moaning quietly and rocking side to side.

"Mom," Lacey said again, kneeling down and raising her mother's face. Linda looked confused for a moment, then recognition dawned on her face and she smiled.

"Lacey," she said.

"It's ok Mom," Lacey said gently. "I'm home."

Taking her Mother's hand, Lacey helped her rise to a standing position. Turning, Lacey led her out the door of the bedroom and opened the door of the room she shared with her sister. Liane was sitting on her bed, legs crossed, sucking her left thumb and tugging on her earlobe with her right hand. As always, Lacey was struck by the sight of her twin sister. Their features were identical, but looked so different on Liane. It was almost as if Liane was a drawing of Lacey, but someone had tried to erase some of the details. Lacey crossed quickly to Liane and wrapped her arms around her.

"What happened?" Lacey said.

Liane let go of her ear, reached behind her back, and produced a hammer.

"I smashed the noise," she said. Lacey gently removed the hammer from her sister's grip.

"You sure did, baby. You sure did," she said.

Two hours later, mother and sister fed and tucked into bed, Lacey sat in the living room and contemplated her options. Her mother had not been diagnosed, but Lacey was sure she had the beginnings of dementia. Chronologically Liane was twenty-three, but had diminished mental development. From the time Lacey had graduated high school she had worked full time, while her mother had stayed home to care for Liane. After the events of this evening, Lacey was not sure how much longer this arrangement could continue.

Tuesday found Loyal, still dressed in yesterday's clothing, snoring gently in his recliner. The detritus of a night spent drinking was scattered around him; nearly empty bourbon bottle, half finished glass of amber liquid beside it, remains of a frozen pizza on a paper plate on the coffee table. Loyal snored and slept as the sun slowly rose. His kitchen window faced East and the sun's rays eventually landed full on his face. The bright light drew his consciousness slowly upward. His mind swam to the surface, and he awakened. He sat still, eyes closed, and gently untangled his memories of the previous day. Lacey dead, Hammond threatening, lunch with O'Keefe, the old couple waking him on the beach, the night spent trying to forget. His mouth was dry, his head pounding. He mentally assessed his heart. It seemed to be beating properly, no chest, back, or shoulder pain. He hadn't had a drink since the heart attack. This morning he remembered why. He felt like shit.

Eventually Loyal rose and walked slowly to the bathroom. He stripped off yesterday's clothes, carefully avoiding his reflection in the mirror for the time being. He turned the water in the shower as hot as he could stand, stepped in, and let the hot spray wash away the stink of booze and the grief over Lacey. He remained in the shower until the water started to cool and stepped out into a cloud of steam. He dried, entered the bedroom and dressed in slacks and a Tommy Bahama, then returned to face the bathroom mirror. He wiped a face sized circle and surveyed the damage. He supposed it could be worse. Bloodshot eyes stared calmly back at him, his skin looked a bit gray, he definitely looked older than he had yesterday. He ran his hands through his shaggy brown hair and walked to the living room. He cleared away the night's debris, dumped the dregs out of the glass, capped the bottle, and trashed the pizza remains. He blended a green smoothie and sat at his tiny kitchen table to consider his options for the day.

He decided to start at the scene of the crime. As he was gathering his keys, gun, and wallet his phone made a gentle ping. The text message was from O'Keefe. It read:

Someone dropped off an envelope for you this morning. It is at reception. Come see me in Computer Forensics when you stop by to pick it up.

"An envelope?" Loyal thought. He had no idea what that might be about. He responded to O'Keefe that he had something this morning and would come by the station around one o'clock.

Loyal drove to Batiquitos Lagoon. He passed Shorebird

Lane. The gates were closed. He parked in the parking lot just past Lacey's street and got out of the Altima, carefully tucking his Kahr PM9 in the belly band around his waist. All traces of the crime scene had been removed. The dirt path down to the lagoon was narrow, about twenty-five feet long, and steep. At the base of the path, the trail branched out to the left and right. Loyal shuffled down and stopped at a small wooden frame that held information about the lagoon. He plucked an information card from the frame, looked at it briefly, then held it by his side as he read the large plank next to the frame.

Batiquitos Lagoon Ecological Reserve

The information presented explained that this lagoon was one of only a handful left in the state of California, and that the ecosystem was very fragile. Below the explanations about plants and wildlife there was a list of rules. Loyal let out a small huff as he read the rule that stated no guns, firearms, or other type of weapons were allowed. Lacey's killer had not followed that rule. Loyal looked again at the card in his hand. The front was a lovely picture of the lagoon and the trail. He flipped it over and saw a map depicting the lagoon's location in relation to the streets and freeways near it. Beneath the map were a few paragraphs containing information about the lagoon, and below that contact information for the Batiquitos Lagoon Foundation.

Loyal slipped the card in his pants pocket, turned right, and started down the trail. He could smell the sage that grew around the lagoon as well as the rotten egg smell produced by the bacteria in the marsh as they drew sulphur from dead animals and plants.The sun shone from behind him, casting his shadow forward about three feet, his shadow self leading his real self. He saw the shadow approaching from behind him just about the same time as he heard the pounding feet. He swiveled quickly, just in time to glimpse a woman, ball cap and sunglasses obscuring her face, jog past him. He followed her progress, watching her slender strong form, noting the ginger-cinnamon color of her ponytail. She followed a curve in the trail and disappeared from view.

Loyal rounded the same corner, although at a much slower pace, looked up and to his right, and realized that Lacey's street butted right up to the lagoon trail. He pulled out his phone, did a quick search on her address, and concluded that one of the large homes he was looking at from down below was likely hers. He searched a real estate web site, found an arial view, and clumsily maneuvered the images until he felt he had located Lacey's house in relationship to the trail. He walked slowly forward, comparing the image on his phone to what was in front of him, and stopped when he felt he was below Lacey's home. He pocketed his phone and looked up at the house on the hill above him. It was two stories, large, red tile roof, with a stone wall surrounding its perimeter. Wrought iron fencing atop the stone wall virtually doubled the height of the protective barrier. Loyal climbed the hill as far as he could, and snapped a picture of the rear of the house. He zoomed in on the picture, which revealed little. Palm trees in the back yard protected the windows of the house. One empty balcony was visible, little else. Loyal stepped carefully down the hill, took one more look around the lagoon trail, then returned to his car.

Loyal pulled into the Carlsbad Sheriff's Department parking lot a few minutes before one o'clock. He spent a moment in his car looking at the large white building. He hadn't been inside since last August when Captain Williams had suspended him for thirty days. He thought about O'Keefe in the newly formed computer forensics division and wondered how much the events of last August had to do with Captain Williams applying for the grant to fund it. He breathed in slowly, let the breath out, exited the car, and walked toward his former place of employment.

The sounds, sights, and smells of the Sheriff's Department hadn't changed at all, and Loyal was transported back in time the moment he stepped inside. At this moment he realized just how much he missed it all. He turned to the left and the reception desk. Fatima was behind the counter as usual. She was in her mid thirties, long black hair, dark brown eyes, round face, and easy smile.

"Detective Truesdale," she said with a large smile. "I was going to call you today. A man dropped off an envelope for you." She rummaged around on the desk and brought forth a large cream colored envelope.

"Thanks Fatima," Loyal said as he reached for the envelope.

"Looks like an invitation," Fatima said, clearly interested in seeing what was inside the envelope.

Loyal tucked it in his pants pocket and said, "I'd like to

say hello to Detective O'Keefe. He told me he is in a new division."

"Yes, computer forensics," Fatima replied. "Upstairs and to the left. Next to your old office. I'm sorry detective, but I have to issue you a visitor badge." She handed him the badge, paused a moment, then said quietly, "Hope to see you back at work soon Detective."

"Thanks," said Loyal. "Me too."

Loyal took the stairs slowly, turned left, and entered O'Keefe's new office. The furniture was sparse. O'Keefe sat behind a modern metal desk, laptop open, his head bent in concentration. Loyal waited a moment, then quietly cleared his throat and O'Keefe looked up.

"Did you get the envelope?" he asked Loyal.

"Yep."

"Here's another one," O'Keefe said quietly, half rising from his seat and holding out a plain white business envelope. Loyal took it, felt that it contained an object that was about two inches long, folded the envelope and put it in the pocket with the envelope Fatima had given him.

"Just wanted to stop in and say hello," Loyal said.

"Great to see you man," O'Keefe replied.

Loyal nodded, turned, and walked out.

9

TRINITY GLASS

T rinity Glass ran the entire length of the Batiquitos Lagoon three times. Her observant eyes took in everything and everyone along the 3 mile trail. She paid special attention to anyone near the home of Bertrand and Lacey Roberts. On her second pass she ran past a middle aged man wearing slacks and what looked like a Tommy Bahama shirt. After she rounded two corners, and was out of his line of sight she slowed, then stopped, hands on knees, feigning being out of breath. She straightened slowly, then turned and walked back toward a curve in the trail. Leaning on a tall tree as if for support, she glanced back at the man on the trail. She watched him peck at his phone for a few minutes, occasionally glancing up towards the back of the Roberts' house. Trinity pulled out her own phone and quickly snapped a picture of the man, then watched as he climbed the hill behind the Roberts' house and took a picture of the back of their large home. When he turned and began his descent she spun around and continued her run. She didn't know his identity yet, but it was simply a matter of time.

10

L oyal did not open either envelope until he reached his apartment. He set them both on his kitchen table, unsure which one to open first. He decided on the unknown, and opened the large cream colored envelope Fatima had been so curious about. Elsie and Phil's smiling faces looked at him from the heavy card stock invitation in his hand. The words *Please Join Us* floated above their heads. Loyal turned the card over and read:

Elsie Davenport and Phil Gillespie request the honor of your presence at their wedding to be held on Friday, April 19, 2019 at 6:00 pm in Borrego Springs California. Please plan on staying the night. Accommodations will be provided, along with a celebration breakfast Saturday morning.

. . .

An address Loyal recognized was listed. There was a hand written note from Phil apologizing for the late notice and asking Loyal to please be there. Loyal flipped the card back over and looked at their smiling faces again. He stood, walked to the trash can in the kitchen, then paused and returned to the table. He'd consider it, he decided. He then turned to the other envelope. It contained a small Sandisk USB drive.

Loyal went to his bedroom and retrieved his laptop. He carried it out to the dining room and sat at the kitchen table. When he opened it nothing happened. Loyal tapped at a few random keys, then realized the computer battery was likely dead. He found the charging cord in a kitchen drawer and plugged the laptop in. He made himself a turkey sandwich on sourdough, giving the computer a few minutes to start to charge, then sat in front of it and turned it on. He held the red plastic drive in his hand between his thumb and forefinger for a moment, then with a deep sigh, plugged it in.

Hammond was good about entering his notes into the computer, and O'Keefe had managed to get copies of everything. Hammond noted the time of his arrival, and the direction from which he had entered the scene. Photographs were included and Loyal recognized the path he had been on earlier in the day. He scrolled down, and the photographs of Lacey appeared before him. She lay on the ground, flat on her back, hands flung out to either side of her torso. Loyal felt his stomach drop and he pushed the unfinished sandwich out of reach. The initial pictures were taken from some distance away, but as Loyal scrolled down the close-ups emerged. The damage inflicted was devastating. Loyal had to force himself to look at Lacey's battered face, blood was everywhere. There was emotion in this murder. Hammond's notes indicated that he felt the same way. The perpetrator was likely someone who knew Lacey well.

Loyal stood and walked to the sink. He ran some water into his hands and splashed his face. He opened the refrigerator and grabbed a water bottle, which he opened and gulped from. He then returned to the electronic murder book. The notes that followed the horrific pictures of Lacey were thorough and detailed. Hammond recorded every person at the scene, and their reason for being there. The name of the medical examiner and their time of arrival was noted. The removal of Lacey's body was detailed, the autopsy noted as pending. The search for evidence was conducted by Detective Mejia. Loyal knew him and considered him to be meticulous. Evidence collected had not yet been recorded. This fact caused Loyal to pause. O'Keefe had copied this information at great personal risk. Asking him to do it again when the autopsy results and evidence had been recorded wasn't something Loyal felt he should do. He put this complication on the back burner for now and continued reading.

. . .

There was only one witness listed. One Donald Blomgren, white male, age 39 had called 911. According to his statement, he had passed Lacey on the trail. He had run to the end of the trail, turned around, and retraced his steps. He doubted more than 15 minutes could have passed from the time he saw her alive to the time he found her battered body on the trail. Blomgren was former military. He had touched Lacey briefly to determine if she was alive, then called the emergency line. He had stayed on the line with the operator until Officer Potter arrived, and remained at the scene until he could be interviewed by Hammond. He had no visible defensive wounds or blood spatter and had not been hesitant to show the Detective his hands and arms. Blomgren lived in Vista, nearly 15 miles Northeast of the lagoon. He claimed to train at the lagoon often. Loyal remembered the dense fog that morning. He copied Blomgren's details into his notebook.

The last bit of information concerned Lacey's next of kin. Her husband, Bertrand Roberts Jr. was listed first. Apparently Lacey also left behind a mother and sister. The mother, Linda Barnett, was in an assisted living community in Southwest Escondido. The sister, Liane, lived on Shorebird Lane with Bertrand and Lacey. Loyal pushed back from the table and went to stand at the kitchen window. He rubbed his hands over his face, attempting to push away the images of Lacey's body. She had never, in all these months of working with him, mentioned her mother and sister. Loyal had told Lacey all about Stella and his long deceased mother. He had even told her about his father, with whom he had not had contact for over 46 years. If Walker Truesdale was alive he would be 87 years old. Loyal supposed he was likely dead, didn't care one way or the other. Why then, had Lacey never mentioned the sister who lived with her, or the mother in Escondido?

11

The bell on the pharmacy door tinkled as Lacey pushed through. John, behind the pharmacy counter, glanced up, registered Lacey's return from lunch, then looked down again. Lacey crossed the small pharmacy and took her place behind the counter beside John.

"He took you to lunch again?" he asked.

"Yes."

"You two have been seeing a lot of each other." A statement, not a question.

"Yes," Lacey said. "Does that bother you?"

"He's only been widowed six months Lacey. And he's probably got twenty years on you," John said. "He's closer to my age than yours."

Lacey put her hand on John's forearm. He sighed and looked at her.

"John, your opinion matters very much to me," Lacey

said. "Bertrand and I enjoy each other's company. He is kind and he makes me feel safe."

"What about the future?" John asked. "Children? Someone to grow old with?"

"I haven't told anyone yet John. Bertrand took me to Lake Tahoe last weekend. We flew in a Gulfstream and stayed at this resort called the Granlibakken. We ate at this fancy restaurant called Edgewood. Everyone up there knows Bertrand. I feel like a princess when I'm with him."

John looked down at the pills he was counting and remained silent.

"Please John, try to be happy for me....for us," Lacey said, her hand still on John's forearm. "We are getting married. He's going to take care of my Mom and Liane."

John turned his head and looked at her. Her eyes were filled with tears. He pulled her in for a quick hug.

"Of course I'm happy for you Lacey," he said.

They separated at the sound of the bell. Lacey looked and saw Len Hammond approaching the counter. She stepped forward to greet him, wiping a stray tear from her cheek. She no longer dreaded waiting on him. Six months of police academy training had produced dramatic changes in the man. Polite conversation had replaced the rude and suggestive comments. His gaze was steady, strength and maturity shining out of his dark eyes.

"Lacey, are you ok?" he asked. "Are you crying?"

"I'm fine," she said, "just allergies."

"There should be something here you can take," he said with a smile as he handed the usual pack of gum to Lacey. "I'm graduating next Thursday. I was wondering if you would be my guest."

"Oh," Lacey said, "that is so exciting and it is so sweet of you to invite me. I'm sorry though, I can't."

Hammond's shoulders slumped.

"It isn't that I don't want to," Lacey said. "I just don't think it would be appropriate. I just became engaged this past weekend."

His dark eyes flickered, and for a moment Lacey had a glimpse of the old Hammond, the Hammond that frightened her. Just as quickly the old look disappeared. Hammond smiled at Lacey and said, "Congratulations. I'm sure you will be very happy."

The bell announced another customer and Lacey looked past Hammond to see Bertrand striding through the pharmacy. His smile was wide, his eyes sparkling. He walked up to the counter, leaned across, and kissed Lacey full on the lips.

"I've got it worked out Lace," he said. "The Granlibakkin on New Years Day. The start of our life together."

"Bertrand, that's wonderful," Lacey said, leaning over the counter to embrace him. When her cheek reached his shoulder she turned her head to the right and found herself looking directly into Hammond's dark and dangerous eyes. At six o'clock that evening, as she and John were locking up and walking to their cars, she could have sworn she felt those same dark eyes watching her.

L oyal read the electronic murder book three times then shut his computer down. He had hand-written pertinent information in his notepad, which he shoved into his pants pocket. He picked up the wedding invitation Phil had delivered to the Sheriff's Department. Phil and Elsie's images smiled out at him. He was once again considering throwing it in the trash when his phone chirped. The text message was from Mitch.

You free? Want to fly drones? San Dieguito Park in one hour?

In the months following Loyal's heart attack his daughter, Stella, had kept herself busy thinking of activities intended to keep her father upright and moving. One of her many suggestions had been that Mitch teach Loyal how to fly recreational drones. For just over $500 Loyal had purchased a DJI Phantom 3 quadcopter. He joined the Academy of Model Aeronautics, or AMA, and registered with the FAA. He and Mitch liked to frequent local parks with lots of acreage and hiking trails. San Dieguito Park was located between Del Mar and Solana Beach on Lomas Santa Fe Drive. It boasted well over 100 acres and five miles of hiking trails. Loyal texted back.

Yes.

Twenty minutes later, after confirming the batteries were charged and packing the drone into the trunk of the Altima, Loyal left Roosevelt Street. He drove to Interstate 5 and headed South. He parked in a parking lot off Lomas Santa Fe, paid the required $3.00, and opened the trunk of the Altima. He carefully lifted his Phantom 3 drone and controller. Just as he was closing the trunk, Mitch's white Nissan Frontier pulled up and parked a few spaces away.

"Hey Loyal," Mitch said as he stepped out of the truck.

"Mitch," Loyal replied, "looks like a good day for flying."

"Yeah. I was thinking we could practice maneuvering in tighter spaces today," Mitch said.

"Sounds good," Loyal said. The two men attached their I Phones to their controllers and chose their desired settings for their cameras. They walked down a long dirt path. The smell of sage filled their nostrils, and they stepped carefully, avoiding the spiky wild cucumber and wild artichoke native to the area. Several varieties of tall oaks and some lower growing manzanita lined the trail. They crossed a suspended rope bridge and found themselves in a clearing.

"This look good?" Mitch asked.

"Yep," Loyal said, "don't see anyone around."

Each man set his drone on the ground. They pressed the power buttons on the controllers and the drones. Each drone buzzed to life. They calibrated the compasses of their drones by turning 360 degrees in each direction. When given the signal, the quadcopters rose to a height of about four feet and hovered.

"I'll go South," Loyal said. Mitch nodded and directed his drone in the opposite direction. Loyal spent a few minutes practicing orientation, then flew his drone towards a line of trees. Maneuvering the drone took all of Loyal's concentration. He was surprised when the low power warning came on. Had 20 minutes really passed? With a quiet sigh he reluctantly directed the small aircraft to return to him.

The two men gathered their drones and retraced their steps to the parking lot.

"You are getting pretty good Loyal," Mitch said.

"Thanks. I'm surprised by how much I enjoy it," Loyal said. "How's Stella?"

"She's good."

"I'm sorry about Sunday," Loyal said. "The whole getting married thing."

"If I had my way we would be married already," Mitch said. "Stella doesn't want to."

"Yeah, I know," Loyal said. "I ordered a bunch of baby stuff. Should come in the next few days."

"Thanks," Mitch said. "You should call her tonight. She's usually home by 5:00."

Loyal gave Mitch's hand a quick shake. "I'll do that," he said.

Loyal returned home, showered, and made a large salad for dinner. He thought about the bottle in the pantry. He hadn't returned it to its home in the garage. Despite the hungover start to the day, the desire for a drink was strong. He stood and walked to the pantry. Staring at the bourbon bottle, he actually felt his mouth watering. He closed the pantry and called Stella instead. Voicemail. He supposed she was still angry with him. He left a message asking if she was available Wednesday evening. He'd like to come over to her place if that was ok. He set the phone down, walked toward the pantry, then abruptly turned and went to the kitchen table. He spent the next half hour reviewing the drone footage from earlier in the day. Mitch was right, he was getting better at guiding the nimble little craft around obstacles. He thought about his inability to see the house on Shorebird Lane, then thought about his drone. He knew he was not supposed to fly the drone anywhere that people had a reasonable expectation of privacy, and that he should maintain a minimum of 25 feet distance from all people and property. Still, the idea formed.

Surveillance of Lacey's home could be conducted from outside those protective walls.

Loyal put the drone's batteries into the DJI charging station. He set his alarm for 5:30 am. He wandered around the small apartment realizing he was only delaying the inevitable. He retrieved the bourbon bottle, took a glass from the cabinet, and sat down in his recliner to drink.

13

After her long run in the morning, Trinity had returned to her condo to shower and change clothes. She spent an hour reviewing all her notes and photos. The man taking pictures on the trail was not in any of them. She logged on to her employers database and uploaded the photo she had taken of him. Powerful facial recognition software delivered his identity moments later. Loyal Truesdale, age 57, resident of Carlsbad, California. Occupation, homicide detective with the Carlsbad Sheriff's Department. Interesting, Trinity thought, the name she had been given as lead detective was Hammond. A bit more searching gave her the answer. The Detective had been on paid leave and suffered a heart attack prior to his return date. Currently he was on disability. "What is his connection?" she wondered out loud to herself.

· · ·

She set to work on her computer, and two hours later had unbelievable details about an incident Truesdale had been involved in the previous August. Trinity ran her hands through her long hair and stared at the screen in disbelief. How in the world had he redirected a satellite? He had been accused of multiple national security issues, and of launching a RF attack during DEFCON, a hacker convention held in Las Vegas. Initially held by the FBI, Truesdale had eventually been cleared, and the case closed. Details of the resolution required an elevated security clearance. "What the hell," Trinity mumbled to herself. "Case closed and I can't see the resolution? And why can't I access the details with my security clearances? What kind of connections does this guy have?" Trinity printed up all the information she was able to access and began a file on Loyal Truesdale. Glancing at the digital clock beside the bed, she saw that it was 3:30 already. She stood and stretched, then headed to the closet. The meeting was set for 5:30 in La Jolla.

An hour later Trinity was dressed in a slate gray Saint Laurent business skirt and blazer with a black silk blouse beneath. She wore red Christian Louboutin pumps, 1/2 carat diamond stud earrings, and her bright hair was carefully pulled back in a chignon at the base of her neck. She exuded money and power. With a final look in the full length mirror, she turned and left the condo. She crossed the parking lot and slid into the black Mercedes e class her employer had leased for her. There was no need for her to enter her destination into the navigational system. Trinity knew where she was going.

14

L oyal's alarm followed his instructions, sounding loudly at 5:30 am on Wednesday. Loyal reached his arm out from under the covers, searching for the button to silence it and wondering why in the hell he had set it. He searched through the fog in his head, eventually stumbling on the memory and his idea of drone surveillance of Bertrand Roberts' house. He got out of bed and dressed in sweat pants and a t-shirt, splashed some cold water on his face without really looking in the mirror, and laced up his walking shoes. The drone batteries were fully charged. Loyal had followed Mitch's advice and purchased two. Each battery gave him about 20 minutes flying time. He opened the front door to a wall of dense fog. It wasn't quite as thick as the fog had been on Monday when Lacey had been killed, but definitely thick enough to impede his planned surveillance. He hesitated, then took a long breath and plunged into the gray mist.

. . .

The drive to the parking lot above Batiquitos Lagoon Trail was treacherous. Visibility was ten feet at best. Loyal's hands were shaking badly, his brain not yet free of the bourbon induced fog, trickles of sweat dripping on his forehead despite the cool morning. He deeply regretted his decision to drink the previous night, but knew at the same time that he would feel differently when night rolled around again. He began the turn into the deserted parking lot above the lagoon then felt some hidden instinct not to park there. Instead he traveled several football fields further past the parking lot and parallel parked on the street. The fog had not dissipated at all. In fact, it was thicker here nearer to the water. The surveillance mission would likely be a bust. He was here, however, so he decided to give it a try.

Loyal glanced at his phone. 6:15. He gathered his drone and controller and inched carefully toward the parking lot, then down the steep incline that led to the trail. He walked slowly towards the spot below the house he had determined to be Lacey's. He held the drone in his hands and did two 360 degree turns to calibrate the compass, then set it on the ground in front of him and powered it up. He flew the drone very slowly and deliberately up the long slope and over the wall and fencing surrounding the house. Visibility was no better 100 feet above than where he was standing. The fog swirled in front of the camera, gray and white wisps obscuring visibility. A palm tree, which Loyal narrowly avoided, morphed out of the fog. Loyal paused the drone's forward motion and turned it slowly in a circle, searching the gray for anything, unsure what exactly he was looking for. He started a second circular sweep, then paused the machine. The light in the direction it was facing was different somehow. He inched his flying craft slowly forward. He was almost upon it when he realized what he was seeing was a lighted window. He paused the drone again and pondered the ethics of using the drone to look in the window of a private home, then eased it slowly forward. The blinds were open. He hovered the drone right outside the window, nearly touching the glass. He sucked a sharp breath in as the individual in the room became visible. Lacey? It couldn't be. He hovered the drone and squinted at the image he saw on his iPhone. The sister, it must be her. She sat facing an easel, paint-brush in her left hand, her profile visible. She dabbed the brush on the easel, pulled her hand back and studied what she had done. Loyal could see now that her movements were different than Lacey's; jerky, less fluid. As if she felt his eyes on her she turned suddenly toward the window. Loyal instantly raised the drone three feet straight up, grateful now for all the orientation practice Mitch had insisted on.

Loyal paused the drone again and waited for his slamming heart to slow. He then pulled the drone away from the house and searched for any other glowing windows. He realized now that the sister's room had been on the first floor of the giant house. He raised the drone a few feet higher in the air and stared at the swirling fog on the screen in front of him. There. Up and to the right a bit. Another faintly glowing rectangle. He eased the drone toward the dim light, eventually reaching the window. It was a bedroom. A single lamp on a bedside table glowed. The comforter of the kingsized bed was rumpled, the bed empty. A figure entered his field of view. Bertrand, Lacey's husband. He wore a white bathrobe, his dark hair was damp. He entered a large walk-in closet and reappeared a few moments later with clothing in his arms. As he set the items on the bed he glanced up at the window. His body went rigid for a moment, he straightened, then rushed at the window.

Loyal directed the drone straight backwards as he dropped into a crouch beside the brush that lined the trail. He hit the return to home button and moments later the drone landed itself gently on the trail. Loyal swooped the aircraft in his arms and ran towards the steep hill up to the parking lot. Bertrand had seen the drone. Would he risk coming out in the fog to look for the operator? Loyal decided he might, and continued past the trail to the parking lot, moving further along the lagoon trail. He heard a rhythmic slapping sound coming from above. He paused to listen; footsteps, coming quickly. Loyal looked around for somewhere to hide. Daylight was coming, but visibility was still very poor. He walked as quietly as he could along the trail, eyes searching for shapes in the mist. He sensed something large to his right and inched that direction, hand outstretched. His fingers brushed against something wet. Palm fronds. Thick and close to the ground. He plunged into them and huddled near the trunk.

TRINITY GLASS

T rinity woke early on Wednesday and dressed for a run. When she opened the door of the condo she was met by a wall of impenetrable fog. She closed the door and spent an hour practicing yoga instead. When she felt sufficiently stretched and relaxed, she took a quick shower and dressed in form fitting jeans and a black T-shirt. She whipped up a quick breakfast and sat down to eat. On the way back from La Jolla the previous evening she had stopped by Loyal Truesdale's apartment and placed a tracking device on his Altima. A similar device had been placed on Bertrand Roberts' car two days ago. She looked at her phone now, fully expecting both men to still be at home, and was surprised to see that Loyal's Altima was parked on the street above Batiquitos Lagoon. She looked out the window. The fog was still very dense. She glanced at the clock. 7:15. She would wait it out for now, she decided, and placed her phone on the table so she could keep an eye on the red dots.

. . .

Trinity opened her computer and reviewed the notes she had entered late last night. She had followed Bertrand Roberts to his dinner meeting at The Marine Room in La Jolla. She sat at the bar and nursed a martini, watching Bertrand out of the corner of her eye. He had sat alone for about fifteen minutes waiting for his dinner companion. Trinity still didn't know what to think about the man who had eventually arrived. She had seen him before in meetings, but never actually spoken to him. Why the hell was Bertrand meeting with Jack Williamson from Space and Naval Warfare?

L oyal inhaled through his nose to try to slow his ragged breathing. He had never been on this end of a chase before. He had always had the power of the badge and the strength of the Sheriff's Department behind him. He had broken the law with his early morning surveillance mission. If Bertrand found him he would be in deep trouble. Especially when Hammond found out. Loyal's ears strained, listening for any sounds. Nothing. Then he heard it again, the rhythmic slapping sound of footsteps. The person came even with Loyal's hiding place, continued slightly past it, then paused.

"Goddamn fog," a male voice said. The slapping foot-steps came back toward Loyal. He held his breath as they continued past the palm tree. Loyal risked a peek out just as the man passed. It was Bertrand, still in the robe, flip flops on his feet. In his left hand he carried a baseball bat.

.   .   .

An hour later Loyal was back home on Roosevelt Street. After Bertrand had walked away, he had waited another twenty minutes, then slunk back to his Altima and driven home. He was cold, frustrated, and more than a little embarrassed. He plugged in his phone and the drone batteries, wiped the drone down, and sat down in his recliner. Five minutes later he was back up. He changed for the gym, unplugged the phone, and drove to JK's.

Adelle was in her usual place at reception. The gym was busy. Loyal nodded to Adelle then spent the next hour on his circuit. Before he left the gym he approached reception.

"Hi Adelle."

"Hi Loyal."

"How's everything going?" Loyal said.

"About the same. Everyone is still in shock," Adelle said. "That annoying Detective Hammond was here earlier. He asked for a list of Lacey's clients."

"I suppose I was on that list?" Loyal said. Then seeing the look on Adelle's face he quickly added, "I would expect to be on it of course."

Adelle leaned over the counter and whispered "Are you still investigating? Do you want a copy of the list?"

She held out her hand and handed Loyal a piece of paper that had been folded multiple times. He palmed it.

"Thanks Adelle," he said. "And yes, I am."

Loyal unfolded the paper as soon as he was in his car. The list read:

- James Amberton 2765 Newland Court
- Loyal Truesdale 1761 Roosevelt Street #1
- Sonia Rosales 3616 Hillview Court
- Gladys Kramer 1435 Shorebird Lane

Loyal's eyes stopped and held on the address on Shorebird Lane. Perhaps this was a way past the locked gates?

The ringing of his phone interrupted Loyal's thoughts. He glanced at the screen and saw a number he did not recognize. He dismissed the call and returned to thoughts about Gladys Kramer and Shorebird Lane. Less than one minute later his phone pinged. Voicemail. Loyal contemplated his phone. He appreciated its usefulness, but disliked having what he considered to be an electronic leash. He tapped phone, then voicemail, and held his leash to his ear. Len Hammond's voice entered his head.

Mr. Truesdale. This is Detective Hammond of the Carlsbad Sheriff Department. I need to speak with you regarding an urgent matter. Please contact me immediately. Thank you.

Hammond rattled off his contact information and disconnected. "Asshole," Loyal thought as he deleted the voicemail. He looked at the list of Lacey's clients again. Hammond was undoubtedly working his way down the list, probably had started with Loyal, and was enjoying having the upper hand. There was no way Loyal was sitting down with Hammond without some type of representation. He spent a few minutes considering the best type. Union rep? Lawyer? He made a mental note to contact someone before the end of the workday. He returned to thinking about the client list and realized that starting with these names could be counterproductive. Hammond was clearly working on this angle and Loyal did not want to cross paths with him. He made the decision to start with Blomgren in Vista.

Loyal drove home to get prepared for surveillance. He google mapped Vista, and Blomgren's address specifically. A real estate site revealed that the home was a two bedroom, one and a half bath; 1,311 square feet. Unbelievably, the estimated value was over $400,000. Loyal did a double take when he noticed there was a large green section of the map very close to Blomgren's home. Another search quickly turned up Brengle Terrace Park. Loyal changed out of his workout clothes, putting on some cargo shorts and a faded Tommy Bahama. He placed some granola bars and a few water bottles into a backpack, hesitated, then added an apple and a banana. You never knew, he might actually eat the fruit. He gathered his PM9, the fully charged drone equipment, shouldered the backpack, and walked out the door. Loyal loaded his backpack and equipment into his Altima, sat down, and started the car. As he pressed play for the cd player he remembered that he was listening to the last disc of *Dark Sacred Night.* Rather than heading straight to the freeway, he turned North on Carlsbad Village Drive and drove to the Georgina Cole Library.

Trinity followed Loyal's progress from Batiquitos lagoon to his apartment. He was there less than ten minutes, then on the move again. His destination this time proved to be JK Gym. Perhaps this was the connection Trinity had been looking for. Bertrand's wife, Lacey, had worked at the gym. It was entirely possible that they knew each other, making Truesdale's interest in Lacey's murder personal rather than professional. Loyal's red dot stayed stationary for just over an hour, then returned to his apartment. Just as Loyal was arriving home on Roosevelt Street, Bertrand's red dot began to move. Trinity was curious about Loyal Truesdale, but Bertrand Roberts was her primary concern. She quickly slipped on her Keen Whisper Sandals, pulled a black ball cap onto her head, grabbed her purse and keys, and left the condo.

L oyal parked and walked into the spacious and airy building. Pre-heart-attack Loyal had not known much about libraries. He had met Angela at a poetry slam at The Dove Library, but that was about the extent of his library experience. Post-heart-attack Loyal was a frequent visitor to the library. Sandy, one of the green shirted librarians, had taken him under her wing. She smiled at him now, and waved him over to the information desk.

"Hi Loyal," Sandy said. She was 5'2" and petite. Her white blond hair, always perfectly coiffed, shone under the florescent lighting. Her quick smile revealed sparkling white teeth. "I have a few new authors for you to try. Have you finished the Connelly yet?"

"I'm on the last disc," Loyal smiled. "What have you got for me?"

"I have two authors I think you should try," Sandy said. "Both are prolific, so if you like them they can provide entertainment for you for quite some time." She reached down behind the counter and came up with two audio books. "James Lee Burke," she said handing him the first one, "and T. Jefferson Parker." She handed him the second. Loyal looked at the audio books. *Rain Gods,* was by James Lee Burke. He liked the look of the cover, a man in a hat and raincoat in the foreground, lightning striking in the background. The T. Jefferson Parker, *L.A. Outlaws,* looked interesting as well. The cover showed a dark figure walking down a stormy street.

"I'll take them," Loyal said, pulling out his library card.

Five minutes later Loyal was settled in the Altima and listening to the last disc of the Connelly novel. He drove North on Interstate 5 then transitioned onto Highway 78 East. He exited on Vista Village Drive, followed the instructions from Google maps, and soon found himself at the mouth of Blomgren's small cul-de-sac. Pressing stop on the car stereo, he turned onto the street and slowly drove past Blomgren's house. It was small and neat. There was a tiny patch of lawn in the front yard. No car in the driveway. As Loyal reached the base of the small street and began his u-turn he noticed a young mother and her two small children playing in the front yard of one of the houses. The woman looked up, saw the unfamiliar vehicle, and called her children to her. As Loyal drove away, he could see her in his rear view mirror. She stood, children's backs against her legs, an arm protectively around each child, watching him drive away. Loyal was disheartened by her response and wanted to turn back and tell her that he posed no danger. He wondered, as he drove away, about her reaction and the fear that permeated today's society.

Loyal's next destination was Brengle Terrace Park. He had noted a footpath linking Via Christina, the street that Via Pedro branched off of, to the park. In order to drive in and park, however, he had to loop around the majority of the open space and enter from a street called Vale Terrace. Loyal parked the Altima in the East end of the parking lot and walked once around the entire park. It was large and more hilly than he had expected. He found the footpath and saw that it was actually a gated easement for the city of Vista. The gate was low and easily climbable. The park had plenty of acreage. There was certainly space for Blomgren to exercise here. Loyal went back to his car and retrieved his drone. He chose to attach his tablet to the controller this time as it provided a larger viewing screen. He walked across the park and back up a hill to an empty area just past the Vista Garden Club Memorial Grove and Gardens. This area backed up to Via Pedro. He turned two 360's to calibrate the drone's compass and set the aircraft gently on the grass. Within moments it was operational and flying. Loyal flew a few passes around the area he was standing in, hovering the drone at twenty-five feet. He raised the altitude to 60 feet and directed the drone over Via Pedro. He located Blomgren's house and flew a few circles around it. He did not lower the drone or attempt to look in any windows. The memory of this morning's near disaster, Bertrand Roberts in his bathrobe and flip flops, baseball bat held casually in his left hand, was still fresh in his mind.

Loyal's phone vibrated, then rang in his shorts pocket. He paused the drone and pulled the phone out. Stella. Loyal quickly tapped return to home on the drone app, set the controller on the ground, and answered his daughter's call.

"Stella," Loyal said.

"Dad." She sounded upset.

"What's wrong?" Loyal asked, watching the drone land gently at his feet. He powered it off and turned his full attention to Stella.

"A Detective Hammond left me a message today," Stella said. "He says he needs to talk to me about an urgent matter."

"God damn it," Loyal said. "Don't call him back Stella. He called you to get to me. I'll handle Hammond."

"What is this all about, Dad?" Stella said.

"Can I come over tonight?" Loyal asked. "It's easier to explain in person."

He heard her sigh. She was still upset with him.

"Sure Dad," she said at last. "Come over around 6:30. We can have dinner."

"I'll be there," Loyal said and disconnected. He quickly made another call and set up an appointment in an hour's time. Loyal gathered his drone equipment and walked back across the park to the Altima. He stowed everything in the trunk, then sat in the driver's seat and chewed on a granola bar, thinking. Hammond had pushed too far this time. Loyal worked on setting his anger aside for the moment as he came up with a plan. When he had finished the granola bar and washed it down with water, he started his car and drove back towards Carlsbad.

19

L acey stood in the enormous kitchen of her new home on Shorebird Lane. She turned a slow circle, taking in once again the granite countertops and gleaming new appliances. It looked like a picture from a magazine. The home had been a wedding present from Bertrand. They had been married a week ago in Lake Tahoe and spent a few days there as a honeymoon. It had been just the two of them. Bertrand had planned everything. The only thing she had picked was her dress. In November, Bertrand had sent her dress shopping. He had made it clear that cost did not matter. Lacey had chosen an ivory colored floor-length dress with a sweetheart neckline and tiny lace cap sleeves. She had considered it an extravagance at $495. She had insisted that Bertrand not see it until their wedding day. She smiled now, remembering the look on his face when he had seen her in the dress.

Lacey still marveled at the way things had worked out. Bertrand was kind and generous, fit and active. He clearly adored her. Although he was nineteen years older than her, the age difference did not seem to matter. She had worried initially about physical intimacy, but that had come quickly once they had begun seeing each other. Being together felt natural, their bodies a perfect fit. Just thinking about him made her miss him and wish that he was here. Bertrand traveled frequently for business. He had left again this morning and would return in a few days time.

A noise behind her caused her to jump. She spun quickly and saw Liane standing in the doorway of the kitchen. She walked quickly to Liane and wrapped her arms around her twin sister. Liane giggled, then wiggled out of Lacey's arms. Her left thumb went immediately into her mouth, her right hand reaching towards her ear. Lacey caught Liane's right hand in her own, stopping its upward progress.

"Remember, no ear pulling," Lacey said.

Liane frowned around her left thumb.

"Do you like your new room?" Lacey said.

Liane nodded and tugged at Lacey, pulling her in the direction of Liane's new living area. The fact that Bertrand had agreed to allow Liane to live with them still astounded Lacey. He had given Liane two large rooms and a bathroom on the bottom floor of the new house. The bedroom was pale yellow with a window seat that faced the back yard and pool. The living room was pale green with many windows that filled the area with natural light. Two fluffy bean bag chairs faced a large television, a bookcase lined one wall. Liane wrapped her arms around Lacey and pulled her down into the beanbag, hard. Lacey held back the harsh rebuke that formed in her mouth. She looked at Liane for a long moment. Her sister was squirming into the bean bag cushion. Liane looked back at Lacey, then pulled her thumb out of her mouth for a moment to say, "TV."

Lacey laughed. "Ok, silly," she said as she grabbed the remote and turned the television on. SpongeBob Squarepants filled the screen; Liane's favorite show. Lacey looked at Liane, happily settled in the bean bag chair, thumb back in mouth, right hand tugging once again on her earlobe. How she wished she could go back in time and somehow prevent the accident that had forever changed her sister.

Lacey's phone rang, bringing her out of her memories and back to the present. She rose and ran to the kitchen where her iphone 3GS sat on the granite countertop. Another present from Bertrand.

"Hello," Lacey said.

"Lacey, it's John." The pharmacist sounded tired.

"Hi John," Lacey said. "Are you ok?"

"Can you come back to work Lacey?" John said. "I can't keep up with the volume and haven't found anyone to replace you yet."

"I'd like to John," Lacey said. "Bertrand is out of town. He'll be back on Friday. I'll see what we can work out."

"It would be for one year only, Lacey," John said. "I'm retiring at the end of 2011 and moving to Arizona."

"As long as we can find someone to be with Liane," Lacey said. "My mom is in a memory care facility in Escondido now."

"Ah, I'm sorry Lacey," John said.

"Me too," Lacey said, "but it is for the best. She needs constant care. Hang in there John, and I'll call you on Friday."

"Thanks Lacey," John said and he disconnected

20

L oyal parked outside the law offices of Smith, Horvath, and Lily ten minutes before his appointment. The law offices were located on Palomar Oaks Way, less than a ten minute drive from the Carlsbad Sheriff's Station. Loyal sat in his car for a few minutes. He had noticed a crunching sound coming from his shoes as he walked across the parking lot at the park. Removing his shoes he saw that the soles were populated by dozens of goat heads, the seed pod of a particularly vicious weed. He picked at the goat heads while trying to tamp down his anger at Hammond. The sneaky shit. Calling Stella had crossed the line. Loyal had years more experience than Hammond. Although they disliked each other intensely, Loyal had tried to stay out of Hammond's way. Hammond, conversely, seemed to search for ways to disrupt Loyal's life. Today, thought Loyal, Hammond was about to get schooled.

· · ·

Loyal exited his Altima and crossed the parking lot. He bypassed the elevator, choosing instead to walk up the two flights of stairs to the law firm's entrance. He entered the quiet office and said, "Detective Loyal Truesdale for Maynard Lily," to the receptionist. She was in her mid fifties with short gray hair and sharp green eyes. She smiled at Loyal.

"Have a seat Detective. I'll let Mr. Lily know that you are here." Loyal sat on one of the couches in the waiting room. He flipped through the magazines on the side table, but nothing held his interest. He sat quietly for a few minutes, then heard, "Loyal, great to see you," and turned his head to see Maynard Lily standing in front of him. Maynard was a giant of a man, at least 6'3", maybe slightly more. He was African American. His skin as black as night. His large head was completely bald and glowed in the soft light of the reception area. His voice was deep and full; what Loyal imagined God's voice would sound like booming down from the heavens. Loyal stood and reached out for Maynard's extended hand. They shook warmly.

"Hi Maynard," Loyal said. "Thank you for seeing me on such short notice."

"Sure, glad I had the time available," Maynard said. "Come on back to my office and we can talk."

Loyal followed Maynard down the hall and into his office on the right. Maynard settled his bulk behind the desk and indicated several chairs in front of the desk from which Loyal could choose. Loyal chose one and sat.

"So," Maynard said, "property or divorce?"

"Neither," Loyal said.

"Neither?" Maynard chuckled. "Loyal, I'm a divorce and real estate lawyer. You know that. I've helped you with both."

"I know," Loyal said. "I need your help on something else; a few hours of your time."

Maynard looked at Loyal for a long moment, then broke into a wide grin. "Ok, Loyal. I'll bite. Let's hear it."

Loyal gave a quick summary of his heart attack, placement on disability, and workouts with Lacey. When he spoke her name Maynard grimaced.

"Did you know her?" Loyal asked.

"Socially," Maynard said. "I represent her husband's company. Such a tragedy."

Loyal nodded. There were no words. He explained his relationship with Detective Hammond, and the fact that Hammond had reached out to Stella.

"I want you to come with me to the Sheriff's Department," he said to Maynard. "What's your hourly rate?" Loyal had stopped at the ATM on the way to the lawyer's office. He leaned forward in his seat, pulled his wallet out of his back pocket, and looked at the lawyer expectantly.

"For you, $200," Maynard said. "Minimum three hours," he added with a grin. Loyal counted off six bills and lay them on the desk. "Do you have time right now?" he asked. "I'd like to get this out of the way."

"Let's go," Maynard said.

.   .   .

Maynard Lily drew stares wherever he went and it was no different when he and Loyal entered the Sheriff's Department and walked up to reception. Fatima's eyes widened briefly, then she welcomed the two men and asked how she could be of help.

"Maynard Lily, Attorney-at-Law," Maynard said in his booming voice. "Please let Detective Hammond know that my client," he nodded his massive head toward Loyal, "and I are here to see him."

Fatima glanced at Loyal, who smiled at her and gave her a tiny wink. Fatima smiled, picked up the phone, and dialed Hammond's extension. After a brief pause she said, "Detective, there is an attorney in reception who would like to speak with you." She listened a moment, hung up the phone, and said to Maynard, "He'll be right down."

Two minutes later Hammond came down the stairs. He paused a moment when he saw Maynard and Loyal, then stepped forward to greet them.

"Detective Hammond," Maynard said, "my client has advised me that you requested a meeting with him."

"Yes," began Hammond, but Maynard continued. "We request that Captain Williams be present during our conversation with you."

Hammond's eyes narrowed, then he turned to Fatima. "Call the Captain. Ask him to meet us in Interview Room One. And issue these men visitor badges." He waited while she gave them the badges, then turned away from Loyal and Maynard saying, "Follow me." They followed

Hammond through a door, entering a long hallway. Hammond opened a door on the left, pushed a small button on the wall, and led them in. Loyal looked up above the door once they had entered and saw the small red light that indicated they were being recorded.

"I assume this meeting is being recorded," Maynard said, following Loyal's glance.

"You assume correctly," Hammond said. He waved at the chairs on the opposite side of the table. "Have a seat." Loyal and Maynard sat. Hammond opened the door and stepped out. He returned a moment later with an unhappy looking Captain Williams, who greeted Loyal and Maynard, then sat. Hammond sat as well.

Hammond began by reciting the date, time, and occupants of the room for the record. He then turned to Loyal.

"Mr. Truesdale, what is the nature of your relationship with Mrs. Lacey Barnett-Roberts?"

Maynard jumped in. "Can you clarify the term relationship Detective?"

Hammond tensed. "Are you acquainted with Mrs. Lacey Barnett-Roberts Mr. Truesdale?" he asked.

Maynard interrupted. "Please refer to my client as Detective."

Hammond glanced at the Captain, who gave a slight nod. Hammond then repeated his question addressing Loyal as Detective Truesdale.

"Yes," Loyal answered.

"How did you come to know Mrs. Roberts?" Hammond

asked.

"She is my personal trainer at the gym," Loyal answered.

"Why do you need a personal trainer?" Hammond asked.

Maynard jumped in. "That is not relevant. My client does not have to answer."

"Have you ever spent time with Mrs. Roberts outside of the gym?" Hammond asked instead.

"Never," Loyal answered.

"Captain Williams," Maynard said, "is this how you are interviewing all of Mrs. Barnett-Roberts' clients? I seriously doubt it. It seems to me my client is being singled out by Detective Hammond." He looked at Hammond. "Are you contacting relatives of her other clients as well? Be advised that Stella Truesdale has also retained my services. Any further communication with her or Detective Truesdale is to be done through me." He turned to the Captain again. "Are we done here?"

Loyal looked at Captain Williams. He knew the man well, knew his tells when he was angry. At the moment his lower left eyelid was twitching ever so slightly. Loyal had seen that twitch before, had caused it on a few occasions. Captain Williams was furious.

"Yes, I think we are," Captain Williams replied to Maynard. "Thank you to both of you for making the time to come down to the station." He rose, looked briefly at Hammond, then left the room. Loyal glanced up and saw that the red light was no longer glowing. Hammond followed his glance, then leaned over the table towards Loyal.

"You better watch your back Truesdale," he said.

"Are you threatening my client?" Maynard said.

"Take it any way you want to," Hammond said, straightening. He led Loyal and Maynard back to reception and walked away without another word. Loyal and Maynard returned their visitor badges and said goodbye to Fatima. She smiled and waved goodbye to them. The two men exited the Station and returned to Loyal's car.

As they pulled out of the parking lot, Loyal thanked Maynard for coming with him.

"It's a good thing you brought me," Maynard said. "That Hammond hates you." He reached in his shirt pocket and brought out a small digital recorder. "He threatened you Loyal." Maynard pushed a button and Hammond's voice filled the car.

"You better watch your back Truesdale."

Maynard turned the recorder off and placed it in the drink holder of the Altima. "There's a little insurance for you," he said. Loyal smiled then picked up the tiny recorder and handed it back to the lawyer.

"Could you hang onto it for me?"

21

LOYAL TRUESDALE

L oyal returned home after dropping Maynard at his office. He showered and dressed in fresh slacks and a clean Tommy Bahama. He picked up the nearly empty 750 of bourbon and went out the front door. He walked down the stairs to his garage, opened the lock, and put the bourbon back where he had found it on Monday. He knew that he would be sorely tempted to get it back out when he returned from Stella's this evening. He wasn't making any firm decisions at the moment, he'd cross that bridge when he came to it.

It was 5:15. He wasn't due to Stella's until 6:30. Loyal was hungry and very tired. The early hungover start to his day, hiding from Bertrand, the time spent in Vista, and his meeting with Hammond had sapped his energy. He decided on a protein drink to take the edge off until dinner at Stella's. He set the kitchen timer for 45 minutes so he wouldn't be late for dinner and sat down at the kitchen table. While he sipped he perused the footage taken at Blomgren's house and the neighboring park. Unlike the fog this morning at Bertrand Roberts' house, the sun was shining brightly in the footage from Blomgren's house. Loyal watched as the drone circled the park where he had been standing. Initially it flew at a lower altitude, then ascended to 60 feet and flew toward Blomgren's house. He saw the young mother in her front yard playing with her two children. He felt sad again that his mere presence had been frightening to her. He thought about Stella and wondered if becoming a mother would make her more frightened of the world around her. He supposed it might. She'd have someone to protect.

Loyal returned to the footage. The drone was circling Blomgren's house. Loyal always set his camera to 60 frames per second. Mitch had taught him this trick. This technique allowed him to slow the footage down without getting a choppy effect. He slowed the action now so he could get a better look at the house and back yard. The house on Via Pedro was small, with a postage stamp front lawn, a small cement patio in the back yard sporting a table and a barbecue, and a small metal shed in the corner of the yard. The shed had an array of antennas on it. Loyal had seen antennas like this before. He paused the footage and tried to think where he had seen them. The answer hovered just out of reach. As he reached out to resume the footage his kitchen timer pinged. Loyal turned off the electronics, switched on the outside light for when he returned, and left for Stella's.

As he drove Loyal replayed the events at the Sheriff's Department in his mind. He thought about Captain Williams' anger and wondered what he had said to Hammond after they had left. The Captain knew that Loyal hadn't killed Lacey, surely Hammond knew this as well. Hammond was yanking Loyal's chain, spending time on a dead end, possibly hampering the investigation. Loyal made a mental list of all the players as he drove. Blomgren was a suspect; why was he there that morning? Lacey's husband was a suspect; he'd searched for Loyal with a baseball bat in his hand. Who else? Again Loyal felt the absence of his badge and the resources of the Sheriff's Department. He knew he was missing something, which made him angry, which in turn caused him to miss things. He was caught on a spinning carousel. He needed to get off.

Loyal parked on the street outside Stella's condo. He had his own gate key, so he let himself in and proceeded to her door. Usually he would just walk into her home, but had felt the tension between them on the phone, so he knocked. Mitch opened the door. "Hey Loyal," he said, "you don't have to knock." He stepped aside so Loyal could enter and closed the door behind them. Loyal inhaled deeply through his nose.

"It smells amazing in here," he said.

"Stella's making a stir fry," Mitch said. "Go say hello."

Loyal stepped around the corner and into the tiny kitchen. Stella was at the stove, her long hair pulled up into a messy bun, stray strands hanging down. She looked at him and smiled.

"Hi Dad," she said. Loyal stepped up to the stove and looped an arm around her shoulders. He leaned down and kissed her cheek.

"Hey there kiddo," he said. "Smells great."

"It's ready," Stella said. "Grab a plate and let's eat."

They sat at the dining room table and ate. Between bites Loyal explained about Lacey's death and Hammond's scrutiny. He gave Stella Maynard Lily's business card and instructed her to contact the lawyer if Hammond called her again. After dinner, Mitch cleaned up the kitchen while Stella and Loyal talked. He apologized again for the marriage comment. Stella thanked him for the gifts and card which had arrived that afternoon. Loyal felt the tension roll off of him. He and Stella rarely disagreed.

"There's something I need to talk to you about Dad," Stella said as they rose from the table. She walked over to a glass cabinet, opened one of the doors, and removed a white envelope. She sat on the couch and patted the space next to her. As Loyal sat down she removed something from the envelope.

"Grandma gave me these," she said as she lay three pictures on the coffee table. Loyal looked and felt his gut clench. The first picture was a wedding picture from his first marriage. He and Michelle looked so young. The second was Michelle, very pregnant, beaming at the camera. The third was Michelle holding baby Stella. Loyal looked, saying nothing, as memories flooded his mind.

"I want to know about her," Stella said.

"I don't want to talk about her," Loyal said.

"I'm going to be a mother Dad, I want to know about my own."

"She's gone, Stella. She left us. There's nothing more to say," Loyal said as he rose. "I've got to go."

"Wait, Dad. Please. I carry her DNA and my child will too. Please."

"No Stella," Loyal said. He walked out of the condo without another word.

John locked the pharmacy door and returned to the cash register. He reached under the counter and pulled out a bottle of wine and two glasses.

"Join me for a drink on our last day working together?" he asked Lacey with a small smile.

"Certainly," Lacey said. "What a nice surprise."

John poured and they each sipped, a companionable silence enfolding them. There wasn't anything left to say. John had sold to a chain pharmacy and was leaving in one week to start his life in Arizona. Lacey planned to take time with Bertrand and Liane. Each had promised to keep in touch.

An hour later Lacey pulled her Infinity G37 into her driveway on Shorebird Lane. The car had been another gift from Bertrand, who was away on business yet again.

Lacey let herself in the front door. The house was quiet. She found Gladys Kramer in the kitchen reading a book.

"How was she?" Lacey asked her neighbor.

"She did real well," Gladys responded. "Spent most of the day painting."

Gladys stood and stretched. She was seventy-four years old, energetic and spry, and lived next door to Lacey. When Lacey had gone back to working at the pharmacy she had hired Gladys to be with Liane.

"Come see what she is working on," Gladys said as she walked toward Liane's living room. Lacey followed. An easel was set up near the windows. Books on local wildlife littered the floor. Lacey still marveled that Gladys, a retired art teacher from San Diego State University with a Masters Degree in Art History, had helped Liane discover her hidden talent; painting.

"Its a godwit," Gladys whispered. Blue water was the background for the leggy bird with a long slender bill. Brown marbled feathers rested on a cream colored body. The bird leaned slightly forward, bill in the water, as if searching for a morsel below the surface.

"It is beautiful," Lacey said.

Lacey walked Gladys to the door and watched until the older woman was safely in her own home. She locked the front door and went back to peek at Liane. Her twin was sleeping soundly, thumb in mouth. On her way out of Liane's rooms Lacey stopped at the painting again. What a miracle that Gladys had unearthed this gift; something that Liane could do independently and well. Although completely unorganized in the rest of her life, Liane was meticulous with her art supplies. This fact gave Lacey the smallest glimmer of hope that perhaps, someday, Liane would be able to live a more full life. With a small sigh Lacey left Liane's rooms, scaled the stairs, and entered her empty bedroom.

T rinity had followed Bertrand to his Real Estate office in La Jolla. She watched as he parked and walked toward the small building. Bertrand specialized in high end real estate deals across the Western United States. His office might be small, but the amount of money that moved through it was huge. She noted the change in him since his young wife's brutal murder. The slower pace, shoulders rounded as if they were carrying a heavy burden, eyes downcast. Trinity had many feelings about Bertrand Roberts, most of them negative. At this moment, however, as she watched him unlock the door and enter his office, she allowed a tiny bit of sympathy to trickle into the mix.

Trinity left La Jolla and drove to the lot in Carlsbad that had delivered the Mercedes to the airport. She spent about half an hour with the young man at the counter, then drove away in a charcoal gray Toyota Camry. She returned to La Jolla and parked in metered parking across the street from Bertrand's office. She racked the seat back to its farthest position, giving her long legs some much needed room. Glancing at the tracking app on her phone, she saw that Loyal was now parked in front of a law office in Carlsbad. As she reviewed his track, she saw that he had spent several hours in Vista, most of the time at a local park. She mentally flipped through all of her notes since Lacey's death. Vista rang a bell but she couldn't remember why. She eased her mind away from the problem, it would come to her in time.

Trinity's employer had access to many databases, some legally approved and some not. Opening her computer, she used a backdoor access code to view Bertrand's communication with the charter company that owned the business jet he used frequently. She saw that he would be flying the following day. This did not surprise her, as Bertrand traveled frequently. What did surprise her was the location where he would be stopping for an hour and then re-boarding.

L oyal was angry. Why now, after all these years, did Stella want to dredge up old memories? Why had his mother given Stella those pictures? And when? She had been dead for years. Loyal paced and fumed. The bourbon was calling him. He had driven home from Stella's and raced up the stairs before he had a chance to open the garage. Now he was drinking Bengal Spice tea, tired beyond belief, yet unable to sleep. He finally gave up on the idea of slumber and decided instead to review the drone footage from Bertrand Roberts' and Donald Blomgren's homes. The foggy footage revealed little. The sister holding the paintbrush and Roberts spotting the drone. Opening his phone, Loyal studied the picture he had taken of the back of Roberts' house. He zoomed in on the exposed balcony and saw an antenna array there that he hadn't noticed before. He reviewed the drone footage from Blomgren's house. The antennas on the shed looked very similar to the antennas on the house on Shorebird Lane. He remembered now where he had seen something similar. It was last August, at Maggie Macphearson's house. He should call her. He wondered if she would even answer his call. He looked at his phone, saw that it was 4:57 AM, and decided this probably wasn't a good time to call.

Loyal inserted the USB containing the murder book into his computer and read through the file again. Blomgren bothered him. Why Batiquitos Lagoon on such a dense foggy morning when there was a perfectly good park across the street from his house? Loyal ejected the USB and held the small red piece of plastic in his hand. A surge of anger flowed through his body. Why Lacey? Why such a brutal attack? What was he missing? Impulsively, Loyal exited his apartment and charged down the stairs to his garage. He opened the door, stepped inside, and quickly closed it again. He grabbed a shop rag and his hammer, wrapped the USB in the cloth, knelt over it on the floor, and smashed it with the hammer. He pounded and pounded, his rage driving the hammer fiercely down over and over again. Finally, rage spent, he sat back on his heels and fought to control his breathing. After a few moments, Loyal picked up the rag, exited the garage, and dropped the cloth and destroyed USB in the dumpster. He walked slowly up the stairs and back into his apartment. He looked at his shaking hands and realized he was still holding the hammer. He set it gently on the kitchen table. He needed to move, to act, to be on the offensive.

Fifteen minutes later Loyal was dressed in loose cargo shorts, a faded Tommy Bahama, and tennis shoes. He packed some snacks and water bottles into a soft cooler, gathered his drone, phone, PM9, and tablet, and walked down to the Altima. It was 5:45, the magical time between night and dawn, the faint glow of the sun barely visible to the East, a clear sky with no fog or clouds. Loyal drove slowly through the nearly empty streets. He eased onto Interstate 5 heading North, then transitioned to Highway 78 heading East. He drove to Via Pedro and noted the white Rubicon in Blomgren's driveway. The house was dark. Via Pedro was a short street that hooked onto Via Christina, which in turn connected to Foothill drive. Foothill ran East and West. To the East it connected with East Vista Way and then to the 78. To the West was a maze of residential neighborhoods. Loyal considered his options and turned left on Foothill. He filled the Altima's tank at a Chevron station, and then parked at the Del Taco on East Vista Way. He angled the Altima so he could see the intersection with Foothill and settled in to wait.

Loyal kept his eyes on the intersection, but let his mind wander into the past. The logical side of his brain understood Stella's desire to know more about her mother. The emotional side was another story. Michelle had left them. She had chosen drugs and booze over family. That was over thirty years ago. Loyal doubted Michelle was even still alive. He supposed he owed Stella something. Just as he was solidifying this decision, the white Rubicon appeared at the intersection. Loyal jolted up, started the Altima, and eased into traffic a few cars behind Blomgren. Traffic was heavy. A glance at the dashboard informed Loyal that the time was 7:18. The Jeep stood out and was easy to follow. Blomgren led Loyal West on the 78, then North on the 5.

Plentiful winter rains had ended, for the moment, California's drought. On the heels of the wet winter had come super bloom spring. A green and yellow quilt blanketed the rolling hills of Camp Pendleton Marine Corps Base. As traffic slowed even further through the Border Patrol checkpoint, Loyal had time to admire nature's artwork. He thought of Lacey's sister holding the paintbrush and wondered what she painted. Just past San Clemente traffic started moving. Loyal stayed several car lengths behind the white Rubicon. As he drove he let his mind wander freely. He found himself wondering about Blomgren's financial status. Hammond's report had listed him as ex-military. The Rubicon was an expensive vehicle. How had Blomgren afforded the house in Vista? How was he currently earning money? The more he thought about it, the stronger Loyal's suspicions grew. Nothing about Blomgren made any sense.

Loyal followed as the white Rubicon merged onto the 405 North. Traffic flowed at around 50 mph. Loyal wondered if perhaps Blomgren was heading to Los Angeles International Airport. If he was taking a flight following would obviously become impossible. The exit for LAX came and went. Blomgren drove one lane to the right of the fast lane, steadily moving North. They passed Santa Monica, Westwood, and Bel Air, then merged onto the 101 West in Sherman Oaks. Forty-five minutes later Blomgren took the exit toward Ca 34, then merged onto E Daily Road. Traffic here was very light and Loyal dropped back a few more car lengths. Loyal followed as Blomgren turned into parking lot A for Port Hueneme State Beach. Blomgren purchased a parking pass from a vending machine then parked in the far Western corner of the parking lot. Loyal entered the parking lot, purchased an all day pass from the vending machine, then parked in the far Southern end of the parking lot, angled so that he could watch Blomgren. And the waiting began. Blomgren did not exit his vehicle. After almost 25 minutes had passed, and when Loyal was seriously debating walking over and knocking on the guy's window, a white Toyota Corolla pulled swiftly into the parking lot, bypassed the vending machine, and pulled up next to Blomgren's Jeep. The driver of the Corolla, a man wearing a ball cap and dark sunglasses, exited the vehicle. Blomgren exited his Jeep at the same time, joined the Corolla's driver, and together they walked toward the Port Hueneme Pier. Loyal studied the two men. There was something familiar about the Corolla driver. It hovered just out of his mind's reach.

Movement to his right caught Loyal's attention and he turned to see a charcoal gray Toyota Camry enter the parking lot. It parked in the Northern most edge of the parking lot and a woman slid out. She was tall and slender, wearing jeans, a black hoodie, and a black ball cap. A pair of binoculars swung from a strap around her graceful neck. Long ginger-cinnamon colored hair flowed out from beneath the cap and down her back like a copper river. From the driver's seat of the Altima, Loyal stared. Was this the same woman he had seen on the lagoon trail? Her body was lean and strong. She moved with purpose, her long legs eating up the parking lot pavement as she strode towards the water's edge. She stood still on the shoreline, raised the binoculars to her eyes, and looked toward the horizon. Loyal watched her for a long moment, then shook his head. It couldn't be the same woman.

During a case the previous June, Loyal had purchased three Spytech gl300 mini car trackers. He had solved the case without activating them, and they had sat in his glove box for the better part of a year. He had charged them the previous evening and activated them this morning. He grabbed two now and ambled over to the Jeep and Corolla. When he was between the two cars he casually dropped his keys. As he bent to retrieve them, he placed a tracker beneath each vehicle. He then turned and returned to the Altima.

Port Hueneme Pier was nearly 1000 feet long and reached well out into the Pacific Ocean. A few fishermen were scattered here and there along its length, but at just after 11:00 am on a Thursday in April it was fairly deserted. Loyal retrieved his drone from the trunk, attached the tablet, calibrated the compass, and launched. He set the altitude at 60 feet and flew first over the attractive woman who was still scanning the ocean, then slowly down the length of the pier. Blomgren and his mystery companion had walked the entire length of the wooden structure and were standing still, leaning against the railing and looking out to sea while they spoke. Loyal lowered the drone to forty feet and flew a long lazy circle, then lowered to thirty feet and circled again. He could tell the men's conversation was heating up. The Corolla driver was gesturing forcefully as he spoke. As Loyal executed another sweeping circle, the Corolla driver removed his hat and ran his left hand through his thick black hair. As he was replacing his cap he glanced up at the drone. Loyal took a quick breath in. He recognized the man now. The man in the cap and sunglasses was Lacey's husband, Bertrand Roberts.

Loyal hit return to home and moments later the drone landed softly at his feet. He looked at the pier and saw that Blomgren and Roberts had started walking back towards the shore. Loyal picked up the drone and walked to the Altima. He stowed his gear, then drove out of the parking lot. He took Surfside Drive to South Ventura Road, drove three blocks, then pulled into a crowded Wendy's parking lot and parked. He slid down as far as he could in the seat, eyes grazing the dashboard. He watched the tracker app and saw that both cars were in motion. Moments later the Corolla and the Rubicon glided slowly by. Loyal fell in behind them, leaving plenty of space. At West 5th Street Blomgren turned right and the Corolla turned left. Loyal stayed with the Corolla. A mile down the road the white vehicle turned and entered the Oxnard Airport.

25

The Corolla pulled in just past an Air Charter service and stopped at a monitored entrance. Loyal parked a distance away and watched as Bertrand showed ID to the guard and the gate opened. The Corolla drove directly onto the tarmac and parked near a large jet. Roberts exited the vehicle and handed the keys to a young man who jumped in the Corolla and drove it away. Loyal kept his eyes on Roberts, who was greeted by the pilot and quickly led on board. Loyal grabbed his note pad and jotted down the N number of the aircraft. He paused a moment, then snapped a photo with his phone. Maybe O'Keefe knew a way to track its destination. Loyal sat in the parking lot as the jet eased onto the runway, accelerated, and launched into the air. He kept his eyes on the white and blue bird as it ascended, the sun reflecting off its shiny exterior, until it was little more than a tiny spark in the blue sky; a blink of light, and it was gone.

. . .

The tracking app showed that the Corolla was driven a short distance, then ceased moving. Loyal realized it was a rental, and kicked himself for not waiting to install the tracker. In preparation for the long drive back to Carlsbad, Loyal fished Rain Gods out of the glove compartment. He inserted the first CD into the stereo and drove out of the parking lot. As he was turning onto West 5th street a charcoal gray Toyota Camry turned into the parking lot. Loyal caught a glimpse of a black ball cap and ginger-cinnamon hair. Loyal pulled into the parking lot for Southwest Community Park, which was located across the street from the airport. He parked so that he was facing the airport and watched as the mysterious woman pulled up to the monitored gate, presented ID, and gained admittance. Loyal's eyes remained on her as she pulled along side a business jet, stepped out of the Camry, and handed her keys to the same young man who had removed Roberts' rental. The pilot of the jet was waiting by the jet's stairs. He escorted the leggy beauty onto the plane. Loyal noted the N number, snapped a picture with his phone, and watched as the plane rose into the clear blue sky. In the same fashion as the previous jet, it twinkled, blinked, and disappeared from sight.

Loyal stayed in the park's parking lot for a short time after the second jet vanished into the ether. He ejected the CD and sat in the quiet of the Altima processing what he had just witnessed. Roberts and Blomgren knew each other. He pondered the nature of the relationship between Lacey's husband and the man who had discovered her battered body. He had no ideas about the mystery woman, but did not believe in coincidences, and was convinced she was somehow connected. Loyal felt the familiar surge, the excitement of the hunt, for the first time since his heart attack. He turned his left hand over so the palm faced him. The scar was faded, but visible. It tracked across his palm, from the base of the thumb to the base of his smallest finger. An arrest many years ago had turned ugly when the suspect pulled a knife. Loyal's Training Officer had tackled the perp, but not before he had slashed Loyal's palm deeply, nearly severing his smallest finger. During the recovery necessary following the surgery to restore full use of his hand, Loyal had realized that if something were to happen to him Stella would be, for all intents and purposes, an orphan. In that moment Loyal had felt his first jolt of true fear. Determined never to feel that way again, he had started taking Jiu Jitsu self defense classes, eventually attaining the level of brown belt. As he studied the faint white line that crossed his palm, Loyal realized that his heart attack had reintroduced fear into his life. He glanced at his own eyes in the rearview mirror; he was taking his life back.

The drive back to his apartment on Roosevelt Street took just over four hours. Loyal restarted the CD and listened the entire drive home. For those four hours he was transported to a dusty town in Texas where evil forces conspired against the good. Loyal parked in front of his garage. He listened for ten minutes more, stopping the CD at the end of the chapter. James Lee Burke was a winner. He'd thank Sandy next time he was at the library.

The black escalade pulled to a stop in front of the house on Shorebird Lane. It was just past midnight and Lacey and Bertrand were returning home from yet another event. This evening's offering had been the KPBS Celebrates Gala; the theme Downton Abbey. Lacey was wearing a floor length, sleeveless red sheath. Long white gloves covered her hands and arms. She was in the process of removing the gloves, plucking at the tips of her fingers to pull them off. Bertrand turned off the engine but made no move to exit the vehicle.

"What is it Lacey?" he said. "You didn't speak the whole way home."

"I've been telling you for months now," Lacey said, "you don't listen. I need more than parties and fancy clothes. You are gone all the time and Liane is always with Gladys. I want to work, even if it is only part time."

"Lacey, I need you available for me," Bertrand said. "I

can't go to these events alone. Besides, I miss you. I want to be with you as much as possible when I'm home."

"I need something Bertrand. I'm going crazy," Lacey said. "Joe at JK Gym is offering me a part time job as a personal trainer. I already got my certificate. I'll only work a few hours in the morning."

Bertrand ran his fingers through his thick black hair, saying nothing.

"I'm taking the job," Lacey said as she pushed her door open and stepped out. "Whether you like it or not."

27

L oyal sat at his dining room table, salad and a glass bottle of Perrier to his right, and studied his notes. What was the connection between Blomgren and Bertrand Roberts? Who was that woman with the fiery hair? He went back to Lacey's employee file. She listed only one reference; John Herrera from the pharmacy. An address in Prescott, Arizona was listed, along with a phone number. Loyal glanced at his phone. 5:20. Not too late to call. He dialed, listened to ringing and a generic voicemail prompt, then left a message indicating he wanted to talk about Lacey, and reciting both his name and phone number. He texted O'Keefe, hoping his wife wouldn't mind, asking if he had time to meet up tonight. O'Keefe's affirmative response came quickly. He suggested Grand Avenue Bar and Grill in Carlsbad at 8:00. Loyal agreed.

· · ·

Loyal finished his salad and water, rinsed the dishes, then went into his bedroom. He opened his closet and pulled out his gi, the traditional outfit worn when practicing jiu jitsu. Loyal removed the clothing he had worn throughout the day and put on his gi. He returned to the living room, pushed the recliner and side table to the wall, and spent the next thirty minutes going through his solo jiu jitsu routine. He was rusty. Some of the moves felt clumsy, especially the rolls. Loyal kept at it and was pleased that it all came back fairly quickly, his muscles falling right back into the familiar patterns. He was getting his old life back and if felt good.

Loyal showered, dressed in slacks and a Tommy Bahama, and headed out to meet O'Keefe. He arrived a few minutes after 8:00 and found O'Keefe seated in a booth at the back of the restaurant, a glass of pale ale in front of him. Loyal slid in opposite O'Keefe. A waitress appeared immediately, took Loyal's order and dropped the cold beer off quickly.

"Thanks for meeting me Pat," Loyal said.

"I've only got about half an hour," O'Keefe said. "I don't know if I told you, Olive is pregnant again and wants me home at night."

"Congratulations," Loyal said. "This shouldn't take too long. Do you know if there is a way to look up N numbers from aircraft to see who the owners are? Also wondering if there is a way to access flight plans to see where planes are going?"

"Yeah, that's pretty easy," Pat said as he stood. "Let me

borrow a pen from the waitress and I can walk you through it.

Pat returned moments later with a pen. He sat and took a long swig from his beer. He swallowed slowly while he wrote some things on a napkin then turned it so Loyal could see what he had written.

"Your best bet for tracking flights currently in the air in California, and parts of Arizona and Nevada, is thebaldgeek.net," he said. "Just Google the site and play around with it for a while. You'll see what I mean. If you just want to look up an N number, go to this FAA site." He pointed to the next line he had written, registry.FAA.gov. "This one is simple, just enter the N number and you will see the details about the plane and owner."

"Thanks Pat," Loyal said as he folded and pocketed the napkin. "I appreciate you coming out tonight. Don't worry about the check," Loyal said as he noticed Pat looking for the waitress. "It's the least I can do. Give Olive a hug for me."

"Will do," Pat said as he stood. "You making any progress on the case? Hammond is next to impossible to be around. I don't think I've ever seen him as angry as he was after your "interview"." He made air quotes as he said the word interview.

"Yeah, I could tell he was mad," Loyal said." Not much progress yet." Loyal paused, then added, "I'd sure love to get my hands on evidence and autopsy reports."

"I'll see what I can do," Pat said.

"Don't put yourself in a bad position," Loyal cautioned.

An hour later, wearing T shirt and sweatpants, Loyal could be found at his kitchen table, laptop open in front of him. He started with the FAA registry, which was as simple as O'Keefe had indicated. He entered the N number from the plane Bertrand had boarded and received results immediately. The plane was a Gulfstream G550. Loyal Google-imaged the plane and found a YouTube video by AINtv. He learned that, along with leather seats, wide windows, and wine refrigerator, the G550 was ideal for long flights and landings on short, high elevation runways. Loyal clicked back to the FAA registry. The Gulfstream was owned by Blackstock LLC. Loyal was not familiar with this corporation and made a note to research it.

Loyal entered the second N number into the registry system. A Lear 35. He watched a YouTube on this business jet. It was smaller and older than the Gulfstream, but still way above Loyal's pay grade. The mystery woman, he was debating calling her Ginger or Cinnamon because of her hair, was flying in style. Back at the FAA registry he received a shock when the plane's owner was revealed. Loyal closed his laptop, leaned back in the hard wooden chair, and ran the fingers of his right hand along his jaw. While Loyal knew precious little about Bertrand, he was aware that the man owned B.Roberts Realty, a company that specialized in high end properties. Who the hell was

Ginger/Cinnamon? And why was she being flown by this entity?

Loyal pondered these things and, getting nowhere, moved onto thebaldgeek.net. Straightening and re-opening the laptop, he accessed the site. The home page sported a photo of the bald geek, a guy named Ben. He sat, looking straight at the camera, arms folded across his chest. His T shirt sported the message *I Void Warranties*. Loyal smiled, he liked this guy already. Baldgeek was more complex then the FAA registry page, as Pat had suggested at the restaurant. Loyal read the list of choices then clicked on *aircraft*. He read the new page that popped up carefully, then clicked on *flight air map*. Up popped a map of Southern California, and moments later the screen was populated by tiny black aircraft that represented all flights currently in the air. Loyal found he could hover over a tiny plane and its N number, and flight plan if available, would be revealed. He also learned, by clicking on *explore*, then *aircraft types*, that he could search by type of plane. He searched Gulfstream G550, and found the N number of Bertrand's ride. It had landed in South Lake Tahoe this afternoon. He searched Lear 35 and found Ginger/Cinnamon's jet had landed in Tahoe as well, about ten minutes before Bertrand's.

28

L oyal woke on Friday morning feeling rested and ready for action. He dressed in exercise clothes, blended a quick smoothie, and drank it as he drove to JK's. He completed his circuit and stopped briefly at the front desk to speak with Adelle. She informed him that Lacey's funeral was the next day. She wrote down the address of the church, and the time of the service. Loyal promised he would be there.

Returning home, Loyal showered and dressed in slacks and a Tommy Bahama. He sat at the kitchen table, planning to make some phone calls and to review all the information he had collected thus far. His first call was to Maggie MacPhearson. Loyal had driven to Maggie's house in Valley Center the previous August hoping to interview her. She had not been home, but he had walked the perimeter of her house and noticed an antenna array similar to what he had seen at Bertrand's and Blomgren's. He had questions and hoped that she had answers. Actually, he hoped she would just answer the phone. He dialed, and was pleasantly surprised when she answered with, "This is Maggie."

"Mrs. Macphearson, it is Detective Truesdale. We met briefly last Summer."

"Yes Detective, I remember you," Maggie said.

"I was wondering if I could ask you some questions about antennas," Loyal said. "It is in regard to a new case I'm investigating."

"I'm not sure how much help I can be Detective," Maggie said. "But I'm happy to help if I can."

"Could we meet?" Loyal asked. "I have some pictures I'd like to show you."

"I have some time this morning," Maggie said. "Can you come to me in Valley Center?"

"Absolutely," Loyal said. He listened as she gave him the directions he already knew, told her he would be there in a little over an hour, grabbed his phone and tablet, and headed out the door.

The drive to Valley Center took Loyal along the outskirts of Escondido. He thought about Lacey's mother in the memory care home, and decided he would stop there on the way home. He reached Maggie's house, which was located at the end of a long dirt road, in just over an hour.

She came out of the front door as he drove up, and greeted him as he exited his Altima.

"Hello Detective," She said as she extended her right hand.

He grasped her hand and shook. "Hello. Thanks for agreeing to see me."

"As long as we don't talk about last Summer," She said with a wide smile.

"All I'm going to say is that you look much happier and healthier than you did in August," Loyal said. "I hope that didn't come off as rude," he added as an afterthought.

She smiled again. "No offense taken. You look about twenty pounds lighter yourself, no offense intended." She laughed, then added, "Come on inside." She turned toward her house and he followed her to the front door. She turned her head towards him as she reached for the knob.

"I have a dog now. He's very protective, but also very well trained. He won't hurt you."

She opened the door and he followed her into the house, then stopped. A giant black and tan German Shepherd was sitting on its haunches in the entryway. It looked at him with intelligent deep brown eyes, its head cocked slightly to the right.

"Storm, stay," Maggie said. "It is okay Detective," she said motioning Loyal forward into the living room.

Loyal walked past the watchful canine and sat on the faded brown couch Maggie had indicated with a wave of her hand. Maggie sat beside him. Storm settled at her feet, and both looked at Loyal expectantly. "How can I help?" Maggie said. Loyal showed her the picture of Bertrand's antenna array on his phone, then the drone video of Blomgren's similar array on the tablet. "Can you tell me anything about what these antenna might be used for?" he asked. Maggie studied the images a second time, then a third. "I can give you some basic parameters," she said as she stood. "Come on into the radio room and I'll explain as best I can." She led Loyal into a room filled with radio equipment. He stood still, taking it all in, while she pushed a few buttons and toggled a few switches. Green, red, and yellow lights blinked on. A table, approximately 4' x 8', was against one wall of the small room. It was full of what Loyal assumed was radio equipment. Additional black boxes were stacked on one side of the table. Maggie sat in the chair in front of the table and indicated a similar chair slightly behind and to the right of her. Loyal sat. Maggie reached down beneath the table and retrieved a few antenna of different lengths. "Ok," she said, "antenna lesson 101. First thing, antenna size matters. Antenna are made in different lengths to serve different purposes. A short one like this," she held up a four and a quarter inch antenna, "is used on UHF. A longer one like this," she held up another approximately 19 and 1/4 inches in length, "will pick up radio waves on VHF."

Loyal said nothing. Maggie waited a beat then said, "Radio waves are on a spectrum Detective. Different length antenna receive different length waves. The antenna that you showed me are short, so, I'm guessing here, are UHF low, or federal bands. I can't be sure."

Loyal held up his hand. Maggie quieted and looked at him.

"I guess what I want to know is can these two people be talking to each other and is there a way I can listen?" he asked.

Maggie swiveled in her chair so that her back was to Loyal and began rooting around in a pile on the table.

"Yes," she said, "they absolutely can be talking to each other. What you need to know is the frequency they are talking on. Then you can listen."

Maggie swiveled back and handed Loyal a small box about the size of a deck of cards. A small antenna poked up from the top.

"This is a frequency counter," Maggie said. "You have to get close to the antennas and the frequency needs to be active, meaning someone needs to be using their radio. If you can manage that, the frequency counter will tell you what frequency they are using, then you can listen in. Do you think you can get close? Maybe peek in a window to see if the radio is being used?" Loyal looked at the small box in his hand and thought for a moment. "Yes," he said, "I think I can."

Lacey sat in her truck in the parking lot of JK's. She had finished with her clients for the day, but dreaded going back to the house on Shorebird Lane. Bertrand was traveling again, and all Liane wanted to do was paint, watch TV, or hang out at Gladys' house. Lacey called Gladys' cell phone.

"HI Lacey," Gladys said after two rings.

"Hi Gladys. How is everything going?"

"Great. We are at my house baking muffins," Gladys replied.

"That sounds fun," said Lacey. "Hey, do you mind if I go to the beach for a bit before I come home?"

"Sure," Gladys replied, "have fun."

Lacey sighed as she disconnected. She hated to admit it, but she was lonely. Going to the beach was simply a distraction. She had few friends besides her clients and

Gladys. She and Bertrand had been married over six years now. Her mother and Liane were well taken care of, as was she. Bertrand was an exciting man and she enjoyed her time with him when he was home. The problem was, he was gone a lot.

She started the Nissan Frontier Crew Cab, another gift from Bertrand, and exited the parking lot. When she looked in the rearview mirror she could see the fins and the tail of the surfboard she had purchased on a whim. She had watched some YouTubes about surfing, and read some blogs. Today, she decided, would be the day she would actually try.

Lacey drove to Swamis Beach in Encinitas and found a rare parking spot in the lot. She changed from her exercise clothes into her bathing suit in the cab of the truck, then hopped out and grabbed the board from the back of the truck. It was large and awkward to carry, but she managed to make it down the steep wooden stairs to the beach without incident. The beach was crowded on this hot Summer day. Lacey worked her way North and found a small spot of sand where she could sit. She carefully set the board down, spread out her towel, and sat down to gather her courage. She thought about the YouTubes she had watched. She understood about body position and center of gravity, had practiced cupping her hands to move water while she paddled out, as well as the motion of going from a prone position to a standing position. It all looked so easy.

Realizing that it was now or never, Lacey stood, grabbed her board and headed into the ocean. Twenty minutes later, disheveled and embarrassed, she was back on her towel. She had tipped over while paddling out, recovered, then simply fallen down every time she attempted to stand. She sat, watching surfers riding the waves, and felt tears threatening. She jumped when she heard a voice to her left.

"Don't give up, surfing is worth it."

She turned and found herself looking into big blue eyes. The man's hair was white blond, his face a deep tan.

"I can help you," he said.

Friday morning found Trinity, dressed casually, boarding the Lear 35 for the flight back to Carlsbad. She had tailed Bertrand around Lake Tahoe the previous evening. He had had several meetings with local big wigs, then a dinner with two hard hitting real estate agents. More of the usual for Bertrand. She found herself thinking about Truesdale. She had known he was heading for Point Hueneme, had watched his red tracker dot follow the same path she herself had been traveling. She had seen him watching her at the pier, and knew that he had seen her at the small airport. What she didn't know was who Bertrand and been meeting 1000 feet from shore on a pier above the Pacific Ocean. She had been paying too much attention to Truesdale, and neglected to snap a picture of the mystery man's license plate. She did recall he drove a white Rubicon, and she knew that Loyal had started his trip up the coastline from Vista. That thought about Vista was still niggling her mind. There was something to that.

There was also something to Loyal Truesdale. Trinity had to admire his tenacity. She was intrigued by him, wondered what he knew about this case, and was curious as well about his experience in Las Vegas the previous August. Her phone buzzed. She glanced at it and saw it was her immediate supervisor.

"Glass," she said as she accepted the call.

"You have anything new to report?" Douglas Caldwell didn't waste any time getting to the point.

"Nothing yet," said Trinity. "I'm close though, I can feel it."

"You know I try to give you as much freedom as possible," Caldwell said, "but I can't let this go on forever without solid results."

Trinity began to speak but Caldwell's voice overrode hers. "One week. That's it." The connection ended before Trinity could respond.

Less than two hours later Trinity's plane was on the ground in Carlsbad. She deplaned, located the new rental provided by her employer, and drove straight to the condo in La Costa. Once there, she took an extra long shower and then dressed in leggings and a T-shirt. She poured herself a large glass of sparkling water and settled down in front of her computer. She reviewed what she had written the previous evening regarding Bertrand's activities. More of the usual, nothing suspicious. Her mind wandered back to the Marine Room in La Jolla and Bertrand's meeting with Jack Williamson. That was suspicious. Trinity sat up straight, reached her arms toward the ceiling and stretched. Time to research SpaWar and Jack Williamson.

Loyal spent about an hour at Maggie's house in Valley Center. She had agreed to loan him Federal Government Frequency Assignments. This was a book he could look the frequency up in once he had gotten the frequency counter close to the antennas. As he was leaving she mentioned that Bruce and Winnie Meyers, who had lent Loyal a dune buggy the previous August, regularly ate breakfast on Saturday mornings at The Lake Wohlford Cafe. "Everyone arrives around 7:30," she had said. "You should come."

"That is a strong maybe," Loyal had replied. "I have a funeral to attend tomorrow, but it doesn't start until 1:00. I'll think about it."

Loyal thought about the invitation as he drove through Escondido towards the facility where Lacey's mother lived. The time spent with Maggie had been enjoyable and he would like to see Bruce and Winnie again. Loyal pulled up to Magnolia Manor and parked in visitors' parking. He entered the office and was greeted enthusiastically by a middle aged woman wearing a royal blue business suit. Her gray hair was closely cropped, her eyes a deep brown. "Hello!" She exclaimed. "Welcome to Magnolia Manor. I'm Deborah." She stood and leaned across the wooden desk behind which she was seated and held her hand out to Loyal. They shook, then she indicated several chairs on Loyal's side of the desk. "Have a seat. How can I help you?" she said. When Loyal explained that he was interested in visiting with Linda Barnett her smile faded. Ms. Barnett, Deborah explained, was in a locked ward and Loyal would need immediate family's permission to gain access to her. Loyal pushed back a bit, but Deborah was firm. No access without permission.

Loyal left Magnolia Manor and worked his way towards the 78 freeway. He drove home, grabbed the frequency counter from the passenger seat, retrieved a few tools from the garage, then took the stairs to his apartment. He had an idea and was excited to give it a try. Less than an hour later Loyal was back in the Altima and heading East on the 78. He drove back to Brengle Terrace Park. He parked and removed everything from the trunk. He walked back to the spot where he had previously flown his drone when doing reconnaissance on Donald Blomgren. Loyal took a moment to admire his clever handiwork. He had attached the frequency counter to his drone. The small screen where the frequency would be displayed was facing the drone's camera. Loyal had configured it so that he would still have half a screen of visuals so that he could steer the drone correctly. The frequency counter was very light and Loyal was hoping it would not affect flying performance adversely.

Loyal completed the drone's pre-flight activities and launched. The quadcopter flew fine, and soon was in the airspace above Blomgren's house. On the half screen Loyal could see the white Rubicon in the driveway. Blomgren was home. He flew above the house at 50 feet. The backyard looked empty. Loyal eased the drone down and peeked in the sliding glass doors. An empty living room was revealed. He piloted to the left and found himself looking in the kitchen window. Blomgren sat at the bar, his profile visible to Loyal. He was eating a sandwich. A radio sat on the bar as well. Blomgren was not using it. Loyal raised the drone up to sixty feet and flew a few passes around Via Pedro. He returned to Blomgren's house and dropped back down to the kitchen window. Blomgren had the radio in his hand and was listening intently. Loyal didn't hesitate, he simply flew the drone across Blomgren's backyard and hovered right above the antennas. The screen of the frequency counter, which cycled continuously, froze when it was near the antennas. Loyal memorized the numbers: 419.9750.

· · ·

Loyal tapped return to home and the drone landed softly at his feet moments later. He packed everything back into the Altima's trunk and drove home. He rushed up the stairs to his apartment, eager to look the frequency up in the book Maggie had let him borrow. He sat at his kitchen table and flipped the book open. He found the section near the back titled *Frequency Order*, and began the search for 419.9750. He ran his finger down the long columns of numbers; the 416 section, 417, 418, and finally 419. He found 419.8750 and 419.9250, then the number jumped to 462.3500. "What the hell?" Loyal muttered. Where was 419.9750? He leaned back in the chair and ran his hands through his shaggy hair, then leaned forward for his phone. He tapped the number for Maggie Macphearson, then leaned back and awaited her answer.

SpaWar, or Space and Naval Warfare Systems Command, had gone through numerous evolutions. Its new name, Trinity learned as she researched, would be Naval Information Warfare Systems, and would take effect this coming June. There were two centers in the United States, one in South Carolina, and one in San Diego. The San Diego center employed over 4,700 scientists, engineers, and support personnel. These folks were partnered with more than 200 active duty personnel and had worldwide connections and partnerships with private industry and academia. Currently SpaWar was housed in a huge building on 70 acres of prime real estate off Interstate 5 near the San Diego Airport. In October 2018 the navy had announced plans to renovate or redevelop the property, which was old and in disrepair. A request was issued to recruit possible private sector partners, as the navy had no budget to replace the building. The hope was that a developer would come up with a mixed use development concept and the navy would get a new SpaWar facility at free or reduced cost in exchange for providing a longterm lease for the current property.

Trinity rolled her shoulders, then stood and stretched her arms toward the ceiling. This information was interesting and could prove to be useful. Bertrand was likely working behind the scenes with Jack Williamson to land the lucrative contract. "Can I come at him from this angle?" she wondered out loud. She reached for her phone to check the tracking app. Truesdale had been active today. She traced his route from Valley Center, where he spent just over an hour, to Escondido where he stopped for less than fifteen minutes. Trinity checked the addresses. The house in Valley Center belonged to a Maggie Macphearson, while the address in Escondido was listed as Magnolia Manor, an assisted living and memory care facility. Loyal had returned home for a brief time, then proceeded to Vista, stopping at Brengle Terrace Park, where he spent over half an hour. Currently he was back home on Roosevelt Street. "Why do you keep going back to Vista?" she asked Loyal out loud. She next turned her attention to Bertrand's tracker. His movements all made sense. He had spent some time at a church in Carlsbad, likely taking care of last minute details concerning his wife's funeral the next day. Currently he was at home on Shorebird Lane.

· · ·

Trinity turned her attention back to her computer. Through her employer she had back door access to pretty much any information she wanted. This was one of the reasons Bertrand Roberts frustrated her so much. He had some impenetrable firewalls that she had yet to figure out a way to get around. At this moment, however, she was interested in Truesdale. Trinity decided to operate on the assumption that his interest in Bertrand Roberts was through his relationship with Bertrand's wife, Lacey. She hacked into the Carlsbad Sheriff's Department and downloaded Lacey Robert's murder book. As she read, she learned the relevance of Vista. Truesdale must be investigating the one witness, Blomgren.

L acey lay in the bed, her arm draped loosely over the warm body beside her. She breathed quietly and tried not to move for fear of waking him. His blond hair was long and tickled her nose, which she wiggled in an effort not to sneeze. It was 2:00 in the afternoon and she was at Van's apartment in Luecadia. They had been surfing together for nearly ten months, sleeping together for four. She had felt the tug of attraction the first time she had looked into his blue eyes. The pull had intensified as he gave her surfing lessons, her skin tingling each time he touched her to adjust her body position on the board. Lacey had tried to deny the attraction, but in the end had given in to it. She knew it was wrong and felt guilty about it every time she was with Bertrand.

She felt Van's body move and realized he was waking. He rolled over and wrapped his arms around her, pulling her close. Lacey breathed in deeply. How she loved the smell of his skin. She relaxed into him for a moment, then spoke the words they both dreaded. "I have to leave soon," she said.

"Please stay Lacey," Van said, "just a little longer."

"I can't," she said as she kissed his chest then raised up on one elbow and tenderly kissed his lips. She slid out of the bed and walked to the tiny bathroom. She showered quickly, dried, and slid back into her clothes. Van remained in the bed. She leaned over him and gave him one last kiss. Then turned and walked out the door.

On her way back to Shorebird Lane, Lacey stopped at the Chevron station just North of La Costa Avenue to fill the tank of her Toyota Tacoma, another present from Bertrand who had some big deal in the works and was rarely home. She went inside to pay, then returned and began fueling her truck. Just as she was replacing the gas cap she heard a voice beside her. "Hi Lacey." She flinched, then turned and found herself looking up into the dark eyes of Len Hammond. "You are a busy woman," he said, glancing at the surfboard in the back of her truck. "Your husband know how much you've been surfing?" Lacey quickly turned, slid into her truck and drove away. In the rearview she could see Len Hammond laughing and watching her, growing smaller as she increased the distance between them.

M aggie answered on the fourth ring. "This is Maggie," she said.

"It's Truesdale," said Loyal.

"Did you get the frequency?" Maggie asked.

"Yes," said Loyal. "It is 419.9750, but I can't find it in the book. The frequencies jump from 419.250 to 462.3500."

"Ah," said Maggie, "they are using an itinerant frequency."

"What does that mean?" asked Loyal.

"I'm trying to think of the best way to explain it," Maggie said with a sigh. "Think about the UHF spectrum as a whole object, divided into parts, which are the bands. Different portions of the band are assigned to different entities like FBI, CIA, Police and Fire, things like that. To keep transmissions from bleeding into each other, space is purposefully left between each assigned band. These guys are transmitting in that space."

"Ok," Loyal said slowly, "that makes sense. Why would they choose to use this particular portion of the band?"

"I can speculate that they don't want to be heard, and this is a section that most people rarely scan. It is right above the more secretive government agencies and right below the HAM radio band."

"Can I listen to them on the itinerant frequency?"

"Sure," Maggie said. "Shoot, I should have given you a radio to use. I don't suppose you have one?"

"Nope," said Loyal.

"Tell you what," Maggie said. "Come to breakfast tomorrow morning at the lake. I'll bring you a radio that will work in the range you are interested in, and show you how to use it."

"Ok," Loyal said. "I'll see you in the morning."

Loyal disconnected the call and sat still in the chair for a moment. A rumbling from his stomach reminded him that he had not yet eaten today. A quick glance at his phone informed him it was nearly 5:30. "Pizza Port," he said out loud. Pizza and a beer sounded really good and it was just a block away from his apartment so he could walk. He pocketed his keys and phone and headed out.

Ninety minutes, two slices, and one delicious beer later Loyal was back home. The entire time he was at Pizza Port he had been thinking about Ginger/Cinnamon. Who was she? How was she connected? He had seen her on the trail, then at Port Hueneme, then at the airport. She had to be involved with Bertrand somehow. And how had her plane taken off after Bretrand's yet landed in Tahoe a short time before him? Loyal looked at the tablet sitting on the table. He pulled it towards him and opened it up. He opened the footage taken at Port Hueneme. He slowed the footage down and watched as Ginger/Cinnamon came into view. He wished now that he had spent some more time filming her. He paused the footage and peered at her image. Her legs were long and looked strong and lean in the form-fitting jeans. She had the binoculars raised to her eyes, her face completely obscured by the lenses and the ball cap on her head. Loyal put the scene in motion again. The long pier came into view, then Bertrand and Blomgren. Loyal slowed the footage down again and watched as the two men talked, calmly at first, the conversation becoming more and more agitated. Bertrand removed his ball cap and ran his hand through his thick hair, then glanced up at the drone. It was at this point that Loyal had hit the return to home button and stopped looking at the tablet's screen. He watched now as the drone turned and made its way back to the parking lot. It traveled over the blue Pacific and right above the mystery woman. Loyal watched as she appeared, binoculars down, head raised, watching the drone fly by. He paused the footage and saw her face for the first time.

Trinity stayed in on Friday night. She watched both her trackers, neither man left their home. She spent her time digging into the backgrounds of Loyal Truesdale and Donald Blomgren. She typed and read and printed. Now, at 10:30 on Friday night she had fairly complete bios on both men. Truesdale was a pretty straightforward guy. Born April 7, 1961 at Palomar Hospital in Escondido. Parents Walker and Rita Truesdale. Raised in Fallbrook, California by both parents until their divorce in 1972. His father had moved, Loyal and Rita had remained in Fallbrook. Loyal graduated high school and college, earning a degree in Criminal Justice from SDSU. He completed the police academy and was hired by Carlsbad Sheriff Department in 1984. He married Michelle Franklin in 1988, their daughter Stella was born in 1989. In 1990 Truesdale and his mother, Rita, purchased a condo in Encinitas together. He and Michelle divorced in 1992. Truesdale moved up quickly in the Sheriff's Department;

from jail to patrol, to robbery, to narcotics, to homicide. He was married again in 2013 to Angela DiStefano. They divorced in 2016. Loyal's daughter, Stella, was the owner of the condo now. Her Grandmother Rita had deeded her half to Stella, then Truesdale had deeded his half as well. He had lived in the apartment on Roosevelt Street for the past three years.

Blomgren's history was a bit more convoluted. He was born July 3, 1980 in Ames Iowa to Carl and Vera Blomgren, the fourth of five children. The family owned a working farm which, according to tax records, rarely showed a profit. Blomgren was a star athlete during his high school years. Trinity found some articles from the town's local paper that described his athletic talent in both baseball and football. Upon graduation in 1998 Blomgren signed up for the US Army and was sent to Fort Benning in Georgia for basic training. Blomgren excelled in the Army, quickly moving up the ranks. When he turned twenty-one he requested and received promotion from E4 to E5. He continued to excel, eventually training at Camp Williams in Utah to become a Counterintelligence Special Agent. Blomgren traveled the world, ultimately ending up in Afghanistan in 2004 during *Operation Enduring Freedom*. This is where Trinity's access to his actions began to be blocked. She was unable to track his movements from 2004 to 2011, when he abruptly was honorably discharged, purchased a home in Vista, and basically disappeared. Trinity accessed his tax records from 2011 to the present.

Since he was only active duty for 13 years, Blomgren's retirement benefits were small, a faction of the $83,000.00 he had earned prior to retirement. He reported no other sources of income.

Trinity pushed back from the computer and table. She stood and walked to the kitchen window of her rented condo. Truesdale made sense. Blomgren did not. How was he living in Southern California on the pittance he received from the Army? How did he purchase the house in Vista, which he had paid off over a five year period? Trinity laced her fingers together behind her neck and stretched. An idea popped into her mind. She went back to the computer and pulled up Blomgren's DMV information. Blomgren owned a 2015 Jeep Wrangler Unlimited Rubicon. Was it Blomgren that Bertrand had been meeting at Port Hueneme? If so, what was their connection?

L oyal's alarm woke him at 5:30 on Saturday morning. He rose, donned his gi, and spent 30 minutes on Jiu Jitsu. He showered, dressed in slacks and a Tommy Bahama, and was out the door and into the thick fog by 6:45. As he drove he listened to Rain Gods. He was about half way through, had listened to some parts more than once, and was loving it. He took Interstate 5 North then eased onto Highway 78 East. As he drove East the fog faded away, bright sunlight and blue skies replacing the gray. He drove through the edges of Escondido, then turned right at the base of Valley Center Road to wind up the hill towards Lake Wohlford. He found the cafe across the street from the lake and parked next to a royal blue dune buggy. Just as he was exiting the Altima, Maggie pulled in and parked her yellow dune buggy a few spaces away. Loyal waited for her to slide out of her buggy and they walked toward the cafe together. The outside was chipped and fading white paint. The inside resembled a cabin, with wooden walls and ceiling. A large swordfish was suspended from the ceiling, a pool table took up the left hand corner. The buggy group filled the corner to the right. They had pushed several tables together to accommodate the dozen or so people who were attending. Laughter and animated conversation filled the air. Loyal spotted Bruce and Winnie sitting together at the corner of one of the tables. There were no spaces next to the popular couple, so Loyal gave them a wave. Bruce waved and said with a warm smile, "Hey Winnie, there's the detective we tricked and sent to Mexico. Remember, he was looking for Maggie? Looks like he found her." Loyal laughed at Bruce's comment, then sat down with Maggie at the opposite end of the tables. He had just picked up the menu when the waitress arrived. She started with Bruce and Winnie, so he had a few moments to peruse the offerings. Not a lot of heart healthy fare, although he wasn't surprised by this. He settled on oatmeal and coffee and placed his order when prompted.

As the waitress eased away to place their orders, Maggie said, "Hey everyone," in a slightly raised voice. Conversation stilled and the occupants of the tables turned their attention to her. "I just want to introduce my guest. This is Loyal," she said waving her hand in his direction. "Loyal," she said as she waved her hand towards the rest of the table, "this is the breakfast group." There was a round of greetings from the group, then they all returned to their previous conversations. Loyal relaxed back into his chair and took up one of his favorite activities; people watching. A man and two women sitting across from him were telling Maggie that they were going to be heading out to Borrego after breakfast to pre-run for an upcoming buggy event out there. They were planning on going to a place called "the squeeze" and another called "the drop off." It was their first time and Maggie, who was clearly familiar with the areas, was giving them advice.

As the waitress was bringing the steaming plates to the table the man seated to Loyal's left said hello and introduced himself as Verne. Loyal returned the greeting. Verne looked to be in his late thirties or early forties. He had shaggy blond hair and green eyes. "You have a buggy?" he asked Loyal, who shook his head no. "You should come to the buggy events anyways," Verne said. "There are always empty seats you can get a ride in. I've been coming to events for years. Finally bought a buggy last year."

"You didn't have to build one?" Loyal asked after he swallowed a bite of oatmeal.

"Nah," Verne said, "keep your eyes out and you can find one for sale."

Breakfast passed quickly and before he knew it Loyal was saying goodbye to everyone and walking with Maggie out to her buggy. She leaned in, reached under her seat, straightened, and handed Loyal a radio. "This is a very special Motorolla, an APX9000. It covers the portion of the band you are interested in and automatically switches from analog to digital. Find a place near one of the homes, tune into the frequency you discovered, and you should be able to listen in," she said as she handed it over. She paused a moment, reached in the buggy again, and handed him another radio. "This is a frequency scanner. Just leave it turned on and on your passenger seat and see what it locks onto."

"I know exactly where I'm going to go to listen," Loyal said. "Thanks again Maggie, for everything."

Trinity Glass and her brother Randall, two years her junior, had won the parental lottery. Edwin and Eleanor Glass were an Architect/Interior Design team that traveled the world designing, remodeling, and decorating luxury homes for the small percent of the population who could afford their services. Both Edwin and Eleanor were only children themselves, and neither could bear the thought of being separated from their children, so Trinity and Randall traveled as well. The family's home base was Bellingham, Washington, but they were rarely there. A tutor traveled with them. The children were educated as they traveled the globe.

On October 15, 1997, when Trinity was just beginning her third year at University of Maryland and Randall had just begun attending University of Washington in Seattle, tragedy struck the family. Colombo World Trade Center, in

Sri Lanka, was the scene of a terrorist attack. A truck load of explosives was detonated in the car park of the Galadari Hotel located next to the Trade Center. Fifteen people were killed, 105 injured. Among the dead; Edwin and Eleanor Glass. In a single moment Trinity and Randall became orphans.

As a child Trinity had been a dreamer. Not the head in the clouds type of dreamer, but a literal dreamer; at night when she was sleeping. Her dreams were not happy or fun. The dark and disturbing images frequently woke her, her heart pounding and eyes wide open as she lay in the dark. As she matured Trinity learned to control her dreams. If she was falling off a cliff, she grew wings; drowning, she could breathe under water; buried beneath the earth, she became worm-like and slithered to the surface. Following the death of her parents Trinity had one recurring dream that she was unable to alter. Her parents were sitting at a table for two, enjoying a morning in Sri Lanka. An explosive laden truck pulled up to the table beside them. They appeared not to notice. Edwin leaned over and whispered something in Eleanor's ear, she smiled and kissed his cheek. The detonation woke Trinity every time.

The detonation woke Trinity on Saturday morning. She sat straight up in bed, hands trembling, breaths coming in short ragged bursts. She rose and dressed in loose fitting workout shorts and a tank top. She spent an hour at the

Resort's well equipped gym, then showered, and dressed in blue leggings, a loose T-shirt, and running shoes. She brewed her own coffee, ate a banana, and packed some granola bars and water bottles in a small cooler. By 9:00 she had traded in her rental yet again, this time for a white Mazda CX-5, and she was making her way towards Vista, one Donald Blomgren firmly in her sights. The vestiges of the dream remained with her. Forward motion was the only way to leave them behind.

Trinity had mapped out the area around Blomgren's house on Via Pedro the previous evening. He lived on a short cul-de-sac which made parking and observing from the car an impossibility. Someone would surely question her presence. A female out jogging, however, would not stand out. Trinity parked her new ride at Brengle Terrace Park. She snapped a black fanny pack containing phone, keys and a tracker, around her waist. She did a quick lap around the perimeter of the park, then backtracked to the City of Vista easement that connected to Via Christina, of which Via Pedro was an offshoot. She climbed the fence easily, then jogged North East on Via Christina, then South on Via Pedro. Blomgren's house was easy to locate. The white Rubicon was parked squarely in the center of the driveway. Trinity jogged slowly, sightly annoyed by the crunching sound coming from the soles of her shoes. She waved at a young mother playing with her two children in their front yard, and received a wave and a "Good morning," in return. When she was in front of Blomgren's she stopped, unzipped the fanny pack, and pretended to take a call. When putting the phone back in the fanny pack, she let it slip from her fingers. It fell directly behind the Rubicon. As she retrieved her phone she planted the tracking device just below his back bumper. Trinity then straightened and began jogging slowly out of the neighborhood. She retraced her steps back to the easement off Via Christina and jogged through the park, ending up back where she had started. Trinity settled in the Mazda, drank a water bottle, and opened the tracking app on her phone. She checked the bottom of her shoes to determine the source of the annoying crunching sound and found dozens of puncture vine seed pods. Trinity removed her shoes and began carefully picking the seed pods out of the soles, keeping her eyes on the tracker app while she plucked.

38

L oyal drove from the Cafe straight to Via Pedro. He noted Blomgren's Rubicon in the driveway, then proceeded to Vale Terrace and parking for Brengle Terrace Park. He parked, then, radio in hand, made his way to the North East corner of the park that was closest to Via Pedro. He dialed in 419.9750, then sat down with his back against a tree to wait for a transmission. He glanced at his phone. It was just past 10:00 am. The funeral was at 1:00 in Carlsbad. He figured he could sit here about an hour, then he would need to leave if he was going to make it to the church on time.

Loyal was patient. Detectives had to be. As he sat waiting, hoping for a transmission and the content of the conversation, he let his mind wander down whatever path it chose. His thoughts flitted from Lacey to Bertrand to Blomgren to

Ginger/Cinnamon. Eventually they settled on Stella. How could he explain what had happened between her parents all those years ago. He thought about the night he had come home and found seven month old Stella alone in an unlocked apartment, crying, soiled, and hungry. Then Michelle coming home, the fight, his ultimatum, and her decision. Loyal had done his best to keep track of Michelle after her departure. It wasn't as easy in the pre-internet days. She moved in with a man in Escondido who Loyal suspected to be a drug dealer. He caught sight of her now and then when he had the opportunity to drive by. Once, a little over a year after their split he had followed them to an Italian restaurant on Grand Avenue and cornered her near the bathroom. In this close proximity, he was shocked by her haggard appearance. She had shrugged off his offers of rehab, peeled his fingers from her forearm, and walked away.

Loyal was brought back to the present by a sound from the radio in his hand. It wasn't voices, rather a scratchy static-filled sound. The sound ended abruptly, then began again. Loyal pulled his phone out, noting that the time was 11:08, and recorded the sound. The pauses between the bursts of sound made it fairly clear that a conversation was being conducted. Unfortunately for Loyal, the content was not able to be heard.

"What the hell is going on?" Loyal said out loud. "I thought this radio could do anything." He leaned to his right and leveraged himself up and into a standing position. He brushed the dirt off his slacks, turned off the radio, and began the walk back to his car.

"What the hell?" Trinity said out loud when she saw Truesdale's tracker. He was here, in Brengle Terrace Park. Had he figured out who she was and followed her here? Could it be possible that he was conducting surveillance on her? She scanned the parking lot and quickly found his Altima. She slid down in the driver's seat of her CX-5. It had a high dashboard and tinted windows so she was fairly certain she could not be seen. Less than five minutes passed before she saw him coming down the pathway. He had something in his hand. She squinted, trying to make out what the object was. When Truesdale was halfway across the parking lot, and about twenty feet from the Mazda, she was able to see that he held some type of radio. "What are you up to Truesdale?" Trinity whispered to herself as she watched him slide into the Altima then drive away.

.   .   .

Trinity remained in the park's parking lot for over an hour. During this time she noted Truesdale's arrival at his apartment, and Blomgren's inactivity. She knew that Bertrand had ordered a limo to take him to the funeral, so was not surprised that his tracker did not move. She watched the trackers until Truesdale arrived at the church for Lacey's funeral. She figured she had three solid hours to implement her next plan.

L acey used her left hand to scoop some guacamole onto a chip and delivered it in one smooth motion to her open mouth. Her right hand was entwined in Van's left hand as they sat on the couch in his apartment. It was 2:15 pm. Lacey had worked at JK's in the morning then joined Van for some surfing when she had finished with her new client, who she was in the process of describing.

"He's a homicide detective with the Carlsbad Sheriff Department," she told Van between bites. "He had a heart attack about a month ago. He's on disability until the doctor says he can go back."

"He probably has some good stories," Van said.

"He might," Lacey agreed. "I doubt he'll be with me long. He's in decent shape. He's practiced jiu jitsu for over twenty years."

"What about me Lace?" Van said as he turned to face her. "Am going to be with you for very long?"

Lacey pulled her hand from his and stood. "I don't want to have this conversation again Van," she said.

Van stood as well, reaching out for her upper arm and gently turning her so that she faced him. "I do," he said quietly.

Lacey shifted away from him and walked to the window that looked out on the railroad tracks that paralleled the coast highway.

"I can't just leave him Van," she said. "He already lost one wife, and he supports my Mom and my sister."

"Are you in love with him?" Van asked, "or me?"

Lacey turned to face him. "I love you Van. I care deeply for Bertrand, I don't want to hurt him."

Van took a deep breath in and slowly let it out. "So you hurt me instead. You need to make a choice Lacey," he said. "I can't keep going this way. It hurts too much."

"I know," Lacey began, but Van cut her off.

"I love you Lacey, but I can't do this anymore," he said. "The only time I can be in public with you is when we surf. I want more than that. I want to go to restaurants with you, concerts, movies. Hell, I'd just be happy to walk down the street holding your hand." Tears sparkled in his blue eyes. "If I can't have all of you, I think it would actually be less painful to have none."

41

L oyal arrived at the church at 12:45. The parking lot was already full and he was forced to find street parking several blocks away. He parked then hustled back to the church, arriving just as the first strains of "Amazing Grace" filled the air. Extra folding chairs had been set up in the back of the church in antici-pation of the large crowd. Loyal spotted an empty one next to a man with wavy blond hair and sat just as the minister began to speak.

Lacey and Bertrand did not have any serious religious affil-iation, therefore the minister did not know her well. He spoke mostly in platitudes. Loyal felt he, himself, could have done a better job of projecting the beauty and vitality Lacey had possessed. A slideshow followed the brief state-ment. Lacey as a child, teenager, and young woman. Some photos from her wedding to Bertrand were included, as well as pictures taken on vacations around the world. One of the last pictures was of Lacey at the beach. She wore a dark blue one piece, her hair was tousled, her eyes bright. She stood just at the water's edge, her feet below the surface, holding her surfboard. Her smile was full of joy. The man next to Loyal stifled a sob, stood, and walked from the room. Loyal followed.

Loyal watched as the crying man walked across the narthex and into the restroom. He waited about 30 seconds then followed the man in. He was standing at the sink splashing water on his face.

"How did you know her?" Loyal asked, causing the man to jump. He dried his face with a paper towel, then turned to face Loyal. "I taught her how to surf. How about you?"

"She was my personal trainer," Loyal said reaching out his hand. "Loyal Truesdale."

"Van Winters," he answered as he shook Loyal's hand. "You must be the detective?"

"Guilty," Loyal said. "You knew her pretty well?" he asked.

Van sighed. "Yeah, pretty well."

"Has a detective reached out to you yet?" Loyal asked.

Van shook his head.

Loyal took out his phone. "Why don't I take your info?" he asked. "Just in case."

. . .

When Loyal returned from the restroom, and his chat with Van, the service had ended and the receiving line had begun. Loyal spent a moment watching Bertrand greet the mourners, then slipped back out into the narthex. To his left he saw an older woman leading a younger woman towards the exit door. Loyal hurried to catch up with them.

"Allow me," he said as he held the door for the women. Looking at their faces he saw the younger one was Lacey's sister.

"I'm Loyal Truesdale," he said as he stepped outside with them. "Lacey was my personal trainer."

"She was mine too," said the older woman with a sad smile, "and my neighbor and friend. I'm Gladys Kramer," She added. "This is Lacey's sister Liane."

"Sorry to meet you under such sad circumstances," Loyal said. "I was actually hoping to talk with you," he added.

"Really, why?" asked Gladys.

"I'm a detective with the Carlsbad Sheriff's Department," Loyal said. "I'm actually on leave at the moment, but am looking into Lacey's murder." He glanced at Liane. She had her left thumb in her mouth and her right hand was tugging on her right earlobe.

"We are heading to my house," Gladys said. "Why don't you follow us and we can talk there?"

Several months before her graduation from University of Maryland with a double major in Criminal Justice and Psychology, Trinity was approached by a gentleman by the name of Chet Forrester. One of her professors, Dr. Brantley, had suggested Trinity as a possible candidate for a position with the Air Force Office of Strategic Investigations. Forrester was honest with Trinity. While she was recommended because of her intelligence, athleticism, and imaginative approaches to problems, the Air Force was also trying to place more women in investigative positions. Trinity took no offense to this, she saw the opportunity she was being given, and agreed. She enlisted the week after her graduation. Her brother and only existing family, Randall, had not attended her graduation. He had dropped out of college after the death of their parents and joined the army. The change in his personality had been instantaneous and dramatic. Trinity kept tabs on him as best she could and was aware that he was stationed in Germany, but the once inseparable siblings had little contact.

During her nearly twenty years with OSI Trinity had learned many means of gathering information. Methods had changed dramatically during her tenure, especially in the last ten years. Things she never could have imagined were possible now. For the average person, something called Wireshark was available. This was basically a way to hack people's security cameras. Trinity had a much more sophisticated program, which she was using now. Bertrand had an extensive security system in place in his home on Shorebird Lane. Trinity simply needed to disrupt communication between the system, the monitor in his La Jolla offices, and the app on his phone. When he reconnected, she would have access to his password and could see the same images that Bertrand was seeing. Trinity had hesitated in using this technology as it wasn't legal and wouldn't stand up in court. At this point, however, she needed more on Bertrand, so she was taking the risk. Trinity disrupted the connection and was surprised when communication was re-established within sixty seconds. Perhaps he had an automatic reconnect. Trinity didn't care. Whatever the reason, she had received the electronic handshake and was now able to see inside the home on Shorebird Lane.

Bertrand had cameras in every room of his home, as well

as exterior cameras monitoring the house on all sides. Trinity began her virtual tour with the interior cameras. She started in the entry way. The white marble flooring led to two staircases which wound up in opposite directions to a wrought iron balcony that overlooked the entry. The kitchen, also marble floored, boasted a large granite island, all white cabinetry, and top tier appliances. The house had a formal dining room with wood flooring and a large glass chandelier above the rectangular table, as well as a formal living room where black leather couches faced a large stone fireplace. The two other rooms downstairs were a bedroom with a large television and beanbag chairs, and a rounded morning room that contained an easel and many painted canvases, and was flooded with natural light. Upstairs were two bedrooms that were clearly guest rooms, a closed door behind which there was no camera, and the master bedroom. Trinity found it unusual that Bertrand had a camera in the master suite. She thought about his wife, and the fact that he traveled constantly. Trust issues perhaps? Trinity gazed for a moment at the elegantly appointed room. King sized bed, sitting room to one side, giant bath with sunken tub to the other. She thought about what money could buy; and what it couldn't.

Loyal felt a weight lift off of him as he followed Gladys Kramer through the gates of Shorebird Lane. "Finally," he said out loud. The cul-de-sac was wide, deep, and shaped like a tear drop. Gladys Kramer drove straight to the bottom of the drop and parked in the driveway of a pale yellow one story house. Loyal executed a turn and parked on the street. The front yard was a blaze of color. Flowering plants with blossoms of red, yellow, purple, and blue were growing in a seemingly haphazard way. A small stone path wound its way through the plants to the bright red front door. Gladys unlocked the door, allowed Liane to enter first, then motioned Loyal in.

"Let me get Liane set up in the living room," she said to Loyal, "then we can talk in the kitchen. Go on in and make yourself comfortable." She pointed to her right, indicating a swinging door that led to the kitchen. Loyal watched the elderly woman gently take Liane's hand and lead her in the opposite direction, then pushed through the swinging door.

Gladys' kitchen was as colorful as her front yard. The walls were painted bright yellow, the cabinets and center island a bright white. An oversized red teapot sat on the stove, bright red dish towels hung from the oven's handle. A large window looked out to the back yard where a cream colored wooden deck, housing two chairs and a small table, was surrounded by more flowering plants. A bar separated the kitchen from the dining room. Loyal sat on a bright yellow barstool to wait for Gladys.

"She's all set for a while," Gladys said as she entered the kitchen. "Let's have some tea and scones outside on the deck." Loyal waited as she prepared the tea and placed some scones on a plate. All this was placed on a bright red tray which she handed to him.

Loyal set the tray on the small table and settled in one of the chairs. "Your house is beautiful," he said as Gladys sat.

"Thank you," she said as she reached for a cup of tea. She took a small sip then asked, "What did you want to talk about Detective?"

"Could you tell me about Lacey?" he asked. "Anything that comes to mind."

Gladys closed her eyes for a moment. "Lacey was such

a caretaker. She had to be. She took care of Liane and her mother for years. You know, I really felt for her Detective, I'm sure it was difficult." She glanced back towards her house. "Liane is a child, and her mother has been deteriorating for years. Lacey held everything together."

"Can you tell me about Liane?" Loyal asked.

"I don't know all the details of her accident," Gladys said. "I believe the girls were around seven or eight. The family took a trip to the Kern River up above Bakersfield. They were kayaking. Lacey was with her mother, Liane with their father. There was an accident, the kayak carrying Liane and her father flipped. Their father died. Liane was under water for a short time and hit her head on a large rock. She was in a coma for over a month and had to learn how to do everything all over again." Gladys let out a slow sigh. "She's come a long way Detective, but she'll never be able to take care of herself independently."

Loyal and Gladys sat quietly for a moment, sipping. "What did Lacey do besides working at JK's?" Loyal asked.

"She spent an awful lot of time surfing," Gladys said. "And she was with Bertrand when he was home of course, although that wasn't often. The man travels a lot."

"Did she have friends over?" Loyal asked, "or go out?"

"No," Gladys said. "She worked at the gym, surfed, and was home."

"Seems like a lonely life," Loyal said.

"Yes, I suppose it was," Gladys said. She paused, then

added, "I have to say, during the last six months or so I noticed a change in Lacey. She seemed restless, distracted."

"You have any idea what was causing that?" Loyal asked.

"I suspect it was more of a *who* than a *what*." Gladys said.

Trinity finished her virtual tour of the inside of Bertrand Roberts' home. She took a moment, before accessing the outside cameras, to stand and stretch. As she was sitting back down she glanced at her tracker app. Bertrand's vehicle was in the driveway of his home on Shorebird Lane, while he was undoubtedly still at the church. She recalled the limo that had delivered him to Lacey's service. Blomgren was still at home, and Truesdale was at "Shorebird Lane?" she said out loud. "What the hell are you doing?" Turning back to her computer, Trinity accessed the cameras on the outside of Bertrand's house. The backyard came into view first. A large pool and covered outdoor kitchen dominated. It appeared that there was a swim up bar joining the pool and the kitchen. A small lawn covered the area between the pool and the wall surrounding the property. Several palm trees were strategically placed as well. Surprisingly, Bertrand had cameras facing from the wall towards the house, as well as cameras from the house facing the wall. Every inch was surveilled. Trinity peered at the house. There, on the balcony of what she guessed was the room that had not had a camera in it, she saw an array of short antennas. Trinity leaned back in her chair for a moment. She closed her eyes and conjured up a picture of Loyal Truesdale from the park earlier. He had been carrying a radio when he had emerged from the park trail and headed towards his car. "Who the hell is this guy?" she muttered. "Perhaps Blomgren has antennas as well? Has Truesdale figured out a way to listen?"

Trinity manipulated the security system so that she was seeing the front of Bertrand's house. Several cameras were located on the upper exterior of the house, providing a view of the entire cul-de-sac. It didn't take Trinity long to locate Truesdale's Altima parked in front of the home to the West of Bertrand's. She left this view open and carried her lap top with her to the kitchen. She kept her eye on the screen as she made a turkey sandwich and poured herself a glass of coconut water. She sat at the kitchen table, watching the screen and slowly eating her lunch. Although Bertrand was her focus, Truesdale definitely had her attention. The guy was everywhere. She wondered what resources were available to him, and why?

Movement on the screen drew Trinity's attention. She watched as Truesdale walked through the neighbor's front yard and approached his Altima. He paused at the driver's door, and stood looking at Bertrand's property. He sat inside his Altima for a moment, then slid out and walked towards Bertrand's home. He paused by the black suburban in the driveway, knelt down and reached under the back bumper, then stood and returned to his Altima. He slid in and moments later was driving away. Trinity reacted immediately to what she was sure she had just witnessed. Truesdale had placed a tracker on Bertrand's Suburban. She quickly deleted the images of Truesdale from the security system saying a silent thank you for the electronic handshake she had received earlier.

L oyal's mind was spinning as he drove home from Gladys Kramer's house on Shorebird Lane. He thought about Lacey being the provider and stability for her mother and Liane for all those years. What a relief she must have felt upon marrying Bertrand Roberts, the weight of responsibility that must have been lifted from her shoulders. He wondered about Van Winters, the grieving surfing instructor, and pondered the true nature of their relationship. He was grateful that he had gotten the man's contact information, another conversation was definitely going to be necessary.

Loyal's phone rang as he was pulling into the parking space below his apartment. He shifted into park, then lifted the phone from the console and looked at the number. Prescott, Arizona. "Yes," he thought, this must be the pharmacist returning his call. He quickly hit *accept* and answered. "Loyal Truesdale."

"Hello," came the reply, "This is John Herrera returning your call. You said that you wanted to ask me about Lacey. Is everything ok?"

Loyal sighed. The man didn't know that she was dead.

"Actually, no," Loyal said. "I'm very sorry to be the one to tell you this, but Lacey passed away last Monday."

There was a sharp intake of breath, a momentary pause, then, "What happened?"

"She was attacked on her morning walk," Loyal said. "I'm a detective involved with the case. I was hoping to talk to you about her."

"Well detective, I don't know how much help I'll be," Herrera said. "I moved to Arizona over eight years ago and Lacey and I haven't really kept in touch beyond Christmas cards each year." He paused a moment then added, "Strangely, she did come to visit last December. Only stayed for a day."

Loyal glanced at the dashboard. It was just after three o'clock. "Is it possible for me to meet with you in person Mr. Herrera?"

"You want to drive all the way out here to ask a few questions?" Herrera asked.

"Yes," Loyal said.

"I'm an early riser," Herrera said. "Anytime after six tomorrow morning works for me. It is about a seven hour drive Detective."

"Would you mind texting your address to this

number?" Loyal said. "I'll be there tomorrow morning." He thanked the pharmacist for his time and disconnected.

Loyal did the math and decided to leave at 10:00 that evening. He turned off the still running Altima and went up to his apartment. He spent just under an hour making notes about everything that he had learned at the funeral and at Gladys Kramer's house. He checked the tracker he had applied to Bertrand's Suburban, no motion there. At 4:30 he called Maggie.

"This is Maggie," she answered.

"Loyal Truesdale," he said.

"Ah, Detective," Maggie said, "were you able to hear any transmissions?"

"All I got was a kind of whiny scratchy sound," Loyal said. "It was as if a conversation was taking place, but I couldn't make out the words."

"They are probably using encryption," Maggie said. "You won't be able to beat that." She paused a moment then asked, "Have you spent any time with the scanner I gave you? That might give you another clue."

"I think it is broken," Loyal said. "It has been in my car all day and has been stuck on the same frequency."

"It hasn't scanned at all?" Maggie asked. "That is pretty strange. Have you heard any transmissions?"

"Nope," Loyal said, "only static."

"Let me ask my radio friends about that," Maggie said. "Can I call you back?"

"Sure," Loyal said, "any time."

46

L acey stood on the shore, hand shading her eyes, and scanned the ocean waters. A group of surfers was out there catching waves, but she could tell that Van was not among them. It had been over a week since he had told her their relationship needed to be all or nothing. She had not seen or spoken to him since. His ultimatum had caught her off guard, her silence had given him the answer he was seeking. He had, with tears in his eyes, quietly asked her to leave his apartment.

Standing on shore now, looking out to sea and searching for him, Lacey felt her own tears threaten, then spill. This was agony. Her heart felt raw; punished. She turned away from the blue expanse and walked slowly back to her truck. She lowered the tailgate and climbed into the back, leaning against the bed of the truck below the windows of the cab. She was trapped. She loved Van, she knew this without a doubt. She cared for Bertrand, and didn't want to cause him pain. There was also the issue of Bertrand's support for her mother and Liane. If she were to leave Bertrand, what would become of them. She and Van could probably take care of Liane, but her mother, who no longer even recognized her own daughter, needed round the clock care. She could never afford that.

So caught up in the merry-go-round of her thoughts was Lacey that she didn't realize he was standing next to her truck until he spoke.

"Not surfing much lately Lacey," he said.

She flinched then turned her head to see Len Hammond standing there.

"Are you crying?" he asked when he saw her face.

"Leave me alone," she said.

"I can help you Lacey," he said

"I don't want your help," Lacey said as she slid out of the bed of the truck. She closed the tailgate, walked to the drivers side, and got in. "You are always around, watching me," she said before closing the door. "I don't like it, leave me alone."

Maggie called back as Loyal was making an early dinner. His plan was to eat, sleep for a few hours, then leave for Prescott at 10:00.

"I think I have an idea about what is going on with the scanner," Maggie said, "but you are not going to like it."

"What is it?" Loyal asked.

"There is a possibility that a tracker has been placed on your vehicle," Maggie said. "The scanner isn't picking up anything else because of its close proximity to the source, which is likely a tracker."

"What the hell?" Loyal said. "Why would anyone be tracking me?"

"Go out and check your car detective," Maggie said. "Take the scanner, remove the antenna, walk around your car, and look in the place where you are getting the strongest signal. Look under the frame, in the wheel wells, anywhere a small device could be attached."

"Thanks Maggie," Loyal said. "I'm on my way out to the car now."

"Let me know what you find," Maggie said. "This is getting more interesting by the moment."

Loyal set the food he was preparing aside and walked down to his Altima. The scanner was on the passenger seat. He removed the antenna and began slowly moving around the car. He started by the passenger door, went around the front of the Altima, passed by the driver and rear passenger door, and moved toward the back of the vehicle. As he neared the back left wheel well, the signal strength increased from one-half to three-quarters. Loyal stopped moving and bent down. He couldn't see much from that angle, so he sat down on the asphalt, then lay down on his back and poked his head under the car. He saw it in moments, a small metal box nearly identical to the one he had placed on Bertrand Roberts' Suburban earlier in the day. Loyal reached out and pulled the small box off the Altima. He rolled to his knees, then stood. He paused a moment and studied the small box that surely held a tracking device. It looked to be smaller and more sophisticated than the one he had used. He turned and went back up to his apartment.

Loyal called Maggie first, told her what he had found, and thanked her again. She was interested and wanted to talk more, but Loyal was on a schedule and it had just gotten a hell of a lot tighter. He assured her he would call her as soon as he could. Loyal considered several options, quickly deciding on his plan of action. He texted O'Keefe.

Call me when you can talk.

He looked at the clock; 6:12. O'Keefe should be home. Loyal went back to the stove and finished re-heating some enchiladas from a few nights back. He had just taken his second bite when his phone rang. Loyal checked the caller ID; O'Keefe.

"Pat," he said, "thanks for calling back."

"Sure Loyal. What's up?"

"I want to set up some simple cameras that surveil the front and back of my apartment," Loyal said. "Do you have any time to help me set that up tonight?"

"On Saturday night? Is it that urgent?" O'Keefe asked.

"Yes," Loyal said.

"Ok," O'Keefe said, and then proceeded to give Loyal a list of items to pick up at Fry's. "I'll meet you at your place in two hours," O'Keefe said.

Loyal agreed and disconnected. He grabbed his keys and wallet, looked at the enchilada for a moment and the tracker next to it, then turned and walked out the door.

Trinity Glass believed in forward motion. She slept because it was a necessity. So it was unusual to find her asleep on the couch in her rented condo at 6:00 pm on Saturday evening. Her spontaneous erasing of Loyal's activity on Shorebird Lane had left her edgy. She had put on her gi and practiced jiu jitsu for an hour, then checked the trackers and found Loyal and Blomgren at their respective residences. Bertrand's security system showed that he had been dropped off by the limo and was home. She had checked Bertrand's charter company and found he was scheduled to fly out on the next morning at 10:30 am. No flight plan had been filed. She suspected he was traveling to Tahoe again. She had sat on the couch with a deep sigh. She was damn tired of following Bertrand back and forth to Tahoe with no solid results.

. . .

Without realizing what was happening, Trinity had shifted her lean body so that she was lying on the couch. She lay on her right side, her face towards the cushions. Her long legs had twitched once, and she had dropped quickly into sleep. Her dream was simple. She and her brother, Randall, were riding bikes down a mountain path. The day was clear and bright, the sun a warm yellow against a deep blue sky. Green grass lined the dirt path upon which they rode. Giant fir trees sat about thirty feet back from the path on either side. Randall was in front, Trinity following him. He would glance back every so often and give her his wide, warm smile. Occasionally he would break into laughter, which rode on the wind to her ears. She treasured the sound.

The change happened so gradually that Trinity didn't notice at first that the sky was darkening, the trees getting closer to the path, the ground becoming uneven. Maintaining balance became more difficult. She was falling farther and farther behind Randall. Trinity, unconsciously, attempted to alter the dream. She willed her legs more strength. It didn't work. Soon Randall was out of sight. Pushing hard, Trinity rounded a corner and found herself on the edge of a cliff. She threw herself off the bike, landing hard, and watched as the bike slid to the cliff's edge and tumbled over. She was alone. She stood and looked around. The cliff was in front of her, a dense forest behind. She faced the forest and searched for a trail or path that she could take. She saw nothing and felt panic rising. Movement to her left caught her attention. Peering into the dark she saw a person standing just outside the tree line. "Randall!" she yelled and ran toward the shadowy figure. As she approached, she slowed, then stopped. It wasn't Randall. It was Loyal Truesdale and he was waving her towards him. She moved cautiously towards him. When she reached him he took her hand and, without a word, led her into the woods.

Trinity woke with a start, unsure for a moment where she was. She sat up, looked around the condo, and brought herself back to reality. The dream had left her shaken. She had seen Randall so clearly, heard his laugh as it blew back to her waiting ears. He had been so vital, alive. She knew this to be untrue. Randall was dead. He had died in Afghanistan. Trinity stood and went to the kitchen for a glass of water, which she drank slowly as she stared out the kitchen window. She thought about the last part of the dream, about Loyal Truesdale, who had taken her hand so gently and led her away from danger.

L oyal drove to Frys, an electronics store in San Marcos, purchased two two-way security cameras, and drove back to Carlsbad. He was just opening his front door when O'Keefe pulled into the alley that ran behind his home. He waited as O'Keefe parked and then joined him on the stairs.

"You want to explain what's going on?" O'Keefe said as they walked into Loyal's apartment.

Loyal crossed to the table, set down his purchases, and held up the tracking device. "This is what's going on," he said.

O'Keefe crossed the apartment and took the device from Loyal, looked at it a moment, then handed it back. "Where did it come from?" he asked.

"Underneath my car," Loyal said.

"Any idea who put it there?" O'Keefe asked.

"My top three suspects are Bertrand Roberts, Donald

Blomgren, and Hammond," Loyal said. "I'm leaving for Arizona tonight and leaving the tracker in my garage."

"You must be making some headway in your investigation if those are your top suspects," O'Keefe said. "So you want the security cameras installed so you can see if the mystery person drives by."

"That's right," Loyal said.

"No problem," O'Keefe said. He picked up the cameras. "These are easy to install and connect to your phone. Show me where you want them."

By 9:00 the cameras were in place and connected to Loyal's phone, and O'Keefe was on his way home. Loyal trashed the enchiladas, made two tuna sandwiches, and brewed a pot of strong coffee. His original plan of food and a nap now discarded, he was opting for food and caffeine. He dressed in loose sweats, a T-shirt, and tennis shoes, then gathered slacks, dress shoes, and a Tommy Bahama for the meeting with the pharmacist. One sandwich was eaten, one packed for the road. The coffee was poured into two large travel mugs. Loyal placed the clothes and food in his car, and the tracker in the garage. He practiced checking the cameras again. Satisfied, he slid in the car and drove away six minutes before 10:00. As he drove away he started the CD of Rain Gods. The narrator said "Chapter 21." Immediately Loyal was transported to the small dusty town in Texas where bad things were happening.

.   .   .

Just past 2:00 in the morning, as Loyal exited the 10 freeway for the 60 North, the novel ended. Loyal was impressed by James Lee Burke's storytelling skill. He turned the CD player off, took a long sip of coffee, and reached for the tuna sandwich. He drove along in silence, nothing visible outside the headlights' reach. Exactly one half of the moon glowed against the black sky, illuminating little. Loyal drove and let his mind choose its own path. It didn't take it long to settle on the tracking device. Loyal had lots of questions. Who had put it there and why? How long had it been there? He thought about his top three suspects; Hammond, Roberts, and Blomgren. He supposed Hammond could have placed it there to determine if Loyal was investigating. Roberts and Blomgren had met at Port Hueneme, perhaps one or both of them had seen him there. Ginger/Cinnamon crossed his mind. Who the hell was she, and why was she always around?

After he turned left off the 60 onto the 73 at Aguila Loyal pulled his Altima to the side of the road. He left it idling while he checked his newly installed security cameras. Nothing yet. He set his phone aside and continued North toward Prescott. The flat lands gave way to hills, then mountains. The Altima climbed steadily, gaining distance and altitude. Loyal's thoughts remained on the tracking device. He conjured an image of Hammond's face that day at the station, his words *watch your back* echoed in Loyal's mind. Loyal had known Hammond since the young man had joined the Sheriff's Department in 2011. Loyal had made Homicide Detective in 1989, but still made it a point to introduce himself to anyone new. He had disliked Hammond from the beginning, but tried not to show it. In 2015 Hammond had been moved to Vice and partnered with a detective named Clayton Fields. Fields had been with the department two years longer than Loyal. Joe Gordon, Loyal's TO, had advised Loyal to steer clear of Fields and Loyal had done so. Fields had retired in 2016 after mentoring Hammond for a year. Through his work in vice, Fields had a connection with Michelle that Loyal still preferred not to think about. Hammond had followed Fields' lead, skirting the boundaries of the law when he felt it necessary. Loyal was sure Hammond would have no issues with placing a tracker on the Altima.

Ginger/Cinnamon popped into his head again. She was involved somehow, he was sure of this. Loyal didn't believe in coincidences, and she had been around a lot. He had seen her on the trail, at Port Hueneme and Oxnard Airport, and she had landed in Tahoe mere minutes before Bertrand. He moved on to Bertrand, the husband of the murder victim, and Blomgren with whom he had a clear connection. It was entirely possible that one of them had spotted him outside of their residences, at Port Hueneme, or even at Lacey's funeral. It occurred to him that he had placed a tracker on Blomgren's Rubicon and all but forgotten that it was there. He would check it when he arrived in Prescott and see where Blomgren had been.

· · ·

Loyal made good time and arrived in Prescott just after 4:00 am. Despite the coffee, he was exhausted. He drove past some low slung motels and a gas station, deciding to pull in at the Safeway grocery store. He drove slowly by its darkened entrance, noting that it opened at 6:00 each day. He parked in the far end of the parking lot, racked his seat back as far as it would go, set an alarm on his phone for 5:50, and quickly fell asleep.

50

Trinity finished her water and went back to her computer. She checked Bertrand's charter company and was surprised to see that his flight was originating at Oxnard Airport, rather than Palomar. A flight plan had been filed and he was, as she had suspected, traveling to Tahoe again. She glanced at the clock. 9:32 on a Saturday night and here she was, alone again in a city where she had no friends. Trinity let her face fall into the palms of her hands and just sat there for a long moment. She was tired of it all; the constant travel, the lonely nights, the corrupt people she investigated, the deceit, the lies, the double-dealing and backstabbing. She wanted something good in her life, one thing that was pure and simple and true. There had been relationships over the years. Some short term, some lasting years, but nothing that had stuck. She raised her face from her hands. This line of thought wasn't helping. This was why

Trinity liked to be on the move. Forward motion kept these thoughts and feelings at bay.

Her thoughts returned to Bertrand Roberts. If his flight originated at Oxnard, then he was likely driving there. She thought about his previous meeting at the pier. She was going to have to follow him. She checked her tracking app, the car hadn't moved. She checked his security cameras. The bedroom cameras had been deactivated. She assumed he was sleeping. If he was flying at 10:30, and possibly meeting with someone first, he would be getting an early start. Trinity did the math and figured Roberts would be on the road by 4:30 the next morning. She would have to be as well. She checked the trackers of Truesdale and Blomgren. Truesdale had not moved. He was still at his apartment on Roosevelt Street. Blomgren had gone out earlier, spent half an hour at the Albertsons on East Vista Way, and was back home on Via Pedro.

With everyone accounted for, Trinity started prepping for her early morning drive. She laid out jeans, a T-shirt, a sweatshirt, and a hat. She packed a small backpack with an apple, a banana, an almond butter sandwich, several water bottles, and her gyro-stabilized binoculars. She showered, dried her long hair, set an alarm for 3:30, and was asleep by 11:00. If she had dreams, she had no memory of them when her alarm woke her at 3:30. The trackers all showed no movement, which was not a surprise. Trinity drank a quick cup of coffee, dressed, and was on the road by 4:15. On impulse, she drove by Truesdale's apartment. The apartment was dark, but his Altima wasn't in its usual spot. Trinity put her car in park and peered out the window. Going against all her training, she slid out, grabbing a small penlight she had placed in the storage area below the front console. She shielded the light with her hand, allowing just enough to try to see if she could see through a crack to determine if his car was in the garage. The door fit snugly, she couldn't see anything. Frustrated, she cut the light, returned to the CX-5, and proceeded to the Ralph's on Avenida Encinas. It was located less than three miles from Shorebird Lane and conveniently close to Interstate 5. When Bertrand started his drive, she would be ready to follow.

51

L oyal's phone pinged at 5:50. He quieted the alarm, stretched his cramped limbs, and returned his seat to an upright position. He checked his reflection in the rear view mirror, using his fingers to calm his unruly hair. He grabbed his wallet, keys, and clothes for the day, slid out of the Altima, and headed for the entrance to Safeway. He was the only customer in the store and felt the employees' eyes following him as he passed through the aisles. Loyal changed quickly in the store's bathroom. He purchased a coffee and a breakfast sandwich from their surprisingly well stocked deli, mumbling something about an early morning meeting to the clerk, and returned to his car. While he chewed, he checked the tracker he had placed on Bertrand Roberts' car. He was in motion, heading north on Highway 101 near Thousand Oaks, moving steadily. Heading back to Port Hueneme or Oxnard Airport perhaps?

. . .

He next checked his security cameras from the previous evening. He started at 2:00 am and fast forwarded the footage. The infrared cameras caught a few cats moving through the alley, and one skunk. Then nothing until a pair of headlights appeared at 4:31. Loyal slowed the footage and went back to the moment when the headlights first appeared. He watched as a white crossover SUV eased down the alley and stopped in front of his garage. A moment later the driver's door opened and a woman slid out. As soon as she began to move he recognized the body. Shielding a light with her left hand, she moved towards his garage. She spent less than a minute trying to see inside, then extinguished the light, returned to her car, and drove away. Loyal watched the footage three more times. Yes, he was sure, the woman was Ginger/Cinnamon. "Who the hell are you?" Loyal asked out loud. Was she the person who had put a tracker on his car? Why? He needed to meet her. The long drive home would give him plenty of time to devise a plan.

One of Loyal's great strengths as a detective was his ability to focus completely on one thing at a time. He did this now, putting the flame haired woman out of his mind, and turning his attention to John Herrera. He entered the pharmacist's address into his phone and was rewarded with a map and directions. Herrera lived on Foothill Drive which, according to Google maps, was a mere seven minutes from Loyal's current location. Loyal called the pharmacist, explained where he was, and asked permission to drive to his house. Permission was granted and Loyal was on his way.

John Herrera's house was a single story, set back a ways from the road, and surrounded by trees. Loyal found it easily. He drove down the long driveway, parked, and approached the front door, which opened just before he reached it. A thin, gray haired man in his 70's stepped out to greet Loyal.

"Detective Truesdale?" he asked.

"Yes," Loyal said, extending his hand as he stepped on the porch. They shook. "Thank you for agreeing to meet with me Mr. Herrera."

"Anything to help put the monster who did this to Lacey behind bars," Herrera said. "I read the articles after we spoke last night." He led Loyal into the house. "Let's talk in the kitchen, I have coffee ready. And please call me John, Detective."

Loyal followed. "Coffee sounds great John, and feel free to call me Loyal."

John's kitchen was small, comfortable and spotless. He pointed toward two barstools that fronted a small wooden island.

"Have a seat," he said as he poured two mugs of coffee. He placed one in front of Loyal. "Black ok?"

Loyal nodded, and John sat down.

"How can I help?" he asked.

Loyal placed a small recorder on the island. "Are you comfortable with me recording this?" he asked.

John nodded and Loyal started the device.

"You said Lacey visited you last December," Loyal said. "Let's start there."

John paused for a moment, took a sip of coffee, and said, "She had a lot on her mind and needed someone to talk to. Perhaps I should give you some background? What do you know about Lacey?"

"Not a lot. She was my personal trainer, but didn't share much about her private life."

"And you are allowed to investigate?" John asked. "Isn't that a conflict of interest?"

Loyal sighed. "I'm actually on disability at the moment. Had a heart attack about six months ago."

"So, you are conducting your own investigation?"

Loyal nodded. " I am. I don't trust Hammond to get it right."

"Hammond?" John said. "Len Hammond?"

"You know him?" Loyal asked.

"He's one of the reasons Lacey came to see me," John said. "He's had a thing for Lacey for years. She told me that he'd been following her around. She was thinking about filing a complaint."

Loyal, who had been about to take a sip of coffee, set his mug down abruptly. "What? Hammond has been harassing her?"

John sighed. "Let me take you back a few years." He talked for the next ten minutes, Loyal listened and learned about Hammond's fascination with Lacey that went back many years.

"When she came to see me in December she said he had been following her around, popping up in different places where she was, making suggestive comments that were upsetting her," John said. " I advised her to make a formal complaint. Doesn't sound like she ever did."

Loyal sat in shocked silence. All those workouts with him and she had never said a word, hadn't even hinted that something was wrong.

"Talk about a conflict of interest," John said, breaking the silence. "Hammond should not be investigating."

"Agreed," Loyal said. "Did she talk about anything else when she came to see you? Seems a long way to come for advice you could have given over the phone."

"Lacey didn't have anyone to talk to, Loyal. Her sister has diminished capacity, her Mom is in a locked memory care facility, and Bertrand, well, let's just say things were a little rocky with them."

"Did she mention anyone else?" Loyal asked. "Friends, her surfing instructor, perhaps?"

"I don't want to betray her confidence, Loyal," John said. He ran his hand across his forehead and through his gray hair. "I guess it doesn't matter much now that she is gone." He looked directly at Loyal, holding his gaze. "Can you try to keep this to yourself?"

Loyal nodded. "I'll do my best, but no guarantees."

"She cared deeply for Bertrand, but she was in love with Van Winters," John said. "She was very concerned about what would happen to her mother and sister if she left Bertrand. Especially her mother. The care she requires is very expensive."

Loyal thought for a moment. "Did Hammond know about the affair?"

"Yes," John said, "she thought that he did."

Trinity ate the apple and watched the trackers. Bertrand's began to move at 5:17. She watched his progress to Interstate 5, and fell in about a mile behind him, heading North. She was curious about Roberts' decision to drive himself to Oxnard Airport. It was a deviation from his normal pattern of behavior, just as the meeting with Blomgren in Port Hueneme had been. Trinity had been watching Bertrand Roberts for quite some time. The man rarely deviated.

Traffic was light this early on a Sunday morning. Bertrand drove at exactly 70 mph. One mile behind him Trinity did the same. The sky gradually lightened in the East, daylight arriving fully just before 6:30. Occasionally Trinity glanced at the trackers for Blomgren and Truesdale. No motion yet from either of them. Trinity thought about her impulsive decision to stop by Truesdale's apartment. All of her training cautioned against being seen. Getting out of her vehicle and trying to see in his garage went against everything she had been taught. She silently chastised herself for such a foolish action.

Just South of the city of Camarillo Roberts' exited the 101 on S. Lewis Rd. Trinity did the same and found herself on a two lane road in the midst of agricultural fields. She immediately slowed, doubling the distance between her car and Roberts'. She followed him by tracker only, no visuals, as he passed Cal State University Channel Islands and S. Lewis became Hueneme Road. "Looking for a tail, huh?" she asked out loud. Trinity maintained the distance, following Roberts into the town of Port Hueneme, then West toward Hueneme Beach Park. His tracker indicated he had pulled into parking lot A. Trinity bypassed this lot, parking instead in lot B. She parked facing lot A and watched as Bertrand exited his vehicle, slung a green and black backpack over his shoulder, and walked toward the pier. Trinity opened the car door and stood leaning against it, tracking his progress.

She leaned back in the car and opened the metal case that sat on the passenger seat. She removed the Fraser Volpe gyro-stabilized binoculars, marveling again at how light this new version was. She remembered her original pair, the Fraser Volpe MK-10 which had been far heavier and had lacked the starlight and video capabilities of this latest iteration. She closed the car door, leaned against the Mazda, raised her binoculars, and studied Bertrand as he crossed the sand and purposefully walked the length of the pier. The binoculars brought everything so close and with such clarity that she could read the Cabela label on his fishing backpack. She scanned the handful of people on the pier. Two weathered looking older men were fishing off the North side of the pier. They nodded to Bertrand as he passed, then returned to their poles. A young mother, carrying a baby in a sling, watched as her blond haired young daughter skipped along in front of her. Bertrand passed them as well, walked to the very end of the pier, leaned on the rail and looked out at the blue Pacific. The backpack hung off of his left shoulder and looked fairly empty. He carried no fishing equipment.

"What in the hell are you doing?" Trinity whispered as she hit the video record button. She stayed still, binoculars trained on Bertrand, and recorded the scene. Less than five minutes passed before another man entered her field of vision, his back to her. He leaned on the pier railing, facing the opposite direction of Bertrand. Neither man acknowledged the other. While Trinity watched and recorded, Bertrand set his backpack on the pier and walked back toward shore. Trinity kept her eyes on the backpack. After one full minute, the other man picked up the backpack and turned to walk back toward the beach. Trinity's only reaction when she saw his face was a small intake of air, which she then blew out slowly. The man with the backpack was Jack Williamson from Spa War.

53

L oyal spent a few hours with John. He learned a lot about Lacey as a teenager and young adult. John's narrative matched Gladys's, highlighting Lacey's burden of caring for both mother and sister. John explained a bit more about Liane's accident and recovery; her initial assessment at Kern Valley Hospital in Mountain Mesa, transfer to Bakersfield, then another transfer to Rady Children's in San Diego, the six week coma, learning even the basics all over again.

"Lacey carried a lot of guilt regarding Liane," John had said. "Although they were identical twins, Lacey was the more skilled of the two, both academically and athletically. Liane was always a step behind even before the accident." After a brief pause he had said with a small sigh, "Lacey carried a lot of weight on her shoulders." He had described her mother's slide into early onset Alzheimer's and Lacey's struggle to keep the family together.

"I wasn't thrilled about her marriage to Bertrand

Roberts," he had said, "but it sure did take the pressure off Lacey. And, surprisingly, they seemed to be a good fit." He had answered Loyal's many questions about Len Hammond with patience, making it very clear he did not like the man. Loyal's recorder captured every word.

Just after 8:30 Loyal shook hands with John, slid in the Altima and started the long drive back to Carlsbad. He drove back past the Safeway, the small line of motels, and began the descent from the mountain town. At one point the road split and Loyal found himself on a one way road high above the mirror opposite road that led up the mountain. As he wound down the twisting road, Loyal passed a site labeled *Granite Mountain Hotshot Memorial*. He slowed as he passed the entrance to the site, remembering the tragic story of the nineteen men who had lost their lives fighting the fire above the town of Yarnell. It stuck in his mind, not only because it was such a tragedy, but also because one of the young men had been born in Hemet, California, which was just an hour Northeast of Loyal's childhood hometown of Fallbrook. In Loyal's mind, firefighters were true heroes. He made a mental note to look the memorial up when he got home.

The road straightened and Loyal dropped out of the mountains. It had been dark when he had driven through this area the previous night and he saw now how flat and barren the land was. Manufactured homes sprouted here and there among the bushes and rocks. It was such a contrast to the crowded coastal cities of Southern California. With no audio book to entertain him, Loyal was left with his own thoughts. He relaxed his mind, freeing it to land on whatever topics it chose. Unsurprisingly, it landed on Hammond.

Loyal's training officer when he had first been hired by Carlsbad Sheriff's Department had been a crusty but good natured 20 year veteran named Joe Gordon. The first thing Joe had said to Loyal as they drove away from the station on their first day together was, "I want you to forget everything you learned at the Academy. Your real training begins today." No statement was more true. Loyal considered Joe a partner, friend, and mentor. Joe had a laundry list of sayings he would trot out when he thought they applied. One had been "It's not an issue until it becomes an issue." Looking at him through the lens of the information provided by John Herrera, Hammond had just become an issue.

54

T rinity recorded Williamson's walk down the pier, across the sand, and to the parking lot. He unlocked a black Yukon and slid in. Trinity turned off the video and listened to the gyro on the binoculars spooling down. She slid into her own car and started the ignition. She watched Williamson as he exited Lot A. She fell in behind him, about two car lengths back, and followed as he drove to the 101 and headed South. It was nearly 11:00 and traffic was thick, but flowing. Trinity kept her position behind him and called her boss from the car. Douglass Caldwell answered on the second ring.

"You got something Glass?" he said, wasting no time on niceties as usual.

"Yes," Trinity said. "I'm going to email you some footage when I have a secure connection. I need more time Doug."

"Send me what you have," Caldwell said. "I'll make the determination after I review it."

"Will do," Trinity said, and disconnected.

The long drive South from Port Hueneme gave Trinity ample time to consider what she had just witnessed. Bertrand and Williamson were up to something. Thinking back to her research on Spa War, Trinity recalled the potential redevelopment of Spa War's current location. Turning that prime real estate into a mixed use development was worth a pretty penny. It made sense that Bertrand would be interested in that opportunity. Although the backpack had not been heavy, it could easily have contained a significant amount of money. Trinity had held $500,000 in cash once. Made up of all $100 bills, the bundle had weighed just over ten pounds, which had been a true surprise. If it was cash in the backpack though, where had Bertrand gotten it? A withdrawal that large from any bank would have been reported to a number of different agencies. Trinity had thoughts about another way Roberts could have obtained that much cash, but made a mental note to check financial records when she got back to La Costa.

As she drove, her thoughts turned to Loyal Truesdale. The man intrigued her. Her research on him indicated that he was clever and persistent. His overall solve rate as a Homicide Detective was higher than average, there had been no complaints filed against him by the public. He had been suspended for thirty days the previous August following the incident in Las Vegas. The fact that she was unable to dig more deeply into the details of that incident, despite her high security clearances, aroused her curiosity. She glanced at her tracker app, Truesdale was still at home in Carlsbad. "What are you up to?" she asked the red dot on her phone screen. "What are you doing right now?"

As they crossed the long bridge that joined the 405 to the 5, traffic eased and Williamson sped up. Trinity pushed down on the accelerator to keep pace. She watched the needle inch past 80 mph and the city of Irvine was soon behind them. With her focus on Williamson, Trinity didn't notice the Highway Patrol car until it was directly behind her, blue and red flashing in her rear view mirror. "Damn it!" she swore out loud as she slowed, put on her turn signal, and crossed three lanes of traffic to pull over on the shoulder. She stopped the car, cut the ignition, rolled down the window, and waited for the officer to approach.

When the officer leaned down to her window to request license and registration Trinity silently swore again. He was young, a newbie, probably inflexible. She handed him her documentation and he returned to his vehicle to run her information. She sat quietly, looking longingly down the southbound freeway lanes, Williamson long out of view. She would have to try to track him through traffic cameras, a time consuming procedure. The officer reappeared at her window and leaned down saying, "I'm having trouble accessing your drivers license information ma'am."

"It is a confidential license," Trinity said. "I'm employed by the government."

"In what capacity?" asked the officer.

Trinity hesitated, thinking about the countless number of occupations that were allowed confidential licenses, then replied, "I'm a museum security guard."

The officer gave her a long look, then handed back her documents and said, "I'm giving you a verbal this time Ms. Glass. Try easing up on that accelerator ok?"

"Thanks," Trinity said. "And I will."

She waited until the officer was back to his vehicle, started the car, signaled, and merged back into traffic.

L oyal stopped for gas at a giant Chevron station just East of the California border. He topped off the tank, then drove across the border and back into California, where gas was over a dollar more per gallon. Interstate 10 was crowded, Loyal found himself jockeying for position with trucks towing boats or trailers, cars weaving in and out of traffic, and giant Fed Ex, Amazon, and Swift cargo trucks dominating the two right lanes. Frustrated, Loyal exited at Chiriaco Summit for a stretch and a snack. He parked, slid out, and stretched his arms toward the sky. The day was warm and clear. The springtime sun was embraced by bright blue skies, the desert landscape sparkled in the distance. Loyal thought back to the previous August when he and Phil had traveled this very road on their way to Las Vegas. The thought of Phil reminded Loyal of the wedding invitation sitting on his kitchen counter. He should probably attend.

.   .   .

Loyal strolled into the cafe and took a seat at the corner of the counter where he had a good visual of the main entrance. He ordered a burger and a cup of coffee. While he was waiting for his food he took out his phone and re-watched the footage of Ginger/Cinnamon attempting to see into his garage. He was sure it was her. "Who the hell are you?" he murmured to himself. His thoughts were interrupted by the arrival of his meal. While he ate, Loyal watched the other customers in the cafe. The hum of multiple conversations mixed with the clatter of dishes and the tinkling of the bell on the door. A family of six had taken over a table in the corner. The parents looked to be in their mid thirties and were both preoccupied with their phones while the children, who Loyal guessed were all under the age of twelve, argued noisily with each other across the table. An older couple, wearing matching Grand Canyon sweatshirts, sat at a table for two. Their heads were tilted towards one another and they spoke in quiet voices. Loyal ate his burger, finished the last drops of coffee, paid the bill, and left the cafe.

He slid into his Altima and looked with despair at the crowded Interstate. Just as he was shifting into reverse his phone rang. He checked the caller ID, saw it was Maggie Macphearson, and tapped *accept*.

"Hello," Loyal said.

"Detective, it is Maggie. I hope I'm not interrupting anything, I'm just so curious about the tracker," she said. "Have you figured out who put it there?"

"You aren't interrupting," Loyal said. "I think I know who put the tracker on my car, but have no idea why. I'm actually trying to come up with a plan to catch them following me."

"I know some guys who would probably help you with that," Maggie said. "Want me to reach out to them?"

Loyal laughed. "Sure, why not? I'm on my way home from Arizona, about three hours away from you. Traffic is awful. I think I'm going to take back roads through Mecca, the Salton Sea, and Borrego. Should I stop by?"

"Yes," Maggie said. "I'll see who I can round up."

Loyal terminated the call, drove one exit further West on the crowded freeway, then exited and drove down a winding two lane road and into the desert.

The road to Mecca was just as Loyal remembered it from the previous August. It was one lane in each direction and curvy. The empty road sparkled in the sun and the barren desert stretched for miles in all directions. Loyal relaxed as he drove through the lazy curves, eventually entering an area where steep walls rose on either side of the road. It resembled a mini Grand Canyon, the road weaving its way like a river between the walls. Gradually the formations gave way to flat land again, then irrigated squares of farmland appeared. Loyal maneuvered through the agricultural areas, then through the town of Mecca, past the Salton Sea, and turned West towards Borrego.

·   ·   ·

The land between the Salton Sea and the town of Borrego was known as the Badlands. The area was about twenty miles long and fifteen miles wide. Unbelievably, this land was once covered by an ancient sea and featured many steep sided gullies formed by once flowing water. The parched land looked desolate and dangerous. Although no plants or living creatures were visible from the road, Loyal supposed there was plant and animal life out there hidden from view. Soon the Badlands gave way to flat desert land, and Loyal found himself entering the actual town of Borrego Springs. He passed the small airport and the elementary school, wound through the Christmas Circle roundabout, and headed up Montezuma Grade. By 3:45 he had descended from Palomar Mountain, passed the hulking monster that was Harrah's Casino, and was heading into Valley Center.

Trinity drove at exactly 68 miles per hour until the freeway clogged up just South of Camp Pendleton. The next twenty miles were filled with brake lights, unsafe lane changes, and drivers paying more attention to their phones than the traffic. This was Trinity's seventh day in Southern California and she was absolutely sick of the congestion. When she finally parked her CX-5 in front of the condo, she looked at her hands and realized how tightly she was gripping the steering wheel. She loosened them, unstrapped, and slid out of the car.

A glance at her phone informed Trinity that it was nearly 4:00 pm. She was stiff from spending the majority of the day sitting in her car. She thought about her exercise options, quickly deciding on a run along the beach in Carlsbad. In ten minutes she was changed, back in the car, and heading for the coast. She parked in a parking lot on

Garfield Street, walked one block West to a sidewalk above the beach, and began jogging South. The temperature was in the low 60's and the air was cool and refreshing. Trinity felt the stress of the day blow away on the breeze.

She ran South for about half an hour, then turned around and retraced her steps. She arrived back at her vehicle at 5:40, drove back to the condo, and took a shower. By 6:00 she was dressed in loose sweats and a long sleeve t-shirt, and in the kitchen sipping a glass of red wine and preparing a large salad. When the food was ready she sat at the table to eat and search camera footage for Williamson. Trinity logged into a government site that featured automatic license plate recognition. She entered Williamson's license plate and the gps coordinates for the general area. She received information immediately. The last stoplight camera to record Williamson was on Orange Street in Coronado. He had exited Orange on to Isabella Street. A quick check in a different database disclosed that Williamson owned a home on Isabella Street.

Trinity worked backwards, tracing Williamson's route in reverse. She followed the traffic cameras back down Orange Street to the Coronado Bridge. From there she was able to access Caltrans cctv and track him to just north of Sea World. The length of freeway from this point until just North of Genesse contained no cameras. Similarly, there were blank spots from Solana Beach until the 78 interchange, as well as from just North of the 76 to San Clemente State Beach. The lack of cameras near Camp Pendleton made sense to Trinity, the other two blank spaces did not. Using the time stamps on the images and traffic density information, Trinity calculated that it was likely Williamson had stopped somewhere between Genesse and Sea World for approximately 30-40 minutes. She would have to search stoplight cameras in all the cities that bordered Interstate 5 in that area.

L oyal pulled up to Maggie's house just shy of 4:15. An orange Datsun b210 and a powder blue Chevy luv were parked in a dirt area just to the side of the garage. Maggie's yellow buggy was inside the open garage, and an older model green Ford Taurus was parked behind it. Antenna sprouted like weeds on all three of the unfamiliar vehicles. Loyal parked the Altima behind the Taurus, slid out, and approached the front door, which was open. Maggie's giant German Shepherd was sitting smack in the middle of the opening, facing outward. Loyal stopped about three feet from the canine. For about 30 seconds neither man nor beast moved. Ever so slowly, Loyal reached into his pocket and slid his phone out. With four silent taps he dialed Maggie's number. Moments later he heard her old flip phone ringing with that funky Verizon default ringtone song that was so popular in the early 2000's. Keeping eye contact with the dog in the doorway, Loyal raised his phone slowly, reaching his ear just in time to hear Maggie say, "This is Maggie."

Within a minute Maggie was at the door. She instructed Storm to go lay down on his bed in the living room, then waved Loyal inside. "I've rounded up three guys who are willing to help you," she said to Loyal. "Come on in and meet them." Loyal followed Maggie into the living room. Three men sat on her well worn brown couch. All three wore faded jeans and t-shirts, as did Maggie. Loyal felt out of place and overdressed in his slacks and Tommy Bahama.

"Guys, this is Detective Loyal Truesdale," Maggie said. Pointing at each man as she introduced him, Maggie said, "This is Brian, Chris, and Terry."

"Please just call me Loyal guys," Loyal said. He saw there wasn't room on the couch, stepped to the dining room table and grabbed a wooden chair which he placed opposite the couch, and sat.

"Would you like some iced tea?" Maggie asked. Loyal nodded yes. Maggie stepped away to get a glass for him.

"That's an interesting assortment of vehicles you guys are driving," Loyal said with a smile.

"An old ham is like a hermit crab that doesn't want to outgrow its shell," said Terry. "Once we get our rides set up the way we want, we don't ever want to have to move the equipment."

"Which one is yours?" Loyal asked.

"I'm the Taurus," said Terry. "Don't think I could fit into either of the other vehicles."

"I'm the luv," said Chris.

"I'm the 210," said Brian.

"Maggie said you wanted some help with surveillance," said Chris.

"Yes," said Loyal. "You guys have done surveillance before?"

The three men exchanged a quick glance and smiled.

"You could say that," said Terry. "What's your situation?"

"I've identified an individual who placed a tracker on my vehicle," Loyal said. "I want to try to draw her out. Since she can track me from a distance, I want you guys to find her and track her."

"We can do that," Said Brian. He looked at his friends on the couch. "Should we try to enlist a few more guys?"

Terry said, "I'll make a few calls." He rose and walked into the kitchen, passing Maggie who was returning with Loyal's iced tea and tapping his phone as he walked. Maggie handed Loyal the glass and sat down next to Storm on his dog bed, her hand automatically coming to rest on his head.

"My friend Larry has agreed to drive my car," Loyal said. "He's about my size and I'll put him in one of my trademark Tommy Bahamas. I'd like to ride with one of you guys if that's okay."

"Sure," said Chris.

"I think she has an interest in a guy who has an office in La Jolla so I'd like to make a stop there," Loyal said. "I was thinking about Coronado Island as well. I'd like to go to a few places, with stops at each of about half an hour. Something to grab her attention and draw her out."

By 5:45 two more people had joined the group. Dennis, who drove a Ford Mustang from the 90's, and Dee, who drove a late model Toyota Camry. After some discussion, a plan was hatched. They were en route to Loyal's apartment in Carlsbad to meet Larry and re-attach the tracker to Loyal's car. By 6:30 Larry was wearing one of Loyal's Tommy Bahamas, each driver had a list of destinations, and all the vehicles' tanks were topped off. Loyal was riding with Chris in the Chevy, and the group, which Maggie had affectionately referred to as "The Dark Forces", was on the road.

58

Feeling frustrated with the camera search, and with anger at the newbie cop who had disrupted her surveillance of Williamson on his return trip, Trinity pushed away from the table and stood up to stretch. She glanced at her phone to check the time, 6:41, and took a small sip of the red wine that she had barely made a dent in. Looking at the phone reminded her of Truesdale and the tracking device. She checked it and saw that his red dot was finally on the move again. She wondered again about the fact that he had not moved for over twenty-four hours; food poisoning perhaps? It was a non-issue now that he was mobile again. She took the phone, settled herself on the couch, and watched Truesdale's dot as he headed South on Interstate 5. He exited the freeway at Torrey Pines Road and continued South into the Village of La Jolla. He took a right on East Ivanhoe Avenue, a left at Wall Street, and parked across the street from Bertrand's real estate office.

.   .   .

"What the hell?" Trinity said out loud as she sat straight up on the couch staring in disbelief at her phone. She kept tabs on Bertrand's movements and knew that he was still in Tahoe. She stood up, phone in hand, and began pacing the room. "What are you up to?" she said. She continued pacing for a few more minutes, watching the unmoving tracker. This was insane. What could he be doing there? Impulsively she walked to the bedroom. Tossing the phone on the bed, she opened the closet and removed a black sweatshirt, a black beanie, and a pair of black jeans. In less than five minutes she had changed clothes, laced up a pair of black running shoes, and was heading for the front door, phone and computer in hand. Trinity drove to the Chevron at the junction of La Costa Avenue and Interstate 5. She filled her nearly empty tank and was just merging onto 5 South when the tracker began moving again.

Trinity drove fast; 85 miles per hour. Traffic was fairly light on a Sunday night at 7:30. She kept one eye on the road and one eye on the tracker which was now displayed on the open lap top resting on the passenger seat. Truesdale retraced his path to Torrey Pines Road and followed it North until it intersected with La Jolla Parkway. He stayed to the right and merged back onto the 5 South. Trinity was just passing Sea World Drive when Loyal merged onto the 75, better known to locals as the Coronado Bridge. As she watched his tracker cross the elegant span, she felt a tightening in her chest. Her mind raced as she tried to figure out what Truesdale was up to. Could he be involved with Bertrand and Williamson? Was he in on what she suspected was a bribe regarding the SpaWar property redevelopment? Trinity pressed the accelerator closer to the floor. She was close to 95 mph now and taking a huge risk. If she was pulled over at this speed she would get a hell of a lot more than a warning. She covered the remaining 7 miles in under 5 minutes and was ascending the Coronado Bridge just as Loyal's vehicle was parking on the West Side of Spreckles Park.

59

Despite the cramped quarters in the Chevy luv, Loyal and Chris were having a great time riding together. Chris was telling Loyal about past adventures involving the Dark Forces. These folks were a lot of fun. After the 20 minute stop in La Jolla across the street from Roberts' reality office, they had headed South to Coronado. Loyal had picked Coronado for two reasons. The first was that he knew the layout well, having driven here multiple times while listening to Michael Connelly's novels. The second was that traffic would be light on a Sunday evening. Although Dennis had pointed out that this would make them all easier to spot, Loyal still felt like it was the right move.

Larry parked on the West side of Spreckles Park as instructed. Brian parked on the East side of Spreckles Park which provided him with a clear line of site to the bait car, which the team was referring to as Bravo. Dennis was parked on the South side of the park. The line of sight view to Bravo was a little less clear from this angle, but sufficient. Terry and Dee were both driving in circuits, Dee around the park itself and Terry one block out. All were keeping their eyes open for the target car, which they referred to as Tango. Loyal and Chris were driving a circuit four blocks out. Ginger/Cinnamon knew what Loyal looked like so their car could not get close to the action. Each driver, including Larry, had a radio for communication and had watched the security camera footage taken from above Loyal's garage. He had also shown them the drone footage of Ginger/Cinnamon so everyone had a basic idea about the person of interest. Loyal planned on a thirty minute stop in Coronado. He was hoping she would have taken the bait and come out looking for him. Whether she showed in Coronado or not, he had three more destinations planned in the attempt to lure her out.

Less than ten minutes after they had situated themselves Chris's radio crackled to life. "I've got the eye," Terry said. "Picture is inbound to Truesdale." Loyal's phone pinged a moment later. He opened the message and saw a picture of Ginger/Cinnamon. She was sitting in the car, head turned slightly to her right as if she was looking at something in the passenger seat. She was wearing a black beanie to cover her vibrant hair, but Loyal recognized the delicate angle of her neck and jaw. He had studied all the footage he had of her so many times, he felt he knew her. He looked at Chris and nodded. Chris raised the radio to his mouth and said, "ID confirmed." "Copy," said Terry, and soon each other driver had echoed this word.

Trinity eased up on the accelerator as she made the turn onto the 75 and ascended Coronado Bridge. The view from the apex was stunning. The sun had gone down about half an hour ago. The moon was low on the horizon, exactly half of a circle glowing in the dark sky, the vast Pacific Ocean an inky black beneath the bridge. For a brief moment Trinity felt suspended in time. The descent into Coronado literally brought her back to Earth.

Trinity caught greens on the first two stoplights she encountered, then a red stopped her at the intersection of Orange and 6th. She used this brief stop to glance at the computer in the passenger seat and orient herself to the moving map that was displayed on the screen. She sensed movement on her left and turned to see an older green Ford Taurus in the lane next to her. The driver, a man she guessed to be in his late 60's, was looking at her. Their eyes met briefly, then he looked forward again. The light turned green and as the man accelerated straight ahead Trinity noticed several antenna attached to the top rear of the car. "Interesting," she thought as she turned right. The park was located to her left but Trinity wanted to approach Truesdale's car from behind, so she went right on 6th, left on D, then left on 7th. It was basically a one block u-turn. When she turned left onto Orange she would be behind Truesdale. Unfortunately that plan changed when his tracker started moving again.

Truesdale's vehicle traveled North on Orange Ave then turned right and traveled up and over the Coronado Bridge. Trinity followed the tracker, staying about half a mile behind the Altima. She watched the red dot as it turned North on Interstate 5. Trinity made the same choice at the base of the bridge and began retracing the route she had just traveled. As she drove Trinity thought about all the information she had collected on Truesdale. With the exception of the incident in Las Vegas, nothing unusual had been uncovered. He appeared to be an honest and dedicated detective and father. She just couldn't picture him involved in a shady deal. If he was alone in the car, she decided, wherever he parked next she would approach him. She had to know what he was up to.

L oyal and Chris had left Coronado ahead of everyone else. They drove straight up Interstate 5, listening to the Dark Forces on the radio as they made their way North.

"I've got the eye and three for cover," said Brian. Then a bit later he said, "Setting up to get off the freeway at Rosecrans."

"Copy," said Dee. "I've got the eye and two for cover." Then a bit later she said, "Exiting at Nobel Dr."

"Copy," said Terry, " I've got the eye and three for cover."

They continued in this fashion, rotating so no one was behind Tango for very long. Loyal was impressed with their organization and efficiency. He was sure Ginger/Cinnamon had no idea she was being followed. Chris and Loyal exited Interstate 5 at Carlsbad Village Drive. They parked at Loyal's apartment and listened to the radio communications. Larry, in his role as Loyal, exited on Cannon Road and took Carlsbad Blvd. North to Carlsbad Village Drive and parked in the parking lot of Pizza Port. The last person to report on Tango's location was Terry, who turned into the Pizza Port parking lot and parked so that he had a line of sight view of the CX-5 that was parked across the street.

Loyal and Chris had walked from Loyal's apartment and were in the parking lot of Roosevelt Pizzeria, just South of Pizza Port. When Ginger/Cinnamon's location was reported Loyal walked South to Oak Ave, crossed Roosevelt, walked one block, then turned North on Madison Street. Chris, who Ginger/Cinnamon would not recognize simply walked to Pizza Port. He tapped on Terry's window as he passed the Taurus, and they went inside to join Larry and the rest of the dark forces.

Trinity was trained to always be aware of her surroundings. As she traveled North on Interstate 5 she noticed an unusual pair of circular headlights a few cars behind her. The car exited at Rosecrans, but was back behind her at Via de la Valle. When she exited at Cannon, she saw a car behind her that had small antenna attached to the top back rear. The Taurus from Coronado? She was being followed. Her adrenaline spiked. Who was following her? Williamson from SpaWar? Had Roberts finally caught wind of her? Another agency? Was she putting Truesdale in harms way by following him and leading her followers to him?

She glanced at the red dot. The Altima was parked at Pizza Port in Carlsbad. A public place suddenly seemed like a good idea. She would continue to follow. She needed to talk to Truesdale. She drove past Pizza Port and parked across the street in the Bank of America Financial Center lot. Across the street from her the green taurus with the antenna pulled into the Pizza Port parking lot. A few minutes later a thin guy in jeans and a t-shirt approached the Taurus and tapped on the passenger side window. The drivers' side door opened and a tall older man slid out. Together the two men walked into the restaurant.

L oyal walked into the B of A parking lot. He spotted the CX-5. It was parked and facing Pizza Port. He could barely make out her silhouette in the drivers' seat. His heart was beating a bit faster than normal. He felt like he had in high school when he was getting up the courage to ask a girl out. "Why are you so damn nervous?" he muttered to himself. He took a deep breath and approached her car from the passenger side. He didn't want to scare her so he swung wide and approached at an angle. She was looking straight ahead at Pizza Port when he tapped his knuckles against the passenger window. She barely flinched, just turned her head slowly to look out the window at him, her eyes widening slightly with recognition and surprise. He twirled his finger, the universal sign indicating that she should roll down her window, which she did.

. . .

Loyal's first thought was that her eyes were blue. He smiled and said, "I'm meeting some friends for pizza and beer. Want to join us?"

She waited a beat, then smiled back and said, "Sure, why not."

She rolled up the window, slid out of the car, and stood looking at him across the vehicle's roof. He walked around the front of the car and stood facing her. He held out his hand. "Loyal Truesdale," he said. She took his offered handshake and said, "Trinity Glass."

"I've been wondering abut that," Loyal said. He knew he had a big goofy grin on his face, but didn't really care. She was smiling too, and still had his hand in hers.

T he knock on the passenger window had startled her, but Trinity had been trained to respond calmly and did not show a reaction. Her first thought when she saw who was standing beside her car was one of relief. Her second thought was, "How?". She rolled the window down at his prompt and was surprised when he simply invited her to join his group at Pizza Port. She agreed, rolled up the window and slid out of the car. When he walked around and offered her his hand, she took it, enjoying its warmth and strength. It was only after each had said their name that she realized she had forgotten to let his hand go.

Loyal squeezed her hand gently, then released it. He held her gaze for a moment then said, "I have questions."

"Me too," said Trinity.

A moment of silence passed between them then Loyal

said, "You hungry?" Trinity nodded. "Come on," he said turning toward Pizza Port. "I've got some friends in there. I'll introduce you and buy you a beer."

They crossed Roosevelt and walked through the parking lot. As they passed the Taurus Trinity pointed at it and said, "I made this one." She pointed at the b210 and said, "That one too. Your friends drive cars that stand out."

"Really?" Loyal said. "Both of them? You're good. You some kind of spook?" He opened the door of the restaurant for her and as she passed by she looked up at him and said with a smile, "I can neither confirm nor deny."

They walked inside and found the dark forces gang at a picnic style table in the center of the restaurant. Dee scooted over to make room for Trinity and Loyal.

"This is my stalker, Trinity," Loyal said. Each member of the group introduced themselves to Trinity.

"She's good," Loyal said. "She made the Taurus and the b210."

"The b210 has round headlights," Trinity said. "They stand out." She looked at Terry. "I noticed you at the stoplight in Coronado. Then I saw you again at Cannon. The antennas caught my eye." Her eyes swept the entire group. "You all are good though. What's your story?"

"We started out trying to track jammers," Chris said.

"Jammers?" asked Loyal.

"Basically counterproductive malcontents," said Terry.

"They get a charge out of messing up radio conversations," said Brian. "Some play annoying music, others repeat curse words, some ring bells or honk horns."

"Radio bullies?" Trinity asked.

"You could say that," said Dee. "We learned surveillance techniques so we could track them down."

The conversation continued, pizza and beer were consumed, and the time passed quickly. Larry was the first to leave. "I'll drop your car at your place," he said to Loyal. Dee and Terry left soon after that. Then Brian, Chris, and Dennis. When it was just the two of them Trinity turned to Loyal and said, "I still have questions."

"Me too." said Loyal. He looked around at the nearly empty restaurant, then back at Trinity. "These guys are about to close."

Trinity stood, looked down at Loyal for a long moment, then held out her hand. "Come on, I'll walk you home," she said.

Loyal took Trinity's hand and stood. He kept hold of her hand as they walked to the exit. He didn't want to let go and figured she would break the connection if she wanted to. The night air was cool on his face as they crossed the parking lot.

"Do you want to get your car?" he asked.

"Let's walk," she said.

They walked in silence for a few minutes, then Loyal said, "First question. What is your connection to Bertrand Roberts?"

"I could ask the same question of you," Trinity said.

"His wife was my personal trainer," Loyal said.

"I'm trying to prove he's corrup,." Trinity said.

"Who do you work for?" asked Loyal.

"Uncle Sam," Trinity said. "You investigating Lacey Robert's murder?"

"Unofficially," said Loyal.

. . .

They climbed the steps to Loyal's apartment and he unlocked the door. He motioned her to the kitchen table, pulled two glasses from a cupboard, and a bottle of red from the pantry. He uncorked the wine, poured them each a glass, set the bottle on the table, and sat down beside her. He told her everything about his investigation thus far; the radio communication and secret meetings between Bertrand and Blomgren, Hammond's obsessiveness and apparent harassment, the affair with Van Winters. Trinity listened carefully, speaking only with the occasional question. When Loyal finished talking she said, "Bertrand Roberts is a lot of things, but I don't see him killing his wife, although he's probably not above paying someone else to do it."

"Tell me what you know about him," Loyal said.

"Let me give you a little backstory," Trinity said. She told Loyal about her upbringing, her parents' deaths, and the change in her brother.

"The last time I saw him was in Germany in 2004," she said. "He went to Afghanistan after that. Bertrand and Blomgren were both in Afghanistan too. Blomgren was army. Bertrand was a civilian advisor."

"Doing what?" ssked Loyal.

"The U.S. was handing out millions of dollars to Afghan farmers in exchange for information about the Taliban, and the farmers' promise to stop poppy production." Trinity paused to sip her wine. "Obviously, the military and the CIA could not give out money directly, so that's where people like Bertrand Roberts got involved. Roberts speaks four languages fluently, one being Dari, or Persian. He handled millions of dollars over there. When he came back to the U.S. he started purchasing high end properties and formed his realty company."

"You think he was skimming?" Loyal asked.

"Yes," said Trinity. "And I think that is what got my brother killed."

"What happened?" Loyal asked.

"He was shot by a sniper," Trinity said.

Loyal pulled the cork from the half empty bottle and refilled their glasses. He looked at Trinity for a long moment.

"You must have something more," Loyal said.

"I do," said Trinity. "I travel a lot for work, but my home base is Bellingham, Washington. I was in Virginia when Randall was killed, and stayed on the East Coast until his body could be returned to the States. Then there was the burial at Arlington. I wasn't able to return to Bellingham until nearly a month after Randall was shot. It was then that I found his letter dated six days before his death. He said he was uncovering big things, then mentioned our year in France." She paused for a moment. "We spent a year in France when I was eleven and Randall was nine. We were big into playing imaginary military games. I always insisted that I be the military leader, Randall was always the traitor. We gave ourselves French names, Loyal. I was Lisette Brodeur. Randall was Charlie LeFleur. In the letter he sent to me he referred to himself as Roberto Bertrand."

L acey leaned against the granite countertop, arms tight across her chest. Bertrand stood about two feet away from her, arms at his sides. The tension filled the room.

"I can't keep pretending I'm happy Bertrand," Lacey said. "You are always gone."

"I told you from the beginning that I am an ambitious man, Lacey," Bertrand said. "You knew I would be gone a lot."

"Well, I need more," Lacey said.

"You have everything Lace, what more could you need?"

"I don't want more things," Lacey said waving her arm around the well appointed kitchen. "I need more time, more companionship."

"I'm working a big deal right now Lacey," Bertrand said. "It's huge."

"It won't be enough," Lacey said. "It never is."

Bertrand let out a long, slow breath. He closed the distance between them, took her hands in his. "I know what it's like to have nothing Lacey. I won't ever be in that position again."

"Were you this way with Coraline?" Lacey said. "Was her life this lonely hell too?"

Bertrand dropped Lacey's hands, raised his left, and swung. The slap was quick and hard. "Don't ever disrespect Coraline in this house," he hissed. Lacey raised her hand to her right cheek. A tear slipped quietly down the stinging skin. Without a word she turned, grabbed her purse off the rack by the door, and fled the house. She slipped in her truck, backed hard out of the driveway, and drove toward the gate. A glance in her rear view mirror told her that Bertrand was not following. The tears came faster as she drove with no destination in mind. It wasn't until she was parked in the parking lot that she realized where she had driven. Swami's, the place where she had first met Van. She missed him so much. It had been six weeks since he had given her the ultimatum. There had been no communication since that day.

Lacey slid out of her truck and walked slowly down the wooden stairs to the empty beach below. She sat heavily in the sand and looked at the sky. The night was clear and the full moon floated above the dark ocean. The reflected light cast a long yellow path over the black water. An intrusive thought slid into her mind. She could simply step into the water and follow that floating path straight out into the Pacific. She flung herself backwards and lay in the sand, not caring that she had no towel to lie upon. She ran her hand over her still sore cheek, the tears flowing freely. "What did you expect?" she asked herself in a hoarse whisper. She knew that she had traded love for security. She thought about Bertrand. He had been honest from the very beginning about his business and his ambition. He had not changed. It was Lacey who had changed. Lacey who had decided she wanted more for herself. Lacey, who was tired of sacrificing her time, and freedom, and now love, for two people who never gave back. The guilt flowed in with these thoughts. Neither her Mother nor Liane had asked for the tragedies that had befallen them. They depended on her.

Lacey lay in the sand for over an hour. Eventually she sat up, then stood, brushing the cool sand from her clothing. She leaned forward so her hair hung down, and shook the sand from it as well. The wooden stairs led her to the parking lot. She slid in the truck and drove home. Bertrand apologized for the slap, Lacey apologized for her words. Bertrand postponed his business trip for four days and spent every moment with Lacey. They took long walks down the beach, kayaked in Carlsbad lagoon, and ate quiet dinners at home. On the night before he left he took her to The Marine Room in La Jolla. They dined on lobster and filet mignon and drank two bottles of Pinot Noir. They stayed the night at the La Valencia Spa and Hotel. When they said goodbye at Shorebird Lane late the following morning, each told the other that they felt confident they could leave the past behind.

"It took me a while to figure out the hidden message and make the connection to Roberts," Trinity continued. "I was so bowled over by grief and shock. Once I started investigating I became convinced. I don't think I'll ever be able to prove Bertrand was behind Randall's murder." She looked straight in Loyal's eyes and held the gaze. "But I am going to take him down through his shady and illegal business deals," she said. "I've gotten some incriminating footage. I know he has a burner phone. If I had that, I'd have him." She sighed, glanced at her phone, and stood. "It is nearly 2:00," she said. "I should go." Loyal stood and walked to the door with her. It opened to a wall of dense fog. "Dangerous to drive in this," Loyal said. "You should probably stay."

The next morning found Trinity at the kitchen table and Loyal in the kitchen making coffee. He handed her a steaming mug, then pulled a kitchen chair out and sat down opposite her, a mug of coffee in his hands. "We have different end games," Loyal said after a long sip, "but we seem to be dealing with the same players."

"Yep," Trinity said. "I agree. You thinking we should pool our resources?"

"I do," said Loyal. "After listening to you last night I think Blomgren is the key. I'm going to hit him straight on this morning. Just show up at his house and see what happens."

"I've got to send some footage to my boss. Should have done it yesterday, but I got caught up in following you," Trinity said with a smile. "Roberts is scheduled to return from Tahoe today. I'll be keeping tabs on him." She put her hand on Loyal's arm. "I need to tell you something," she said. "I have eyes on Roberts' house through his security system. I saw you put the tracker on his vehicle. I deleted the image." She smiled and narrowed her eyes. "If you repeat that I will, of course, deny it."

Loyal returned the smile. "You are one incredibly clever woman," he said. "And if you repeat that, I will not deny it."

Half an hour later, as the sun was breaking through the fog from the previous evening, Trinity and Loyal were walking back to her car. They paused at her driver's door and she reached up and brushed his cheek with a kiss. They looked at each other for a long moment, then she slid in the car and drove away. She could see him in the rear view for a moment. He stood still, just watching her go. "Focus Glass," she said out loud to herself. She was finding the focusing difficult. Her mind kept returning to the previous night and this morning. Loyal was an interesting man. There was something so steady and reassuring about him. After Randall had been killed Trinity had felt completely unmoored. Much like an abandoned vessel far out to sea, she had been unable to drop anchor and had drifted in an ocean of uncertainty. Eventually her focus had become Bertrand Roberts, and she had hunted him with the stealth and diligence of a great white shark. Personal relationships had suffered, then ended. For the first time in many years she felt she had met someone who understood her.

The first thing she did when she reached her rented condo was send the images of the backpack exchange to her boss, Douglass Caldwell. She then checked Bertrand's flight information. He was scheduled to leave Tahoe at 1:00 pm and arrive in Carlsbad at 2:30. On impulse she checked baldgeek.net. Loyal had shown her the website this morning over coffee. She was surprised that she had never come across it herself. She pulled up the virtual radar. It was amazing how many planes were in the air. The map of the lower half of California was saturated. She looked at the information presented in a chart on the bottom right portion of the screen. 832 aircraft were currently being tracked. The chart showed a silhouette of each craft, as well as its type, callsign or N-number, duration of flight, altitude, and whether it was military or civilian. Out of curiosity, Trinity began scrolling down the list looking at N numbers. She stopped when she came to one she had long ago committed to memory. The Gulfstream G550 that Bertrand always used was in the air already, and had been for nearly half an hour. Trinity opened a new window and rechecked the flight plan on file. It had not been changed. She stared at the planes on baldgeek.net and said out loud, "What the hell are you up to?"

L oyal watched Trinity drive away, then turned and walked back to his apartment. As he walked he replayed the events of the previous evening in his mind. The Dark Forces, Pizza Port, the evening with Trinity. She was intelligent and creative. "Focus Truesdale," he said out loud to himself with a smile as he climbed the stairs. An hour later Loyal was in Vista making the turn onto Via Pedro. After spending some time thinking, he had decided that direct confrontation was, indeed, the best plan of action. The white Rubicon was in the center of the driveway. Loyal parked next to the curb and walked to the door. He depressed the doorbell and was rewarded with the echoing ring from inside the house. He waited a full minute, then rang again. Still no one came to the door. It had been after 10:00 when Loyal had left Carlsbad, and was probably near 11:00 now. Could Blomgren still be sleeping? Loyal knocked on the door hard; four clear raps.

Still no one answered. He stepped back and looked up. A security camera was trained directly on the front door. He waved his arms; still no response. Loyal's intuition was ramping up. Something was wrong here.

The blinds in the front windows were closed. Loyal walked toward the side of the house. The fence was wooden and about four feet high. Loyal put his foot on the spigot coming out of the house, prayed it wouldn't snap off, and raised himself up. The spigot held, and Loyal was able to slide his right leg over the top of the wooden fence, pivot his body, and slide down the other side. It was not a graceful move, but it did the job. Loyal had done drone surveillance on this house and was fairly sure Blomgren did not have a dog. Still, he walked cautiously. The blinds on the kitchen window were raised. Loyal peeked in and saw nothing. He rounded the back corner of the house, saw the shed with the antenna array on his right, the barbecue and patio, and an open sliding glass door to his left. He used his elbow to slide it open a few feet more, leaned in, and called, "Hello. Is anyone home?" There was no answer. Loyal stepped tentatively into the room, then stopped. The coppery smell of blood was unmistakeable. He backed slowly out of the house. He stood for a moment on the small patio, then leaned down and removed his shoes. He slid the PM9 out and slowly entered the house. He cleared the small living room, dining area and kitchen. There was a closed door near the entry way to his left. He slid his hand into his jacket pocket, and using it as a glove, he carefully opened the door, revealing an empty half bath. To his right was a partially open door. He pushed it slowly with his elbow. The smell was much stronger in this room. Loyal eased through the doorway, entering the bedroom. A kingsized bed monopolized the space. Blomgren lay on the bed, his body under the covers as if asleep, his head a bloody mess. "Fuck," said Loyal under his breath. "This just became a major issue." He knelt down and cleared the space under the bed. He opened the closet door, using his pocket as a glove again, his gun ready. The closet held only clothes. Loyal pushed the door closed with his elbow and turned to look at Blomgren. His head had been bashed, in much the same way as Lacey's had been. Loyal looked up. There was blood splatter on the ceiling. He took out his phone and took a picture of the blood splatter and of Blomgren.. He emailed the pictures to himself, then deleted them from the phone. He took one more look around the bedroom, then backed out of the room and exited the small house. He paused on the patio to slide his gun back into his belly band, and put his shoes back on. He then made his way back to the front, and considered his options.

Simply leaving was not an option. The security cameras likely had recorded his approach to the front door. Besides that, disability or not, he was a sworn officer of the law. His next thought was whom to call. Protocol was simple.

Always call 911 first. Loyal set protocol to the side and thought it through. Obviously Vista, through 911, as this was within their precinct. Carlsbad deserved a courtesy call as Blomgren was a critical witness, and potential suspect, in Lacey's case. Hammond was going to have a fit. "Damn it," Loyal said out loud. The first call he made was to Captain Williams at the Carlsbad Sheriff Department. He then sent a text to Trinity.

Blomgren dead, murdered. Don't reply, will talk later.

He deleted the text as soon as it was delivered. His second call was to Maynard Lily, who agreed to be available if the Vista Detectives took Loyal to the station for questioning. Loyal deleted his call history and then made the third call, which was to 911. Loyal explained who he was, gave a clear description of himself and his clothing, and described the situation on Via Pedro. The dispatcher took the information and asked Loyal to please remain on the phone until an officer arrived at the scene. Loyal agreed and sat down on the curb to wait.

He didn't have to wait long. Two marked units, lights flashing and sirens screaming, arrived in less than four minutes. Loyal ended the call with the dispatcher and stood. The officers cut the sirens, but left the lights flashing and exited their vehicles. They spoke to each other briefly, then walked toward Loyal. Both were young, early thirties, and approached cautiously. Loyal kept his hands visible and said, "My name is Detective Truesdale. I called 911." He indicated Blomgren's house with a small wave of his hand. "I believe there has been a death in this home." The officers were close enough now that Loyal could read the names on their badges; L. Schroeder and K. Delimitros. Delimitros spoke. "Dispatch gave us that intel. Can we see some I.D. please." Loyal reached into his back pocket, pulled out his badge wallet, and handed it over. Delimitros glanced at it, then handed it back. He looked around the cul-de-sac. Curious neighbors were emerging from their homes. "Schroeder," he said, "stay here and protect the scene." He turned towards Loyal. "Walk me through it," he said.

Loyal walked Delimitros through everything; the approach to the front door, the hop over the fence, the open slider, and the entry into the home on sock covered feet. He waited outside while Delimitros entered the home. Less than sixty seconds after he had entered the home, Delimitros was back outside again, his face ashen and his voice shaky as he said, "I need to call homicide in." Loyal looked at the young officer's pale face and recalled the first time he and his T.O. had secured a murder scene together. The victim had been stabbed in the head and neck, and had defensive cuts on his hands. The roommate had called 911, claiming two drug dealers had entered the house and committed the murder. Loyal guessed he had looked much the same way that Delimitros did today. His T.O., Gordon, had looked at Loyal and said, "The dead can't hurt you Loyal. Keep your attention on the living." Gordon was right, it turned out the roommate had committed the murder.

Trinity alternated between monitoring the Gulfstream 550 and checking for an updated flight plan. A half hour after her discovery of Bertrand's deception, a revised flight plan was filed. The jet would be landing at Ontario airport in 25 minutes. Trinity hacked into Ontario's security cameras and watched in real time as the Gulfstream landed and taxied toward the jet center located on the South side of the airport. An orange vested aircraft marshaller used hand signals to guide the jet to its resting spot. Trinity watched as a set of stairs descended from the large plane. A few minutes later the pilot and co-pilot, carrying briefcases, emerged and walked down the stairs. She watched for a full five minutes more, but no one else deplaned. She slapped the table with the palm of her hand, hard. "Dammit," she said, the word harsh on her tongue. Bertrand had given her the slip.

. . .

Trinity stood and began pacing around the living room. Bertrand was in the wind. She stopped, walked quickly back to the table, and checked the tracking app. His vehicle was back at Shorebird Lane. She followed his track backwards and saw that it had left Port Hueneme at 10:25 the previous evening. Her phone pinged and a text message appeared at the top. It was from Loyal and read:

Blomgren dead, murdered. Don't reply, will talk later.

Trinity let out a long, slow breath. Bertrand had gotten back in town just after 2:00 am. She needed the time of death for Blomgren. She wondered if her assessment about Bertrand's ability to kill was incorrect. Perhaps he was willing to get his hands dirty. She was pondering this possibility when her secure email announced an incoming message. She logged on and found a reply from Caldwell.

Looks promising. Dispatching team three. ETA tomorrow 11:00 am. McClellan-Palomar. Do you have details on next meeting?

Trinity responded that she was still working on that, making no mention of Bertrand's duplicity. She spent the next 90 minutes searching traffic cameras in the area between Genesee and Sea World for Williamson's vehicle.

She located him at a traffic light at the intersection of Mission Bay Drive and Garnet. She was able to follow him through traffic light cameras on Jewell, Ingraham, Haines, and Faunel, where he turned right. Trinity studied google maps, then hacked into a security camera located on the Christian Science Building that faced Faunel. She saw Williamson pass by. The next camera she could find was on Pacific Beach Elementary School. Williamson did not show up on that feed. This information narrowed her search to a ten block section of Faunel. Williamson could have turned East or West at any of those intersections, or parked somewhere along Faunel. Trinity reviewed more footage from the traffic light camera on Garnet and Faunel. She located Williamson retracing his route fifteen minutes after he had arrived. With the time frame and grid narrowed, she was able to access satellite footage and soon had found the residence that Williamson had visited. Within minutes Trinity had learned the name of the owner of the house on Faunel; Ann Marie Williamson, Jack Williamson's ex wife.

Trinity memorized the address, studied the map a moment longer, then logged out and closed the lap top. She stood and walked to the kitchen window. She thought about Bertrand, the backpack exchange, and the fact that he was taking more precautions than he ever had before. Trinity was convinced that a deal with Jack Williamson was imminent, and very big. She walked back to her phone and checked the tracker. Bertrand was in motion, the red dot heading west on Poinsettia Lane. Trinity snatched up the phone, slipped on a pair of Blundstone ankle boots, grabbed her purse, and ran out the door.

A black crown vic pulled into the cul-de-sac within six minutes of the officer's call to Homicide. Loyal watched as two women slid out of the vehicle. They spoke with Delimitros briefly, then approached Loyal. One was about 5'4", slender, with dark brown hair cut short to her shoulders. The other was tall, about 6 feet, black as ebony with close cropped hair. Both wore suits and sunglasses, removing the latter as they approached Loyal. The tall one spoke.

"I'm Detective Greene," she said. "This is Detective Sanchez. I understand you are the detective who made the emergency call."

"Yes," said Loyal. "I'm Detective Truesdale from the Carlsbad Sheriff's Department, currently on leave."

"Are you armed Detective?" asked Greene.

"Yes," said Loyal. "My privately owned piece."

"I'm going tp need to see that please," Greene said. She held out her right hand. Loyal reached under his shirt, took out the PM9, and placed it in her hand. "It hasn't been fired," he said, then added, "and this vic didn't die from a gunshot."

Greene examined the gun, then handed it back to Loyal. "Also, I've placed a courtesy call to my Captain," said Loyal. "I believe the victim is a witness in an active murder investigation."

Detective Greene turned to Detective Sanchez and said, "You finish securing the scene." Turning back to Loyal, she said "Show me everything you did and what you touched."

Loyal showed her where he had stood on the front porch, how he had touched the doorbell and knocked on the door. He hopped the fence. She followed easily. He explained about the open sliding glass door, and how he had used his elbow to open it further. She entered the house with him. He retraced his steps and actions. "I'm going to need you to remain on scene," she said.

"I figured that," Loyal said with a sigh.

They returned to the front of the house. Detective Greene asked Loyal to wait with Officer Schroeder, then pulled out her phone and started making calls. Within twenty minutes more vehicles had arrived. The crime scene techs, wearing jumpsuits, booties, hair nets, and gloves, followed Greene into the house. Sanchez had secured the scene. Yellow barrier tape surrounded Blomgren's property and blocked the entrance to the cul de sac. Normally peaceful Via Pedro was a hive of activity. Curious neighbors stood in their driveways and on their lawns. The media arrived soon after the evidence techs and the coroner. Vans from three local stations pulled as close to the action as they could. Smartly dressed reporters called out questions to the officers at the mouth of Via Pedro. Loyal leaned against a marked unit and watched the carefully controlled chaos. He heard a familiar voice behind him and turned to see Hammond arguing with one of the officers securing the scene. After a brief back and forth, Hammond was allowed through. He walked straight to Loyal and Schroeder.

Hammond flashed his badge wallet at Schroeder and said, "I need to talk to the lead detective." Schroeder pointed at Detective Greene who was conferring with a tech on the front lawn. "I'll need to talk to him next," Hammond said, pointing a finger at Loyal. Hammond strode quickly to the edge of the barrier tape and called to Detective Greene. She approached him and they spoke for a moment, then both walked over to Loyal and Schroeder. "Give these guys a minute Schroeder," Greene said. Schroeder nodded and moved about ten feet away. Greene turned and walked back toward Blomgren's house, leaving Loyal and Hammond alone. "What in the hell are you doing here?" Hammond hissed.

"I had a few questions for Mr. Blomgren," Loyal said.

"I told you to leave this alone Truesdale, this is my case," Hammond said.

Loyal kept eye contact, but remained silent.

Hammond took a breath in, then blew it out. His voice was low and filled with malice. "You'll stay the fuck away from my case, Truesdale, if you know what's good for you."

"Is that a threat?" Loyal asked.

Hammond leaned in close to Loyal. His voice a menacing whisper. "I'd go to the Captain on this," he said, "but you'd like that wouldn't you? Loyal the golden boy." He rocked back slightly, then leaned in again. "I'm only going to say this once Truesdale. You better watch yourself. Stay away from my case."

Trinity followed the red dot on the tracker app North on Interstate 5, then East on Highway 78. She stayed about half a mile behind Bertrand. She was feeling edgy about how long she had been driving the CX-5, and decided to swap it out for something else as soon as possible. Bertrand drove through the northern edge of Escondido and went up the grade into Valley Center. He stopped for gas at Valley Center Oil Corporation. Trinity parked across the street at a restaurant called Fat Ivor's and watched while he filled his tank. She glanced at her own gas gauge and realized she only had a quarter tank. When Robert's exited the gas station she drove across the street, filled her own tank, and pulled back out onto Valley Center Road.

As she drove Trinity mulled over the things she had learned from, and about, Loyal the night before. He had been very willing to allow her access to everything he had learned during his investigation. Lacey's affair had been a surprise. Bertrand was not the type of man to take something like that lying down. Trinity wondered if he had been aware that his wife was seeing someone else. Hammond's history with Lacey was interesting as well, as was Hammond's history with Loyal. While Loyal found Hammond to be rude and obnoxious, it was Hammond's TO, Clayton Fields, that Loyal had the real problem with. He hadn't explained in detail, but apparently it had something to do with Loyal's ex wife.

Trinity had not been able to be as free with information as Loyal had been. She had given him as much background on Bertrand as she could. Her high security clearances prohibited her from revealing everything. Loyal had understood this. Trinity thought about Blomgren being murdered. She wondered if Loyal had contacted Carlsbad as well as Vista. He seemed to be honest and forthright, so he probably had. Hammond was going to be livid. She smiled. "Loyal can handle him," she thought.

Bertrand led Trinity through Valley Center, past the enormous Harrah's Rincon Casino, and through a roundabout at the base of Palomar Mountain. He continued East, the windy road increasing in elevation. Just before Lake Henshaw, Bertrand turned left onto East Grade Road. Trinity made the same turn several minutes later, and began ascending the winding road. To her right was a steep drop. The road had no barriers to help prevent a deadly plunge should a driver make an error. To the left the hill rose sharply, rocks and trees dotting the landscape. Trinity drove carefully, keeping a watchful eye on the tracker. Bertrand pulled into parking for the Henshaw Scenic Vista Observation Site. As Trinity passed the entrance she saw that his vehicle was the only one in the lot. She continued on until she found a spot where she could safely pull the car over. It was a tiny stretch of dirt, the right hand tires of the CX-5 were on the edge of a very steep slope. Trinity slid out of the car, grabbed her binoculars and keys, and started walking back towards the observation site.

Hammond walked away without giving Loyal a chance to respond, which was fine with Loyal. He had nothing to say to Hammond. Schroeder walked back and resumed his position near Loyal. Both men watched as Hammond and Detective Greene spoke briefly then turned and walked toward the house. They stood just outside the front door, Hammond gesticulating and speaking forcefully, obviously upset. Greene stood calmly, letting the man have his say, then shook her head. Hammond pulled out his wallet, handed her his card, added a few brusque words, then turned and walked back to his Crown Vic.

Greene spent a few more minutes conferring with evidence techs, then approached Loyal. "I'm going to need you to come down to the station with me Detective Truesdale."

Loyal checked the time on his phone, then said, "I have a prior engagement. I'm going to need to make a call."

"Sure," said Greene. "Make your call then you can ride downtown with me." She turned to walk away, then turned back. "Oh, and I'm going to need that phone after you make your call Detective."

Loyal turned away from Greene and quickly called Maynard Lily. Lily assured him he would meet him at the station. Loyal pocketed his phone and walked to Greene's Crown Vic. Greene and Sanchez took the front seats, Greene driving, and Loyal slid into the uncomfortable backseat. Greene shifted in the driver's seat, angling herself so she could look back at Loyal. She held out her left hand. "The phone?" she asked. Loyal pulled it out of his pocket with a sigh and handed it over. "Why don't I hang onto the gun too?" said Greene. Loyal handed the PM9 over as well.

The drive from Via Pedro to S. Melrose took about fifteen minutes and was completed in total silence. Loyal understood why the detectives were taking him to the station. He would have done the same thing if the situation was reversed, but he still didn't like it. He didn't like the way Hammond was talking to him either. The threats were blatant. Loyal wished he had the PM9 under his shirt. After all his years in law enforcement he felt naked without it.

I t took Trinity about five minutes to backtrack to the outlook. She stopped near some oak trees that she hoped would conceal her presence. She peeked through the branches and took in the scene. Bertrand Roberts stood at the Eastern most end of the observation deck. He leaned nonchalantly against the railing, his gaze seemingly focused on Lake Henshaw and the hills beyond. He was dressed more casually than usual. Trinity raised her binoculars, they brought her so close it was as if she was standing next to the man. She could see the red tag on his jeans, the gold seven indicating the brand and the excessive cost of his apparel. He wore a jacket and had a camera bag slung over his left shoulder. Trinity watched and thought about all she knew about him. The realty company was his main focus, but he also owned a motel in Truckee, a town close to Lake Tahoe. He was intimately involved in the realty business, more remotely involved in the running of the motel. Through tax records Trinity had learned that the motel consistently reported nearly full occupancy. Observation, however, had shown her that the motel was rarely full. She had wondered about the possibility that Roberts was moving cash obtained in Afghanistan through the motel to legitimize it. If this was the case, she wondered, where was he getting the ID's motels were required by law to obtain from guests?

Trinity pushed the record button on the binoculars and watched Bertrand stand still on the observation deck. His gaze remained focused on the blue of the lake and the green hills beyond it. Movement to her right caught her eye and she turned to see a black Yukon entering the parking lot. Williamson was easily visible in the driver's seat. She followed his progress as he parked some distance away from Bertrand's vehicle. He remained in the car. Trinity turned her attention, and the binoculars, back to Bertrand. He had turned and was facing the parking lot, the camera bag was now on the deck by his feet. After a brief moment, Bertrand put his hands in his jacket pockets and walked back to his car. He slid in and drove away without acknowledging Williamson's presence. Trinity swiveled the binoculars to Williamson once again. He exited his vehicle, took a long moment to scan his surroundings, then walked purposefully to the observation deck. He picked up the camera bag, slung it over his right shoulder, and returned to the Yukon. The entire process took less than two minutes. Trinity recorded it all.

Greene led Loyal into the Vista station through a back door. They walked about half way down a hallway, the florescent lights shining brightly overhead. Greene stopped abruptly at a door labeled *Interview Room 4*. She pulled out a set of keys and unlocked the door, motioning Loyal into the room. "Be right back," she said. "Sit tight."

"Detective Greene," Loyal said, and she paused. "My lawyer is waiting for me in reception," he said. "Maynard Lily, big guy, can't miss him." Loyal smiled at her. "Can you make sure he is with you when you return?"

Greene narrowed her eyes. "Sure," she said, then turned and left the room leaving Loyal alone.

Loyal sat at the narrow table and waited. Less than five minutes passed before the door opened and Green, Sanchez, and Maynard Lily entered the room. "I'd like a few minutes with my client please," Lily said. Greene nodded and she and Sanchez left the room. Maynard sat down next to Loyal. "How do you want this to go down?" he asked.

"I'm ok walking them through the events of the morning," Loyal said. "I don't want to talk about my reasons for being there or any connections to Lacey's death."

"Ok," said Maynard as he stood up and walked to the door. He knocked twice, the door opened, and Greene and Sanchez entered the room. Maynard returned to the chair beside Loyal. Greene and Sanchez sat down opposite them. "This conversation is being recorded," said Greene. Maynard placed his own small recorder on the table and hit the record button.

Greene spoke first, reciting the date, time, and names of the people present. "Why were you at Mr. Blomgren's house this morning?" she asked.

"Irrelevant," said Maynard. "My client will discuss the events of the morning. Nothing more."

Sanchez and Greene exchanged a glance. "What phone calls did you make after discovering the body?" asked Sanchez.

"I made a courtesy call to Carlsbad, then called 911," Loyal said.

"Why Carlsbad?" asked Greene.

Maynard took a breath in, but Loyal spoke."It's ok," he said to Maynard. "As I explained at the scene Detective," he said, "Blomgren was a witness and possible suspect in an ongoing murder investigation."

"You are on leave Detective Truesdale," Greene said. "Why were you at a witnesses, and possible suspect's, house?"

"My client will not be discussing that," Maynard said.

"Do you have any thoughts about who would want to hurt Blomgren?" Greene asked.

"No," said Loyal.

The back and forth continued for nearly an hour. Greene and Sanchez were clearly frustrated with Maynard, who interjected frequently. Loyal said little. As Greene was asking again why Loyal had been at the house on Via Pedro there was a quick knock on the door. An officer opened the door and motioned to Greene and Sanchez. They rose and exited the room, coming back in a moment later. "That's all we have for now," said Greene, handing Loyal his phone and gun. "You are free to go Detective. Thank you for your time. Do you need a ride back to your vehicle?"

"I'll drive him," said Maynard.

As Loyal and Maynard crossed the parking lot, Loyal's phone pinged. The text message was from O'Keefe and said:

Hammond is going pretty hard at a guy named Van Winters. He on your suspect list?

. . .

"Dammit," said Loyal. He turned to Maynard. "I'm going to need a little more of your time. I'd like to retain you to represent Van Winters. He's at the Carlsbad station now, being interviewed by Hammond. Go get him and I'll meet you guys at your office."

"On my way," said Maynard.

Loyal walked back into the Vista station. He walked up to reception and said to the man behind the desk, "Looks like I'm going to need a ride after all."

Trinity jogged back to her car, executed a u-turn on the narrow road, and drove back toward the observation site. She caught sight of Williamson's Yukon as it turned out of the parking lot and headed down the hill. She followed Williamson West on the 76, South on Interstate 15, West on the 52, then South on Interstate 5. Traffic was fairly heavy and Trinity stayed several car lengths behind him. She found herself wishing that she had Loyal's Dark Forces gang with her and smiled at the memory of the previous night.

Williamson exited the freeway in Pacific Beach. He drove West on Garnet, then turned right on Faunel. Trinity turned right on Gresham, which was one street before Faunel. She turned left on Emerald, then left on Faunel and drove past Williamson's ex-wife's house. The Yukon was in the driveway. She continued on and parked in the parking lot of a Starbuck's on Garnet. Less than ten minutes later the Yukon passed by. Trinity pulled back into traffic and continued to follow. Williamson drove South on Interstate 5, then exited on Hancock Street. Trinity knew this was the exit for SpaWar, so she did not follow him. Instead she went one exit further, exited, then got back on Interstate 5 heading North. She drove straight back to Carlsbad and exchanged the CX-5 for a black 2018 Yukon Denali.

Trinity drove the Yukon back to her rented condo. She watched the footage of Bertrand and Williamson's exchange of the camera bag again. She was just settling at her computer to research Ann Marie Williamson when her phone announced an incoming text message. It was from Loyal and read:

I'm cut loose from Vista PD. New developments. Going to be busy for a few more hours.

Trinity responded with her condo's address and instructions to come over when he was free, then turned back to her computer. Information about Ann Marie Williamson was readily available and held few surprises. In half an hour Trinity had a fairly complete profile of the woman. Trinity's next step was researching Ann Marie's financials, which proved to be a bit more convoluted. She had alimony from Jack. They had been married for 22 years. Just after their divorce was finalized she had inherited a chain of laundromats from her parents. They were located in some of the poorest and most crime ridden areas of San Diego, yet provided Ann Marie with a surprisingly healthy income. Trinity leaned back in her chair and thought about the backpack and the camera bag that Williamson had delivered to his ex wife. Was she literally laundering money for him?

A patrol officer named Davidson drove Loyal back to Via Pedro. It was still an active crime scene, so Loyal was escorted to his Altima. He slid in and drove away. His head was spinning. Blomgren killed in a manner similar to Lacey, Hammond's unveiled threats, and Van Winters being interrogated. He hoped Maynard had arrived and gotten the young man out of Hammond's clutches, at least for the time being. Loyal was good at reading people and did not think Van was very high on the suspect list. When he parked in front of Maynard's law offices, he took a moment to send a text to Trinity. She responded with her address and the invitation to come by when he could. Her words brought a brief smile to Loyal's face. She was intriguing.

Loyal slid out of the Altima, climbed the two flights of stairs, and sat down in the lobby of Smith, Horvath, and

Lily. It was nearly four o'clock. He had eaten nothing since this morning and his stomach was beginning to complain. He picked up a People magazine. Kristin Bell and Dax Shepard smiled out at him. The main article was about how they made their marriage work. Loyal wondered, again, if Bertrand had known about Lacey's affair. He was pondering this possibility when the door opened and Maynard and a very haggard looking Van crossed the threshold. Loyal rose and silently followed the two men into Maynard's office.

Maynard stripped off his jacket and loosened his tie. He reached into a mini fridge behind his desk and brought out three water bottles. He handed one each to Loyal and Van, then opened his own and took a long drink. Loyal did the same, downing half the bottle in one long swallow. Van simply accepted the bottle and sat down in a chair, leaning forward, elbows on knees, unopened bottle in his hands. His head hung down, long blonde hair obscuring his face. His posture was the epitome of defeat. Loyal took the chair beside Van and looked expectantly at Maynard, who had seated himself behind the desk. Maynard gave a small shrug and said, "This is your show Loyal. I freed the man, where do you want to go from here?" Loyal clapped a hand on Van's shoulder. The younger man straightened slightly and turned his head toward Loyal.

"Thanks for sending a lawyer," he said.

"Tell us everything," Loyal said. "Start with the day you met Lacey. Leave nothing out."

"First you need to formally retain my services," Maynard said, sliding some papers across the desk

Van signed them and slid them back across the desk. He took a deep breath in and slowly let it out. "I met her at Swami's Beach in July of 2017," He said. "She was trying to surf." A smile appeared briefly at the memory, then faded. "I offered to teach her. She accepted." Van spoke for half an hour. Loyal and Maynard asked an occasional question, but were mostly quiet and listening.

"What happened with Hammond today?" Loyal asked.

"He doesn't have anything," Maynard said. "It was a fishing expedition."

"He came to my apartment this morning," Van said. "He told me he needed my help, but when we got to the sheriff's station he switched gears. He was basically accusing me of killing Lacey." Van paused a moment, tears threatening. "I would never hurt her," he said.

"Did Hammond ask about the affair?" Loyal asked.

"He implied it, but I never admitted to it," said Van.

"He knows," Loyal said. He glanced at Maynard. "But he can't say anything." He glanced back at Van. "You did good kid. It's been a long day. How about I give you a ride home?"

Loyal and Van slid into the Altima. Loyal pulled away from Lily's office and after a few moments of silence asked Van, "Where were you the morning Lacey was killed?"

"Asleep in my apartment," Van said.

"I don't suppose anyone was there who can give you an alibi?" Loyal asked.

"I was alone," said Van. "I got up around 8:00 and went surfing. There were guys in the water who saw me, but that was closer to 9:00."

"You right or left handed?" Loyal asked.

Van looked confused at the change in topic, but answered. "Right," he said.

Lacey picked up the backpack, grabbed Liane's hand, and walked her sister next door to Gladys' house. The elderly woman opened the door just as they approached, smiling brightly and saying, "Come on in."

"Thank you again for keeping her overnight," Lacey said. "I should be back midday tomorrow."

"No problem," Gladys said. "I love having the company." She took the backpack from Lacey and pointed Liane in the direction of the kitchen. "Wait in the kitchen, honey," she said, "I'll be right there." She turned back toward Lacey. "You are going to Prescott?"

"Yes," said Lacey. "I'm visiting an old friend."

Gladys gave Lacey a quick hug. "You have fun, and don't worry about Liane. We'll be fine."

Lacey glanced at the clock when she started the truck. 8:15.

She was going to hit morning traffic, but hoped to arrive in Prescott by 4:00. John had sounded surprised when she called to ask if she could visit, but had readily agreed. Bertrand was in Tahoe again. He had driven himself this time, which was very unusual. He was acting strangely, but swore to her that nothing was wrong. He had told her repeatedly that the deal he was working on was the biggest in his career, but refused to tell her any details. "I don't want to sour the deal," had been his exact words.

Lacey thought about that conversation as she drove. The deal that was "soured" for her was their marriage. She just felt so damn guilty when she thought about divorcing Bertrand. He had given her so much, not to mention the care he provided for Liane and her mother. All Bertrand had ever asked from her was her love and loyalty, and she had betrayed him on those two counts. This was one endless loop that flowed through her mind as she drove. The second endless loop was Van. She had not seen or heard from him since October. Lacey had assumed that Van would miss her and give in to the urge to call her. He had not. She understood now that he meant what he said. It was all or nothing. This was one of the things she wanted to talk to John about. The other was Len Hammond.

Loyal drove Van to his apartment in Leucadia and watched as the young man trudged up the stairs and unlocked the door. Van entered his home without a backward glance. Loyal sat in the parking lot for a few minutes and thought about his conversation with Van. He had a few more questions for Gladys Kramer, and decided now was as good a time as any. Loyal pulled out his phone, brought up Gladys' contact info, and dialed. She answered on the second ring.

"Hello Detective," she said.

"Hello Mrs. Kramer," Loyal began, but she interrupted with, "Oh, call me Gladys please."

"Hello Gladys," Loyal began again. "Please call me Loyal. I have a few more questions and was wondering if I could stop by."

"Sure Loyal," she said. "I'm at Bertrand Roberts' house at the moment. Just come here. The gate code is 1421."

"I'm about ten minutes away," Loyal said. He disconnected, started the Altima, and headed toward the freeway.

True to his word Loyal arrived on Shorebird Lane ten minutes later. He keyed in the gate code Gladys had provided and the gate swung slowly open. Loyal parked in front of Gladys' house, took a moment to jot the gate code down in his notepad, then exited the Altima and walked towards Bertrand's house. He was just raising his hand to the doorbell when the front door swung open. Gladys smiled up at him, then stepped back to allow him entry.

"I'm going to have you wait in the kitchen Loyal," she said as she led him through the opulent entryway and into the massive kitchen. "I'm helping Liane pack," she said. "She's going to stay a few days with me."

"Sure," said Loyal, "take your time." Gladys left the kitchen and Loyal looked around. The place was so clean, it looked brand new. Loyal was no slob, but his place didn't compare. The kitchen actually looked unused. His eyes swept the room, stopping on the center of the granite countertop. Two phones lay side by side. One was an expensive Apple iPhone, the other a Tracfone throwaway. Loyal glanced around. He was alone in the kitchen. He approached the Tracfone and pushed the on button. It lit up immediately. Loyal looked around again. Bertrand's car had been in the driveway. These could be his phones. Loyal opened the Tracfone, surprised that there was no code needed. He went to recent calls. Only one number was listed. Loyal pulled out his own phone, took a picture of the throwaway's screen, then shut both phones down and re-pocketed his own.

T rinity sat at the kitchen table, a bottle of Perrier to her left, an open computer to her right. She sipped at the Perrier and watched the screen, which was split into four sections. The top two sections showed baldgeek.net, on which Trinity was monitoring the Gulfstream Bertrand used, and Loyal Truesdale's tracker, which she was monitoring for fun. He was currently on Interstate 5 North, having just left Leucadia. The bottom two sections showed the front and back of Bertrand Roberts' house. The interior security cameras were currently inactivated. Trinity could have turned them on, wanted to in fact, but that act would only reveal to Bertrand that he had an uninvited observer.

She watched as Loyal's tracker turned on Shorebird Lane, then watched through the security cameras as he parked in front of Gladys Kramer's house. He sat in his car for a moment, then exited and walked to Bertrand Roberts' house. She could see his face clearly as he approached the front door and reached out his hand. She couldn't imagine his reason for going to Bertrand's. Just as he was about to press the doorbell, the door opened. Trinity could not see the person who opened the door, but Loyal smiled such a big smile as he entered that she assumed it wasn't Bertrand. She had seen Gladys Kramer enter the residence about fifteen minutes prior to Loyal's arrival and assumed that was who he was meeting. Was he aware, she wondered, that Bertrand was in the house as well? Trinity debated again about turning on the interior security system. How she wanted to have a birds-eye view of what was happening inside the house. In the end she decided to just wait it out. Bertrand was already on edge and acting unpredictably, no sense in making him even more cautious.

80

J ust as Loyal was slipping his hand out of his pocket Bertrand Roberts rounded the corner into the kitchen and stopped abruptly. "Who the hell are you?" he said tersely.

Loyal held his hands out in front of him in a calming gesture and said, "I'm here to see Gladys. She's just getting Liane packed."

"Who are you?" demanded Roberts.

"My name is Loyal Truesdal,." said Loyal. "I'm a friend of Gladys'."

Bertrand looked thoughtful. "I know that name," he said. "Truesdale. You are the detective who Lacey was working with. She told me about you."

"Yes," said Loyal.

Bertrand's gaze passed over the phones on the counter. "You can wait for Gladys outside," he said as he grasped Loyal's upper arm and escorted him to the front door. "I'll let her know you are out here." He closed the door firmly before Loyal had a chance to respond.

Loyal stood outside for just under five minutes. Eventually the door opened and Gladys and Liane came out. Gladys had her left hand on Liane's upper arm and both looked visibly upset. Liane was crying quietly, and sucking hard on her thumb. "I'm going to have to postpone our talk," Gladys said to Loyal. "Bertrand was very angry that I let you in his house." She glanced at Liane. "She doesn't deal with confrontation well." Gladys paused. "Can you call in the morning?" she asked.

"Sure," said Loyal. "I'm very sorry to have caused you trouble, Gladys."

"It'll be ok," Gladys said. "Call tomorrow." She turned to Liane saying, "Come on honey, everything is going to be ok." She then led the crying woman away.

Loyal returned to his Altima and texted O'Keefe.

Call when you can talk.

Next he texted Trinity.

.   .   .

Stopping by my place, then heading to you. Much to discuss. 40 minutes.

Loyal started the Altima and drove through the gates of Shorebird Lane. He hit Interstate 5 North, exited on Carlsbad Village Drive, and drove to Roosevelt Street. It was nearly 7:00 pm, and the fog had returned. It was heavy and wet, swirling in gray spirals and waves, obscuring vision. Loyal parked in front of his garage and exited his vehicle. He had taken two steps when he felt the shock. He knew immediately that he had been hit by a taser. He was familiar with the feeling from his patrol days, when all the young guys rode the lightning at least once. It was a pain one never forgot. He felt the two barbed darts hit his upper and lower back. He lost all muscle control and collapsed to the ground with a grunt. As he lay there he felt the third shock of the gun being depressed against his calf. He was completely incapacitated.

Despite the electricity coursing through his body, Loyal was able to hold onto two concrete thoughts. The first was concentrating on his heart as best he could. He needed to remain as calm as possible. The second was that he was going to kill whoever was doing this to him. The thirty second ride felt like five minutes. When it ended, Loyal lay on the ground, his muscles spasming involuntarily. He lay on his stomach, his left cheek pressed into the rough asphalt. Just as Loyal's arms began responding to his brain's commands, the first kick came. It crashed into his lower right side. He heard footsteps as his assailant walked the perimeter of his prone body. The second kick was brutal. It crashed into his left side with force. Loyal felt ribs break. A grunt escaped his mouth as the pain arced through his body.

A moment later he felt hot breath on his right cheek. His assailant had leaned down and now harshly whispered into his ear.

"I told you to stay the fuck away from this case. You sent that damn lawyer to rescue Van Winters." Hammond's warm breath flowed slowly into Loyal's ear. "This is the last warning. Hate to see you have an accident cleaning your gun." Hammond laughed a short brutal laugh. "And don't think about reporting this. My alibi is crystal clear." Then Hammond was gone, his footsteps fading into the swirling fog, and Loyal lay on the ground; alone.

81

L ess than ten minutes after Loyal entered Bertrand's house, the exterior security footage showed him leaving again. He stood outside the front door for nearly five minutes before a visibly upset Gladys Kramer and Liane entered the frame. Liane was clearly crying. Gladys and Loyal spoke briefly, then Loyal turned and strode quickly to his car, while the two women walked to Gladys' house.

Trinity drained the last drops of Perrier from the bottle, stood, and walked to drop it in the recycle container in the kitchen. Just as she reached the container her phone pinged, indicating a text message. She dropped the bottle and walked back to the table. The message was from Loyal.

.   .   .

Stopping by my place, then heading to you. Much to discuss. 40 minutes.

Something had happened inside Bertrand's house. She would just have to wait for Loyal to get here to find out what it was. She glanced at the time; 6:40. She looked around the condo and decided it could use a little work. She spent the next half hour straightening up and moving sensitive materials out of sight. She felt a small pang of guilt that she couldn't share everything she knew with Loyal. She was fairly sure he had been completely transparent with her. Such was the nature of her job, however, and she believed he understood.

At 7:30, the condo clean and some IPAs chilling in the fridge, Trinity checked her trackers. Bertrand's vehicle was still on shorebird lane, and there was no indication that the jet he usually used was in the air. Surprisingly, Loyal was still at his apartment, the data from his tracker indicating he had been there just over thirty minutes. Trinity waited five more minutes, then grabbed her phone and called Loyal. The phone rang four times, then went to voicemail. She disconnected, waited two more minutes, then tried again. Four rings, then voicemail again. Trinity paced around the small living room. Something felt wrong. Trinity had long ago learned to trust her instincts. She snatched up her purse and keys and headed out the door.

L oyal lay on the ground and conducted an inventory of his injuries. There were some residual tremors from the tasing. His lower right side was throbbing from the first kick. It was his left side, and the broken ribs, that was preventing him from rising. The pain was overwhelming. As Loyal gathered the courage to rise despite the pain, his phone rang. It was in his front left pocket and there was no way he could get to it. Loyal pulled himself into a kneeling position and remained there for a few moments, breathing shallowly. He inched forward and picked up his keys, then managed to turn and sit on the bottom step of the stairs to his apartment. His phone rang again. He did not make an attempt to reach it.

Loyal sat for a few minutes, then slowly stood, using the wall of his garage to steady himself. He began the climb to his front door. He could feel his ribs clicking, the pain so intense it was making him nauseous. He kept his eyes on his feet, placing them with deliberation and care on each of the eleven steps. Eventually he reached the landing, his breath now coming in jagged bursts. He paused to rest a moment, focusing on calming his breathing. As he stood there, headlights swung into the alley. A car pulled up next to his. Was it Hammond coming back for more? Loyal heard a car door open, then close, and footsteps coming up his stairs. Unlike Hammond, whose steps were heavy, these were light. He swung his eyes towards the top of the stairs and was surprised to see Trinity reach the landing.

She paused for a moment, then sprang forward.

"You are hurt," she said. She took the keys from his hand, unlocked and opened the door, and helped Loyal shuffle inside.

"Easy," Loyal said when she moved to wrap an arm around his waist. "Broken ribs."

"Ah, shit," said Trinity. "Recliner?" she asked.

"Taser barbs in my back," Loyal said.

"Let's get those out," Trinity said. She helped Loyal unbutton and remove his shirt and gun. Two barbs protruded from his back, one below his right shoulder blade, and one above his left hip. Trinity grasped the upper barb, turned it ninety degrees and pulled it out. Loyal gasped. Before he had a chance to say anything she had repeated the action with the lower barb. Two small trickles of blood leaked out of the small wounds. Trinity walked to the bathroom and returned with some hydrogen peroxide, a small wad of toilet paper, and two small bandaids. She quickly cleaned and bandaged Loyal's back. In less than five minutes she had Loyal in a clean shirt and settled in his recliner.

"What happened?" Trinity asked as she moved the small end table and pulled a kitchen chair up close to the right side of the recliner.

"Got ambushed," Loyal said. "Need pain meds. There is some old stuff in my bathroom cabinet."

Trinity rummaged through the cabinet and came back with two vials. One held unused Vicodin and the other Percocet. "They are expired," she said.

"Doesn't matter," said Loyal.

Trinity got Loyal a glass of water and fed him a Percocet. "Tell me what happened," she said as she sat back down beside Loyal.

"It was Hammond," Loyal said. "Taser, then two well placed kicks. Second kick broke the ribs. Warned me off the case again." Loyal took a shallow breath. "Hurts like a son of a bitch."

"Try to rest," Trinity said. "I'll be here when you wake up."

L oyal dozed for over an hour. Trinity watched him for a bit, then went into the kitchen in search of something to eat. There wasn't much to choose from. She found some paper in one of the drawers and ate a yogurt while she made a list of things Loyal would need. He was a tough guy, but broken ribs were a bitch. At minimum he'd need a day or two of rest. Realistically he'd need 4-6 weeks. She walked back into the living room and sat down across from Loyal. Even in sleep his body radiated tension. His left cheek had abrasions. She picked up the two barbs she had removed from his back and rolled them around in her hand. She thought about Hammond and wondered what the hell the man was thinking.

Loyal woke with a start. His eyes were wide and he seemed confused for a brief moment. Trinity took his hand in hers. "Hey there," she said. Loyal calmed and attempted a smile.

"How long was I out?" he asked.

"About an hour," Trinity said. "I'll stay tonight, just need to run back to the condo and grab a few things. You going to be ok here on your own?"

"Yeah," Loyal said. "Can you help me out of this chair? Lower the footrest, lean into me, put your head on my right shoulder. I'll reach around with my good arm, you pull on my belt loops." Trinity rolled her eyes at Loyal's play by play instructions, but did as he requested. "Ok," said Loyal, "up on three." With a groan, he stood. "Thanks," he said as he turned and shuffled towards the bathroom.

They used the same motion in reverse to get Loyal back into the recliner.

This chair was going to be his home base for the fore-seeable future. She set the pain meds and the water glass on the small end table she had moved back next to the recliner. She handed him his PM9, which he tucked into the cushions where it was easily accessible. He wouldn't be caught off guard again. She placed his phone on the table as well, then left to get things from her condo.

I t was almost 9:30. Loyal knew it was going to be a long night. This wasn't the first time he had broken ribs. Loyal had spent much of his youth on motorcycles. Fallbrook was rural, and much of the land surrounding Interstate 15 had been undeveloped in those days. Off- road riders in the hills along the freeway were a common sight in the 1970's and 1980's. In his late teens Loyal could be found at Carlsbad Raceway nearly every weekend. He rode hard, raced hard, and, occasionally, crashed hard. Hence the previous experience with broken ribs.

Loyal attempted to adjust his position in the recliner. The smallest of movements produced waves of pain. He opened the two prescription bottles and counted the pills. Seven Percocet and five Vicodin. Enough to get him through the first few days. He spotted the barbs on the kitchen table. Trinity had yanked those things out without hesitation. A small smile appeared on his face at the thought of her, then faded as thoughts of Hammond entered his mind. Loyal flashed back to the moment the taser had hit him. He felt Hammond's warm breath in his ear again. The whispered warning, then the veiled threat.

Loyal forced himself to take a deep breath. A small moan of pain escaped him as his lungs filled with air. He let the breath out slowly and focused his thoughts. He mentally walked himself through the entire day, starting with the discovery of Blomgen, the interview with the Homicide Detectives, the freeing of Van Winter from Hammond's talons, the meeting with Maynard and Van, and dropping Van off in Leucadia. There was something more. It took a moment, but Loyal latched onto it. The visit to see Gladys Kramer and the phones on the counter in Bertrand's house. He opened photos on his phone. There it was, the picture of the only phone number in Bertrand's call history.

Trinity spent about ten minutes at her condo. She packed up some staples from her kitchen, her lap top, chargers for both computer and phone, some toiletries and two changes of clothes. She was in her car and headed back to Loyal by 9:45. The fog was dense and gray, so full of moisture that windshield wipers were necessary. It wrapped its cold wet arms around Trinity as she exited her vehicle outside Loyal's home, sending a chill down her spine. She shook herself, then hurried up the stairs to his apartment. She cracked the door a bit and said, "Don't shoot, it's Trinity."

Loyal was in the recliner. His right hand was not visible, it appeared to be tucked down in the cushions. He brought it slowly out as she entered, crossed the room, and set everything down on the kitchen table.

"I brought some snacks," she said. "You hungry?"

Loyal shook his head. Trinity walked over and sat on the couch across from him.

"How are you doing?"

"Big pain," Loyal said.

Trinity nodded. "Anyone I can call for you?"

"Tomorrow," said Loyal.

At that moment Loyal's phone pinged, indicating the arrival of a text message. Loyal picked up the phone and checked it. The message was from O'Keefe.

Sorry for the late reply. What's up?

Loyal replied.

Can you come by my place tomorrow?

A moment later O'Keefe's reply arrived.

Sure. Morning okay? 8:30?

Loyal replied in the affirmative. He added the suggestion that O'Keefe should announce his arrival then come on in the apartment. He set his phone down on the end table and looked at Trinity.

"What's your plan?"

"I'll stay tonight," Trinity said. "We can call in reinforcements tomorrow."

Loyal nodded and closed his eyes. Trinity placed a blanket over him and checked to make sure his water and pills were within easy reaching distance. She checked Bertrand's tracker and baldgeek.net. Satisfied, she grabbed a blanket and pillow from the bedroom and curled up on the couch. She watched Loyal for a few minutes. He appeared to be sleeping. Trinity closed her eyes and was soon asleep.

86

L oyal kept his eyes closed and his breathing even until he heard Trinity's breaths settle into a steady rhythm. He opened his eyes, looked at her sleeping form, and reached gingerly for another Percocet. He flinched and gasped at the pain in his left side, wondering again what the hell was going on with Hammond. Blomgren's murder had initially pushed Bertrand to the top of Loyal's suspect list, but Hammond's increasingly erratic behavior was causing Loyal to rethink the situation.

Loyal reached his right hand into the cushion of the recliner and rested it on his PM9. The broken rib left him feeling vulnerable, a sensation he did not like. The gun gave him a sense of security. Hammond's attack had caught him completely by surprise. Loyal knew he was a little long in the tooth to still be a working homicide detective.

He felt a tickle of doubt and wondered if he should throw in the towel. He was aware that he was at a disadvantage at the moment; tired, injured, medicated. He felt the Percocet pulling him back into slumber. Rather than resist it, he allowed himself to drift into sleep.

Loyal's eyes moved quickly back and forth beneath his shuttered eyelids. He was riding his Yamaha 250 through a densely wooded area. The narrow path he followed was barely as wide as his tire and wound precariously around trees, over rocks, and through shallow streams. Loyal felt a sense of urgency and was pushing himself to the limit of his riding abilities, but was confused as to whether he was predator or prey. He whipped around the trunk of a large tree and found himself immersed in a bank of thick fog. Visibility was reduced to zero. Loyal stopped his forward motion and turned the engine off. He removed his helmet, his ears straining to pick up any noises, his eyes useless in the dense gray. After a moment he heard the sound of footsteps slightly in front of him and to his left. He leaned the motorcycle against the tree, hung the helmet from its handlebar, and eased forward in the direction of the footsteps. After about 20 feet the fog began to clear. Loyal picked up his pace and began jogging along the trail. He caught a glimpse of movement ahead of him; a jogger, female, with a long dark ponytail. The wooded trail had morphed into the Bataquitos Lagoon trail. Looking up and to his right, Loyal saw the giant house on Shorebird Lane. He started to run full out, but was brought up short by a tremendous pain in his left side. He stumbled, then fell to the ground. He struggled to rise, but was unable. He lay on the ground and watched, immobile, as a shadowy figure emerged from the bushes, raised a weapon above their head and brought it down on the jogger. She crumpled to the ground, her damaged face coming to rest on the damp ground, turned at such an angle that she was looking directly at Loyal. Loyal let out a guttural groan. It was Lacey.

Loyal woke with a start, shifting in the recliner and sending bursts of pain radiating out from his broken ribs. He forced himself to be still, breathing shallowly and waiting for the pain to subside. The dream had been vivid and still clung tightly to his consciousness. He tapped his phone; 3:06 am. These were the brutal hours. The darkness and silence were thick and oppressive, intrusive thoughts attempted to gain purchase in his mind. To keep the negative thoughts at bay Loyal mentally reviewed the investigation, starting from the very beginning. The location, timing, and ferocity of the murder indicated a killer who either knew Lacey or was given information from someone who knew Lacey. Bertrand and Blomgren had been communicating in a suspicious manner, and had met up at Port Hueneme. Perhaps Bertrand paid Blomgren to kill Lacey, then killed Blomgren to clear up loose ends. Possibly Blomgren could have seen Bertrand commit the act and begun blackmailing him. Hammond was an issue. Prior to the attack, Loyal had doubted Hammond could be the killer. Eight hours after the tasing, broken ribs, and threats against his life, Loyal was re-evaluating the possibility of Hammond's involvement. Van Winters was an outlier. His devastation appeared genuine. Loyal kept him near the bottom of the list.

Trinity stirred on the couch, rolled over, and settled back into sleep. Loyal moved his thoughts to her. She had told him that she doubted Bertrand would get his own hands dirty. This added credence to the murder for hire theory. Bertrand definitely had a motive. Loyal wondered again if the husband had known about the affair. Gladys Kramer had suspected something was going on, but when he thought about it, Loyal realized that Gladys had likely spent more time with Lacey than Bertrand had. Loyal sighed, then immediately regretted the action as his rib screamed in protest. Damn Hammond. That second kick had been purposefully placed. Loyal tapped his phone again; 3:58. He closed his eyes and concentrated on slow, even breathing. By 4:10 he had drifted off again.

87

Pale sunlight, filtered through fog and glowing in the kitchen window, woke Trinity at 7:45. She stretched, then glanced at Loyal, who was sleeping in the recliner. Even in slumber he looked uncomfortable. Trinity rose, put the blanket and pillow back in the bedroom, then started a pot of coffee. She looked back at Loyal and saw that he was awake.

"Hey," she said with a slow smile.

"Hey," Loyal said as he made an attempt at a smile.

"Want to get up?" Trinity asked.

Loyal nodded. She helped him up, flinching as he gasped in pain. Loyal eased himself into the bathroom and Trinity returned to the kitchen. She poured two cups of coffee, placing one on Loyal's end table and keeping one in her hands. She checked Bertrand's tracker and baldgeek.net. By all appearances he was at home in Carlsbad. Trinity recalled seeing Liane going to Gladys Kramer's house the previous evening and surmised that Bertrand was likely leaving again soon. Loyal came back into the living room and Trinity helped him get settled in the recliner, then sat herself down on the couch.

"I can stay about half an hour," said Trinity. "And possibly come back tonight. Who should I call?"

"O'Keefe should be here in about 20 minutes," said Loyal. "He can help me get up before he leaves. I'll text my daughter, Stella." He paused to take a shuddering breath. "Can you get my laptop?" he asked. Trinity grabbed it off the kitchen table. Loyal gave her his password and asked her to pull up his email.

"Open the pictures sent from my phone," Loyal said. "Tell me what you think."

Trinity spent a few minutes reviewing the pictures of Blomgren's murder scene.

"Is this Blomgren?" she asked Loyal.

"Yes."

"You know much about blood spatter?" she asked him.

Loyal nodded. "Some," he said. "But I'm guessing you know more."

"Look at this picture of Blomgren's ceiling," she said. She turned the computer screen toward Loyal.

"Judging from the cast off stains I'm thinking left hand-ed," said Trinity.

"I agree," said Loyal.

"Bertrand is left handed," said Trinity, turning the screen back towards herself and studying the picture again.

"Van Winters is right handed," Loyal said.

"What about Hammond?" said Trinity.

"I don't know. He shoots left at the range."

Trinity stood and walked over to Loyal. She leaned down and kissed him lightly on his undamaged cheek. "I've got to go," she said. "I'll try to get back later this evening." Loyal nodded. "That would be nice," he said.

About ten minutes after Trinity left Loyal heard footsteps on his stairs. It was likely O'Keefe, but he slid his hand down to the PM9 anyway. He felt so damn vulnerable. If it was Hammond coming back to inflict more damage, he would be ready. There was a quick knock on the door, then a voice said, "It's O'Keefe."

"It's open," said Loyal. The door opened and O'Keefe walked in. His eyes widened when he saw Loyal's condition.

"What the hell happened?" he asked.

"I slipped and fell on the damn stairs," said Loyal. "Broke some ribs." Loyal took a shallow breath. "That's not why I asked you to stop by though." He nodded at the couch. "Have a seat Pat."

O'Keefe sat. "I need a favor," Loyal said. "And it is a big one. If you aren't comfortable with it just say so, okay"

O'Keefe nodded, his expression serious.

"Can you access stingray for me?" Loyal asked. He was

referring to a controversial cell phone surveillance device. It had a wide variety of uses, including capturing location, data, conversations, and text messages. Police departments across the country had been using it for years. Deployed without the knowledge of, or approval from, the court system, it was basically warrantless tracking.

O'Keefe was silent for a moment. He rubbed his hands over his close cropped hair. "That's a big one Loyal," he said.

"I know," said Loyal.

O'Keefe sighed. "I suppose I could do some "testing" on the portable units," he said, using his fingers to form air quotes around the word testing. "Stingray is part of my department."

Loyal picked up his phone and tapped it a few times. "I'm sending you a screenshot of a phone number," he said. "I need whatever you can get on it."

O'Keefe's phone pinged. He stood, removed it from his pocket, looked at the message from Loyal, then re-pocketed the device. "You are a good friend Loyal," he said. "I have a lot of respect for you. Something about all this," he waved in Loyal's direction, "feels wrong. I'd appreciate the real story one of these days."

Loyal nodded, saying nothing.

"You need any help before I get going?" O'Keefe asked.

Loyal shook his head. "I'm good," he said. "And thanks Pat." He added.

O'Keefe gave a curt nod. "I'll be in touch."

L oyal sat in silence for quite a while after O'Keefe's exit. The kid was right, he thought. He did deserve the truth. O'Keefe had a wife and two young kids; a third on the way. He was risking a lot by helping Loyal. Pushing aside thoughts of O'Keefe for the moment, Loyal picked up his phone and called the other person in his life who deserved more of the truth; Stella. The call went to voicemail, as he had expected it would. He left a brief message asking her to please call him when it was convenient and disconnected. He attempted to shift his body a bit in the recliner and was rewarded with shooting pain from his ribs. "Damn it," he muttered. He reached for the Percocet, swallowed a pill, and sat with his eyes closed, waiting for the effects to kick in. The medicine didn't really make the pain go away, it just changed the way his brain responded to the signals coursing through his nerves.

. . .

An injured and medicated person tends to drift in and out of consciousness. Thoughts are disjointed, swimming in and out of the mind of their own volition. The injured person doesn't so much choose their thoughts, rather their thoughts are chosen for them. Loyal was trying, with little success, to concentrate his thoughts on Hammond, Roberts, and Blomgren. Thoughts of Michelle, his first wife and Stella's mother, kept bubbling to the surface. After she had rejected his offer of help outside the bathroom of the Italian restaurant in Escondido, Loyal had stopped keeping tabs on her. He was busy working his way up in the department and raising Stella. It was more than a year after their last encounter that Michelle turned up on his radar again. It was Clayton Fields who provided the blip.

The Vice Detective had sidled up to Loyal's desk one day, leaned down, and said, "Met your ex the other day, Loyal."

Loyal had glanced at Fields, then looked away, saying nothing.

"She's using her maiden name now, but mentioned you when I was getting ready to arrest her for soliciting."

Loyal's jaw tightened. He made no reply.

"She's living in a dumpy Carlsbad motel," he said with a smirk. "I'm sure you know the one I mean."

Loyal turned his head and looked in Fields pale eyes. "You have a point to make Fields?" he said.

"Just wanted to let you know I did you a solid and didn't arrest her," said Fields.

This was the conversation that popped up unbidden in Loyal's mind. Following the encounter, he had driven by the motel Fields had mentioned several times, seeing nothing. Eventually he had followed Fields to the motel and watched as Michelle opened the door of her room to admit him. Fields had stayed just under 30 minutes. Loyal had no doubt as to what had transpired. He did not approach Michelle's room after Fields' departure. His loyalty was to Stella.

J ust as Trinity closed the door to her condo her phone rang. She checked the caller, saw it was Douglass Caldwell, and accepted the call. Once again Caldwell wasted no time with niceties, instead saying, "I had to redirect team 3 to Texas."

"I need them here," Trinity said.

"Do you have details on another meet?" asked Caldwell.

"Not yet," said Trinity.

"I have a contact for you at the local FBI office," Caldwell said. "If you learn of another meet you can liaise with her."

"I need people I can trust," said Trinity.

"I can vouch for her," said Caldwell. "I'll send you her contact information."

Caldwell terminated the call without waiting for a response from Trinity.

. . .

With a frustrated sigh, Trinity set her phone on the table. She sat down and opened her computer. Bertrand had a flight scheduled to depart from Palomar-McClellan in just over an hour. A flight plan had been filed. He was returning to Tahoe yet again. Trinity checked baldgeek.net to make sure the plane wasn't actually in the air. The N number did not show up on the website. Trinity scheduled a flight of her own, made arrangements to have a vehicle waiting for her in Tahoe and packed a small bag. She texted Loyal to let him know she wasn't coming back in the evening. He didn't respond. She hoped he was sleeping. In less than thirty minutes she was back on the road.

A persistent ringing pulled Loyal out of his slumber. It was work, his consciousness swimming upstream against a Percocet generated current. In the fraction of a second before he was fully awake, he twisted his torso and was rewarded with a burst of pain. He picked up his ringing phone, saw it was Stella, and answered, his voice rough and crackling with sleep and pain.

"Stella," he said.

"Dad, are you alright?" Stella's voice was tight with concern.

Loyal cleared his throat. His next words were steadier. "Yes," he said. "Just drifted off for a moment."

"You aren't a napper," Stella said. "What's wrong. Are you sick? Is it your heart?"

"No, I'm fine," said Loyal. "Was wondering if you could stop by after work."

"Yeah, I can do that," Stella said. "I'll see you around 4:00."

"Great," said Loyal, "see you then."

Upon disconnecting, Loyal saw that he had received two text messages during his nap. The first, from Trinity, informed him that she wasn't going to be able to make it back this evening. The second was from Gladys Kramer asking if he still wanted to talk with her. Loyal replied to Trinity first, letting her know that Stella would be stopping by. He spent some time thinking before he responded to Gladys Kramer. He wanted to talk to her, but not in this injured state. Eventually he sent her a text asking to postpone their conversation for a day or two. Gladys replied in the affirmative.

Loyal sat, phone in hand, and thought about Hammond, and Hammond's investigation, which appeared to be going nowhere. He wondered why Hammond wasn't going at Bertrand Roberts harder. The husband was always the first suspect. As far as Loyal knew Roberts hadn't even been interviewed at the station. He made a mental note to ask O'Keefe about that. The next question Loyal asked himself was whether Hammond could be working for Roberts. Unlikely, he decided, but not outside the realm of possibility.

.   .   .

All these thoughts about Hammond, and the fact that he was holding his phone in his hand, reminded Loyal that he just might have video of the attack on his security camera footage. He logged in and went back to the approximate time of the tasing. He saw his headlights flash as he pulled into his parking spot in front of his garage and turned them off. The fog had been thick that night and the footage of him exiting his car was hazy. Still he could make himself out as he closed the car door and took a few steps. Suddenly his body stiffened, then collapsed. Loyal watched as Hammond walked up, knelt beside Loyal, and pressed the taser gun to Loyal's calf. Hammond then rose and kicked Loyal with intensity in the right side, then walked slowly around Loyal's prone form and launched another kick into Loyal's left side. At this point Hammond glanced around and his face, although slightly obscured by fog, was visible enough to identify. Hammond leaned down and spoke into Loyal's ear, disconnected the taser gun, and strolled away.

Loyal, holding the phone and watching the events unfold, let out a low breath as Hammond exited the scene. The burning anger building inside of him was causing his muscles to tense, which in turn caused more pain to his ribs. He forced himself to close his eyes and breath slowly and evenly. He wasn't sure a word existed in the English language to adequately describe the dark depths of his feelings toward Hammond at the moment. He felt so damned helpless trapped here in the recliner. He made a silent promise to himself that someday in the future he would pay Hammond back for this.

L acey sat in her truck in the parking lot of JK's. She had finished with her last client of the day a full half hour previously, but when she sat down in the driver's seat she realized she really had nowhere to go. Bertrand was away on business and Liane was with Gladys. Lacey's surfboard was in the bed of her truck. The waves in Southern California were the best in the Winter season. Yet Lacey was unable to move. Her visit to John nearly a month earlier had left her with much to consider. His two main recommendations to her had been, in his words, "Report Hammond and divorce Bertrand." These were the words that repeated on an endless loop through her tortured mind. "Report, divorce," echoing endlessly.

With a sigh, Lacey finally started her vehicle and exited the parking lot. She drove aimlessly, no destination in mind. Her subconscious guided her instead, and she ended up parked across the street from Van's apartment building. She closed her eyes and let her thoughts drift; picturing Van at the beach, Van in his apartment, Van in her arms. A tear slid ever so slowly down her cheek. She didn't bother to wipe it away. Eventually, she knew, it would be replaced by another.

A gentle knock on her driver's side window woke Lacey. She was confused for a moment as to where she was. She turned to look out the window and there he was. Van's blue eyes looked at her through the glass. She looked back, wondering if she was still asleep and dreaming. He gave her a small sad smile, then motioned for her to roll her window down. She opened the door instead, causing him to take a step back. Lacey stepped out of the truck and into Van's arms without a word.

Loyal was in the process of attempting to extricate himself from the clutches of the recliner when he heard footsteps on the stairs leading to his apartment. He eased himself back down and slid his right hand into the cushions. There was a quick rap on the door and then it was eased open. He heard O'Keefe say, "It's Pat, don't shoot." A moment later O'Keefe peeked around the door, his eyes settling on Loyal's right hand. He entered the apartment, closed the door, and said, "I assume that's why your hand is in the cushions." Loyal gave a short nod and small smile. He noticed that O'Keefe was carrying a paper grocery bag. "What do you have there? Loyal asked.

"Olive sent some homemade soup for you," O'Keefe said as he crossed the room and set the bag on the kitchen table. "Want some?"

"Sure, in a minute. Can you help me stand up first?"

· · ·

After standing with assistance from O'Keefe and making a trip to the bathroom, Loyal found himself back in the recliner with a steaming mug of soup in his right hand. He sipped slowly, feeling the warm liquid trickling down his throat and settling in his empty stomach. He glanced at O'Keefe who was in the kitchen putting away the rest of the soup. In his mind he always referred to O'Keefe as "kid". Looking at him now, Loyal realized he needed to re-think that description. Pat O'Keefe was much more than a kid. He shouldered lots of responsibility, both at work and at home. The risks he was taking for Loyal were serious, threatening everything that mattered to O'Keefe. At the very least, O'Keefe deserved the truth.

Loyal set the mug down and picked up his phone. "I've got something to show you Pat," he said. O'Keefe walked over to the recliner. Loyal handed him the phone. "Just watch," Loyal said. O'Keefe stood still and watched the video from the security cameras he had installed the previous Saturday. Loyal watched the young man's face which at first registered surprise, then anger, then absolute shock. He handed the phone back to Loyal and sat heavily on the couch. Loyal stayed silent as he watched O'Keefe process what he had just seen. Finally O'Keefe said, "What are you going to do with that?"

"I haven't decided yet," said Loyal. "But this stays between you and me, Pat."

"Going to be hard to look at Hammond without wanting to punch him," O'Keefe said. "Shit Loyal, this is serious stuff. What did he say to you when he leaned down?"

"Told me to back away from the case. Made a comment about me having an accident cleaning my gun," said Loyal. "Also said he had a rock solid alibi. Guess he wasn't aware of the cameras."

O'Keefe just shook his head.

"Listen Pat," Loyal said, "I really need you not to act on this."

Their eyes met. "You got it Loyal."

94

Trinity caught Bertrand's tail at the airport in Lake Tahoe. He was driving a black Toyota 4Runner. Trinity was in a Toyota as well; her model being the Highlander and silver. She followed him North along Ca Route 89, and was surprised when he passed by his usual turn on Granlibakken Road. Instead, he took a left on Lake Road, then reconnected with the 89 and continued North towards Truckee. There was a fair amount of traffic, which made Trinity's job of following reasonably easy. A few cars worth of separation made it easier to maintain cover. Trinity wondered, as she had many times in the past, why Bertrand flew into South Lake Tahoe when there was a perfectly good airport just outside of Truckee. His jet would have no problem landing there, and it would have cut his drive time by two-thirds.

. . .

Bertrand drove straight to a DMV services office. He parked the 4Runner right in front of the structure and went inside. Trinity parked across the street and watched the building. The clock ticked and half an hour stretched into an hour. Bertrand remained in the building.

95

L oyal swallowed another Percocet after O'Keefe left. The younger detective had promised silence for the time being, but was clearly distressed by what he had seen. Loyal debated the wisdom of showing O'Keefe the footage, but when O'Keefe mentioned that he had the portable sting ray in his car, Loyal knew he had done the right thing. Loyal counted the remaining Percocet; four. He still had the five Vicodin as well. There was no way he was going to see a doctor, so he would just have to make them last as long as possible. After they were gone, he would just tough it out.

The sound of footsteps on his stairs sent a rush of adrenaline through Loyal. With as little motion as possible, so as not to disturb his ribs, Loyal slid his right hand down to the PM9. There was a light tap on the front door, then he heard, "It's O'Keefe, don't shoot." A moment later the door opened and O'Keefe stepped inside.

"Sorry man," he said. "I forgot to give you this." He walked to Loyal's side and held out his hand. In his palm was another red USB drive. "Autopsy and evidence," O'Keefe said.

"Thanks," Loyal said with a weak smile. "You should be using my password when you access things like that."

"Oh, I am," said O'Keefe with a smile.

"Can you help set me up with my computer so I can look at everything?" Loyal asked.

"Sure thing."

Ten minutes later, when O'Keefe left for what he swore was the last time that day, Loyal started reading the new reports. O'Keefe had wedged a pillow between the right arm of the recliner and Loyal's lap. The computer, with the USB drive inserted and files opened, was placed on the pillow. With his right hand Loyal could scroll up and down as he studied the new information. The autopsy report was first. Time of death was listed as between 5 and 7 am on Monday April 8. The victim; Lacey Barnett-Roberts, white female, 69 inches tall, 135 pounds. The external examination was first. The coroner detailed everything, the clothes he removed and bagged, the wedding ring, a thin gold chain around her wrist. Cause of death was blunt force trauma. The coroner believed the first blow had struck her neck, in the curve between the chin and throat. This blow likely broke her neck and crushed her larynx, causing her death. More blows, on her face and abdomen, had been struck post mortem. Tiny bits of debris had been found in the wounds, leading the coroner to believe that the weapon had been a heavy branch possibly picked up from the land surrounding the lagoon. There were no defensive wounds.

Loyal skipped the internal examination and went straight to the evidence report. It was sparse. The lagoon trail was used by many people, and the ground was wet and spongy, therefore footprints were not of much use. The weapon had not been found. Bits of trash had been gathered and were listed, with accompanying pictures. Loyal picked his phone up and texted O'Keefe.

Call when you can talk.

He re-read the reports and shut the computer. Getting it off his lap and onto the end table took some time, but he eventually managed it. He wished he would have thought of asking Trinity or O'Keefe to set him up so he could listen to the T. Jefferson Parker novel Sandy had recommended. Loyal closed his eyes and silently cursed Hammond. He sat still, eyes closed, and concentrated on his breathing. Eventually he drifted off, and was awoken some time later by the ringing of his phone. Caller ID indicated O'Keefe and Loyal accepted.

"Hi Pat."

"What's up Loyal? I had to turn Stingray off to make this call. Don't want our conversations recorded."

"I'll make it short," said Loyal. "Why isn't Hammond going hard at Bertrand Roberts?"

"Rock solid alibi," said O'Keefe. "He was on a conference call with three investors in Dubai. He records and date and time stamps everything."

"Could his records have been manipulated?" Loyal asked.

"He allowed me access to his data," O'Keefe said. "I didn't find anything that looked like it had been tampered with. Hammond got statements from all three investors corroborating his alibi."

"What if there was a connection between Bertrand and Blomgren?" Loyal said.

"You find one?"

"Maybe," said Loyal.

"Might be time to go to the Captain with what you have Loyal," O'Keefe said.

"Maybe," Loyal said. "Let me know what you get with Stingray."

T rinity watched the DMV services offices and thought about Loyal. The poor guy was pretty beat up. She thought back to a car accident she had been involved in many years ago. A guy had run a red light and t-boned her vehicle. The doctors said she had been lucky to hobble away with a few lacerations and three broken ribs. Recovery from those broken ribs had been six weeks of torture. Hopefully Loyal had a group of friends who would be willing to help him out.

Thinking about the accident brought up the memory of all the bureaucracy involved in getting the car declared a total wreck and collecting from the insurance company. The thought of bureaucracy brought her back to the DMV services office that Bertrand was still inside. She racked the seat back as far as it would go, and pulled her computer into her lap. It didn't take long for Trinity to identify the owner of the DMV services office; Blackstock LLC, the same company that owned the Gulfstream he flew in. Could Roberts be using drivers license information obtained through the DMV service to register fake guests at the motel? That was a way to make it look full on paper. By using this process he could use his own cash to pay for the rooms and pay taxes on the income. This would be the perfect way to legitimize his illegally obtained cash from Afghanistan.

L oyal napped on and off throughout the day. By three o'clock he was hungry and needed to use the bathroom. Stella was due to arrive around four. He struggled for a moment, trying to get himself out of the recliner. He could feel the broken ribs clicking against each other with each movement. In the end he swallowed another Percocet and decided to wait.

Just after four he heard footsteps on the stairs and slid his right hand into the cushions. There was a quick knock on the door, then he heard Stella say, "It's me Dad." She opened the door, saw Loyal in the recliner, and rushed to his side.

"Dad. What happened?" She gently touched the abrasions on his cheek.

"The cheek isn't so bad," Loyal said. "But I have a few

broken ribs. I'll tell you everything, but can you help me get up first?"

Stella helped him maneuver his bulk out of the chair. He asked her to please heat up two large mugs of Olive O'Keefe's soup, then headed toward the bathroom. Stella did so without any questions, then helped him back into the recliner when he returned.

She allowed him a handful of sips from his mug of soup before she began asking questions.

"What happened Dad?"

Loyal told her everything that had happened in his investigation since he had last seen her. It had been six days, so there was much to tell. Loyal spoke slowly, pausing occasionally to take some shallow breaths. Stella listened without interruption as the story unfolded. The only thing he left out was the Dark Forces and Trinity. Stella's face paled as she watched the security footage of the attack by Hammond.

"Are you taking this to the Captain?" she asked.

"Not yet," Loyal said. When she started to protest he said, "It is leverage. Hammond doesn't know about it. I may need to use it."

"Because you are still investigating," Stella said with a slow smile. "One of the things I've always loved about you, Dad, is your persistence. But how will you continue? You're injured."

"I'll manage," Loyal said.

. . .

Loyal and Stella sat in a companionable silence and sipped their soup. Eventually Loyal spoke again.

"I've thought about what you asked. I'm ready to talk about your Mom." Stella's head popped up. "Just be aware, you might not like a lot of what you hear."

Stella nodded. "Okay," she said.

Loyal was silent for a moment. "I'm not sure where to begin," he said.

"How about the beginning," Stella said.

Loyal nodded, took a breath in and winced as his ribs protested, then began.

Van held Lacey for a long moment. She lay her head against his chest and felt the tears she had been holding in for so long spill down her cheeks.

"Nothing has changed Lacey," he said.

She pushed back and looked up at him, questions in her eyes.

"I love you," he said. "But I want all of you. I can't be with you any other way."

"I miss you Van," she said. "I'm dying inside."

"Then leave him Lacey."

Lacey took a shaky breath. "I don't know what to do."

Van sighed. "Yes, you do."

Loyal started at the beginning and told Stella everything. He described the first time he had seen Michelle, at a bar in Carlsbad called The Crazy Burro, and how he just couldn't stop staring at her. Michelle was vibrant, beautiful, and exciting. He had bought her a drink and they had ended up sitting and talking until the bar closed for the night. He spent every free moment with her for the better part of a year. They had married, and a year later Stella was born. Loyal took on as much overtime as he could so that Michelle wouldn't have to work. He described the night he came home and found seven month old Stella alone in an unlocked apartment. Michelle's descent into drug use and, eventually, prostitution came rapidly after that night.

Stella listened in her usual way, intent on his words and

saving any questions until the end. When Loyal grew quiet she said, "Did you try to help her Dad? Get her into rehab?"

"I did," Loyal said. "She made it clear she didn't want anything from me."

"Did she ever ask about me?" Stella asked. "Try to have contact with me?"

Loyal shook his head. "I'm sorry, but no she didn't."

Stella's brown eyes flooded with tears.

"Eventually I just had to make a choice Stella," Loyal said. "My loyalty was always with you."

Stella remained silent for quite a while. She sat on the couch, her brown eyes focused on something Loyal couldn't see. He waited patiently. Eventually Stella blinked a few times, then her eyes found his.

"Do you think she is still alive Dad?"

"I honestly don't know," said Loyal.

Stella nodded, then stood and walked to Loyal's side. She took his hand in hers.

"Thank you Dad," she said. "I appreciate your honesty."

Loyal squeezed her hand gently. "You deserved the truth."

Stella sighed and gave her head a little shake. She looked back at Loyal. "What can I do for you Dad?" she asked. "Want some more soup?"

Loyal shook his head. "How about telling me all the details about that little grand-baby you've got on board?"

Stella's smile brightened. "Absolutely," she said as she sat back down on the couch.

ertrand spent three hours in the DMV Services office. When he left he drove to the motel he owned, spent an hour in the office, then drove straight to the Granlibakken. The road leading to the hotel was a narrow two-lane that dead-ended in the hotel's driveway. If Trinity followed she would likely raise Bertrand's suspicion, especially if she did not check into the hotel. Instead, she parked in the parking lot of New Moon Natural Foods, which was located at the mouth of the road to the Granlibakken. She went inside and bought a few snacks, then settled down to be ready to follow Bertrand if he left the hotel.

At 9:00, with no sign of Bertrand, Trinity left the parking lot and drove to her Airbnb. It was a tiny one bedroom cabin. She had used it before and liked its location, just over a mile from the Granlibaaken Hotel. Trinity showered, then popped open one of the beers she had purchased at the market. She took a long, appreciative sip. It was nearly 10:00 pm. She considered, then decided it was not too late to call Loyal. He answered on the fourth ring.

"Trinity," he said. He sounded tired.

"Did I wake you?" she asked.

"Nope," said Loyal. "Stella just left about twenty minutes ago."

"You sound tired Loyal."

"We had a long talk about her Mom," Loyal said. "Between that and these ribs I am pretty tired."

"Did it end well?" asked Trinity.

"Yeah," said Loyal. "How's Tahoe?"

Trinity described her surveillance of Bertrand and his stops at The DMV services and the motel. Loyal thought her theory about the money laundering was a good one.

There was a lull in the conversation, then Loyal said, "Tell me something interesting."

Trinity was silent for a moment, then said, "I've had broken ribs twice in my life. First time was a car accident. A guy ran a red light and t-boned me."

"And the second?" Loyal asked.

"You ever heard of The Ranch?

"No," said Loyal.

"It is just outside of Warner Springs," said Trinity. "About an hour and a half from you."

"The navy training facility?" Loyal asked.

"Yeah," Trinity said. "We called it The Ranch; survival, evasion, resistance, and escape training. The acronym is SERE. I was there about 8 years ago on a joint agency special training session."

"Am I cleared for this information?" Loyal asked.

"I might skip some details," Trinity said with a small laugh.

She spent the next few minutes telling Loyal about the training, the accident, and her injuries. She described the unforgiving landscape and terrain at The Ranch, and how she had slipped during orienteering and fallen into a ravine packed with boulders. When ribs met rocks, rocks came out on top. Trinity had suffered two broken ribs, a partially dislocated shoulder, and many scrapes and contusions. Recovery had taken ten weeks.

"So I know what you are going through," she said. "You have someone stopping by tomorrow morning?"

"O'Keefe," said Loyal.

"Good," said Trinity. "I'll check in with you at some point tomorrow." She paused, then said, "I wish I was there."

"I do too," said Loyal. "I'm getting used to having you around."

Trinity could hear the smile in his voice. She smiled as well. "I'm getting used to being around." She said. "Be easy to make a habit of it."

"You won't hear any complaints from me." Loyal said.

Trinity paused a moment before responding. "Sleep well Truesdale." She said, and ended the call.

L oyal set his phone on the end table and plucked another Percocet out of the bottle, noting that only two remained. He still had the five Vicodin, but knew he was going to have to think about getting some more pain meds before too long. He closed his eyes and thought about Trinity. He pictured her smiling blue eyes, her river of copper hair, her lean athletic build. With her image firmly in his mind, he drifted off to sleep.

A muffled thump brought Loyal roughly out of sleep. The living room was dark. He slid his hand down into the cushions and rested it on the handle of his gun. His phone was in his lap, he noted the time as 3:16 am. He remained still and silent in his recliner, his ears straining to hear any sounds from inside or outside his home. After a few moments, and hearing nothing more, he relaxed a bit. He was injured and vulnerable, and this time of night made everything worse. Sounds were always exaggerated in the dark. Dangers felt more real. One thing was for sure, if Hammond came back for more Loyal would be ready and wouldn't hesitate.

He drifted in and out of restless sleep, eventually coming fully awake just past 7:00. The fog outside his kitchen window was thick and gray, the sunlight barely able to filter through and light up the room. At 7:30 he heard footsteps on the stairs. There were two rapid knocks on the door and he heard O'Keefe say, "It's Pat, Loyal. Don't shoot."

"The door is unlocked," said Loyal. "Come on in."

O'Keefe opened the door, entered, then turned and closed it.

"You should lock this," he said as he crossed the room.

"Can't get up to open it," Loyal said. He nodded towards the bag O'Keefe was carrying. "More gifts from Olive?"

"Breakfast burritos," O'Keefe said with a smile. "And decaf. You need some help getting up?"

"Yeah, thanks," said Loyal. "Been a long night."

O'Keefe helped Loyal out of the recliner. He busied himself in the kitchen while Loyal used the restroom. He helped Loyal back into the recliner, placed a burrito and a mug of coffee on the end table, then settled on the couch with a burrito and some coffee of his own.

.   .   .

"I got a hit with the stingray and the number you gave me," O'Keefe said. "It's in an audio file. I emailed it to you last night."

Loyal attempted to sit up a bit straighter and was rewarded with a shock of pain.

"What's the content?" he asked around a bite of burrito.

"I don't understand the relevance," O'Keefe said. "And honestly I'd rather not be involved."

"Understood," said Loyal. "Thanks for everything Pat. I appreciate the risks you have taken on my behalf. I won't involve you any further."

O'Keefe swallowed his last bite of burrito, then stood. "That's probably for the best," he said. "Can I do anything around here before I go?"

"Could you hand me my computer?" Loyal asked.

Trinity woke with the rising sun. She checked Bertrand's flight plans and saw that he was scheduled to take off from South Lake Tahoe at 10:15 am. She arranged a matching flight for herself, then showered, dressed, and dried her long hair. By 7:30 she was back in the New Moon parking lot sipping on a green smoothie she had purchased from the store. Trinity didn't trust Bertrand's flight information. He had tricked her once before, that would not be happening again.

Just after 8:15 Bertrand's black 4Runner glided past the parking lot and turned right, heading South. Traffic was light. Trinity followed at a discreet distance. The day was clear, the skies a cloudless bright blue, the sun shining. Following was simple, as she was fairly sure where he was going. Bertrand did not disappoint, and by 10:30 both

Bertrand and Trinity were in the air and heading back to Carlsbad.

Trinity's Lear made slightly better time, and she landed eight minutes before Bertrand. She passed quickly through the jet center and was waiting in her car, with a view of the jet center door and Bertrand's car, when he exited the large building carrying two briefcases and a small duffle. He strode quickly to his vehicle, threw his belongings in the back seat, and drove away. Trinity followed him on the tracking app, figuring she could catch up with him if he went anywhere but Shorebird Lane. Her guess about his destination proved to be correct, and fifteen minutes later Bertrand's vehicle pulled into his driveway. Trinity shifted the Yukon into drive and left Palomar McClellan. She did not head to her condo in La Costa, instead she drove straight to Oceanside.

L oyal was raised out of his fitful slumber by quick, light footsteps on the stairs. As usual, his hand slid into the cushions toward his PM9, but he did not feel the usual sense of apprehension. He was fairly sure he recognized the steps ascending toward his apartment, and they did not cause him concern. A small smile appeared on his face when he heard the light knock and Trinity say, "It's me Loyal, don't shoot." His hand slid out of the cushions as the door opened and Trinity walked in.

She strode across the room, leaned down and brushed his lips with a light kiss, then stood back and scrutinized him.

"How are you doing?" she asked.

"Could use some help getting up," Loyal said. "I'd like to take a shower."

Trinity helped him up. He walked gingery toward the

bathroom. Getting undressed was painful, but the shower was worth it. He stepped out of the shower, dried himself as best he could, and wrapped the towel around his waist. When he stepped out of the bathroom he saw that Trinity had laid clean clothes across the bed. He could smell the aroma of Olive O'Keefe's soup from the living room.

Getting dressed proved to be a bit more difficult than getting undressed had been. Loyal ended up asking Trinity for assistance. She helped him into his clothes, gently combed his hair, then eased him back into the recliner. He swallowed another Percocet, then took a few sips of the soup she had reheated for both of them.

"Thanks Trinity," he said.

"Whatever I can do to help," she said. "Those bruises on your sides are pretty impressive. How are you feeling?"

"Body hurts," said Loyal. "But I have something for you." He opened his computer and clicked on the audio file O'Keefe had sent him. "Listen to this." Bertrand's voice floated into the room.

"I have the final installment," he said. *"We need to meet one more time."*

Loyal paused the audio file. "I don't recognize the other voice," he said, "I'm hoping you do." He then resumed the playback.

. . .

"*Saturday,*" said the other voice.

"*Same location,*" Bertrand said, "*11:30 am.*"

"*That works.*"

"*And you'll announce my contract with SpaWar the following week?*"

"*Tuesday,*" said the voice Loyal didn't recognize.

"*Good,*" said Bertrand, and the phone call ended.

A slow smile spread across Trinity's face. "You got his burner?"

Loyal smiled right back at her. "I got lucky."

"How?" asked Trinity.

Loyal told her about his moment alone in Bertrand's kitchen and the phones on the counter. He explained about Stingray, leaving out O'Keefe's involvement.

"Do you recognize the other voice?" he asked.

"I know who it is," said Trinity.

"Stingray evidence isn't admissible in court," Loyal said.

"Doesn't matter," said Trinity. "I know where the meet is, Loyal. I can finally get the bastard on something real."

104

LACEY-MARCH 2019

Lacey walked with Loyal to the front door of JK's.

"You know you really don't need a trainer anymore," she said.

"I need someone to be accountable to," said Loyal. "Otherwise I might not show up."

"Makes sense," said Lacey. "I'll see you on Wednesday then."

"I'll be here," said Loyal, and he stepped through the door.

Lacey turned and looked around the gym. It was a little over half full. Adelle stood behind the reception desk and Joe Kagan was chatting with a client. Lacey sighed, she felt so flat lately. Working at the gym had once given her so much pleasure. She was finding it hard to find gratification in anything anymore. Gladys had commented on her mood more than once. Bertrand had even mentioned it yesterday when he had returned from another business trip. Lacey had told both of them it was due to her Mother's continued decline, which they had accepted. She couldn't tell either of them the true reason. She was so damn sad about Van, she just couldn't hide it anymore.

Lacey double checked with Adelle that she wasn't needed at the gym any more for the day, then drove home to Shorebird Lane. Bertrand was at the office in La Jolla, and Gladys and Liane were in what was now referred to as Liane's studio. Gladys was reading a book and Liane was at her easel.

"Hi," said Lacey.

"Hi honey," said Gladys, glancing up from the book in her hands. "How was the gym?"

"Good," said Lacey. "How was everything here?"

Gladys stood and walked towards the kitchen. Lacey followed.

"Is something wrong Gladys?" Lacey said.

"Liane climbed over the back fence today and went down to the lagoon trail," Gladys said. "Gave me quite the scare. I went to the kitchen to get us a snack, and when I came back she was gone. Took me about ten minutes to find her."

"Has she ever done that before?" Lacey asked.

"I don't think so," Gladys said. "I just thought you should know."

Trinity left Loyal's apartment shortly after he played the audio file of Bertrand and Jack Williamson's conversation. She drove straight to the condo and placed a call to Douglass Caldwell.

"Talk to me Glass," He answered on the fourth ring. "You got something?"

Trinity outlined the content of the phone call and the details of the last meeting. "This is it Doug," she said. "I finally have something concrete on Roberts. Williamson is a bonus. I need a team."

Caldwell paused briefly, then said, "I can spare Parker from Team three."

"I need more than one," Trinity said.

"I gave you the local FBI contact."

"I'll reach out to her Doug," Trinity said. "But I need one more."

"Okay, Glass. I'll send Silva too."

"Thanks Doug," Trinity said. "Email me their flight information and I'll meet them at the airport."

"Will do," said Caldwell, then he disconnected.

Trinity sat back, closed her eyes, and imagined Bertrand Roberts in handcuffs. A small smile played at the corners of her mouth. She sat back up and located Caldwell's email with the contact information for the local FBI agent. She placed a call to her, was directed to voicemail, and left a non-specific message asking her to call at her earliest convenience. Her adrenaline was pumping. She was so close to success. She paced around the small condo for several minutes, changed into shorts and t-shirt, and headed for the spa's gym.

An hour later, exercise having helped to dissipate the adrenaline load, Trinity returned to the condo and showered. She dressed in jeans and a sweatshirt,and headed back towards Loyal's. It was nearly 5:00 so she stopped at Pizza Port. She ordered a pizza to go and drank a beer while she waited. Loyal couldn't drink while he was taking the pain medication, but that wasn't going to stop her from enjoying a celebratory beer.

L oyal heard the light footsteps, the knock, and the admonition not to shoot. The door opened and Trinity stepped in bringing with her the enticing aroma of Pizza Port.

"I brought us dinner," she said, depositing the pizza box on the kitchen table, then crossing the room and leaning down for a kiss.

"You hungry?"

"Yeah," said Loyal.

"You need me to help you up?" said Trinity as she pulled plates out of the kitchen cabinet.

"Nope," said Loyal. "I actually got myself out of this chair earlier." He paused, then added, "Hurt like hell."

Trinity handed him a plate with two slices on it, then settled on the couch, a plate in her lap. She took a bite, chewed and swallowed.

"Good you were able to get yourself up," she said. "I want to thank you again for that audio file."

"You get everything set up?" Loyal asked.

"It's in the works," she said.

They ate in silence for several minutes. Loyal had not eaten much since the ambush, and was pleasantly surprised to find that his appetite was slightly improved. He followed the first slice with a Percocet, then ate the second slice. He was just setting the plate on the end table when his phone rang. He glanced at the caller ID, then accepted.

"Hi Maggie," he said.

"Hey Loyal," Maggie replied. "I was wondering if you had any more news on your stalker? I talked to Dee and she told me about your adventures with the Dark Forces gang. Sorry I missed that, it sounded like fun."

"It was," said Loyal. "And my stalker is sitting on my couch at this very moment." He smiled at Trinity.

"Well that certainly is interesting," said Maggie. "Hey, why don't you bring her to the wedding on Friday?"

"Ah, I'm not sure I can make it," said Loyal. "I had a fall and have a couple of broken ribs. And I know for a fact she is tied up that day."

"You have to come Loyal," said Maggie. "Just have someone help you into your car on that end, and we'll help you out when you get here."

Loyal sighed. "Can I get back to you on that?" he asked.

"I promise we can keep you comfortable Loyal," Maggie said. "Just get yourself here, we'll take care of the rest."

.   .   .

Loyal ended the phone call without committing to attend.

He asked Trinity to look over the autopsy and evidence reports, which she did.

"No surprises here," she said when she had read everything.

"I thought the same thing," said Loyal.

"You have anything else I haven't seen?" Trinity asked.

Loyal thought a moment. "Some footage from Port Hueneme. Want to see it?"

"Sure."

Loyal pulled up the footage from the drone and handed his phone to Trinity. He watched her face as she watched the screen.

"We need to know what they are saying," she said.

"I thought the same thing," said Loyal. "You know anyone who reads lips?"

"I work for the government, Loyal. We have someone for every situation." Trinity paused and smiled. "Our lip readers are the best. Even better than the NFL."

Trinity reached out to her contact and then sent the footage from Port Hueneme.

"We should have a transcript by tomorrow morning," she said. "It's already 9:20 back East," she added when she saw Loyal's raised eyebrow.

"So, who's Maggie?" asked Trinity a moment later.

"Just a friend," said Loyal. "She set me up with the people who helped me track you down."

"Sounded like she was inviting you somewhere."

"A wedding this Friday in Borrego," said Loyal. "I think I want to go. She invited you as well, but I'm guessing you are busy."

"You guessed right."

"You think you could find the time Friday morning to help me down the stairs and into my car?" Loyal asked.

Trinity smiled. "I'll make the time."

There was no fog on Thursday morning. The sun shone brightly through the kitchen window, the rays illuminating Trinity's still form as she slept on the couch. The golden light shone on her face and brought her gently out of a deep and dreamless sleep. She glanced at Loyal and saw he was asleep in the recliner. Trinity stretched, then rose. She started a pot of coffee, then sat at the kitchen table with her phone and her laptop in front of her. An email from Douglass Caldwell informed her that Parker and Silva would be arriving at Palomar McClellan on Friday morning at 10:00. Just as she was about to log out, another email arrived. This one was from her lip reading contact. Trinity clicked the message and read the transcript. Bertrand was referred to as *Ball Cap,* Blomgren as *Bare Head.*

> *Ball Cap: You were supposed to be watching her.*
> *Bare Head: She was alive and alone when I passed her.*
> *(Drone passes behind men's heads)*

Ball Cap: This isn't a partnership Don. You work for me.
(Bare Head does not respond)
Ball Cap: I don't need this scrutiny.
Bare Head: I know Bertrand.

Trinity read the brief conversation several times. She rose, carried the laptop over to the recliner, and tapped Loyal gently on the shoulder. He opened his eyes slowly.

"Hey there," said Trinity.

Loyal looked up. "Hey," he said.

"Hope you don't mind that I woke you," Trinity said. "My lip reader got back to me. Want to see the transcript?"

Loyal nodded. Trinity placed the laptop in his lap and he read the exchange.

"What do you think?" she asked.

"Judging by this conversation, it doesn't sound like either of these guys are the killer," Loyal said.

"Agreed," said Trinity.

"So that leaves Hammond and Van," Loyal said. "Or someone completely off my radar."

"But why kill Blomgren?" Trinity asked.

Loyal shook his head. "Maybe Blomgren saw more than he is admitting to," he said. "Or maybe Blomgren did kill her and Bertrand figured it out. Then Bertrand would have a motive for killing Blomgren. You saw the pictures. There was rage in that murder."

Lacey climbed the steps to Van's apartment and knocked on the door. Her heart jumped a bit when he opened it and looked out.

"Hi," she said.

"Hi," Van said.

"Can I come in?" Lacey asked after a moment passed.

Van blinked, then smiled and stepped back. "Of course," he said. "Sorry, you just caught me by surprise. Wasn't expecting it to be you."

"You expecting someone else?" Lacey asked as she sat on the couch.

"No," said Van, "never."

Lacey patted the couch cushion and Van sat beside her.

"I'm leaving him, Van," she said. "We can be together."

Van stared into her eyes for a long moment. "Is this real, Lacey?" he said.

"Yes," Lacey said. "He returns from a business trip tonight. I'm going to tell him tomorrow."

·   ·   ·

Van pulled Lacey into his arms. She relaxed into him, relishing the smell of his skin and hair. She was both terrified and exhilarated at the same time. Telling Bertrand would be painful. She did care a great deal for him. She also had Liane and her Mother to consider. Linda, who's dementia was profound, was completely lost to her. If Bertrand cut off all the funds for her care she would have to be moved to a facility that accepted State assistance. Unless Gladys offered some type of help, Liane would have to come live with Van and Lacey. Lacey breathed out and pushed those thoughts from her mind, concentrating instead on the moment she was in.

Van eased her out of his arms and stood.

"I have something I got for you a while ago," he said. "I want to give it to you now."

He walked to his bedroom and returned a moment later with a narrow rectangular box, which he handed to Lacey. She opened it and removed a thin gold chain. Van took it from her and clasped it around her wrist.

"It's beautiful Van," Lacey said. "I'll never take it off."

Trinity and Loyal spent the morning talking about things unrelated to Bertrand or Lacey. She described her unconventional upbringing, high-lighting the many countries and cultures her family experienced during her childhood. Loyal was fascinated by her tales of exotic locales, and especially enjoyed that her stories took his mind off the pain emanating from his left side. When Trinity fell silent, Loyal took up the narrative. He described his youth in Fallbrook, his love of motorcycles, his races at Carlsbad Raceway and in Baja, the freedom of a dirt trail in the middle of nowhere. It was a pleasant morning for both, no mention of murder or duplicity. The time passed quickly and Loyal felt a pang of disappointment when Trinity eventually announced that she had things to take care of and would be heading out for the rest of the day, promising to return for dinner and to stay the night.

.   .   .

With Trinity's departure, and the emptiness of the apartment, the pain returned. Loyal downed a Vicodin, noting that only four pills remained in the bottle. The Percocet were gone. Fortunately, Loyal had remembered to ask Trinity to set up the CD player. As the Vicodin slowly dulled the pain to a manageable level, he hit play and began *LA Outlaws.*

Trinity's phone rang as she was descending Loyal's stairs and heading to her car. Caller ID indicated the local FBI office. She accepted the call.

"Glass," she said.

"This is special agent Hobbs," the woman on the line said. "You left a message for me."

"Yes," said Trinity. "Thank you for getting back to me. Douglass Caldwell gave me your contact information."

"Caldwell, Huh?" said Hobbs. "Are you in Southern California Agent Glass?"

"Carlsbad," said Trinity.

"Meet me at the Starbucks on Loker Avenue just off Palomar Airport Road in one hour," said Hobbs. "I'm wearing a dark blue suit and have short black hair."

"I'll be there," Trinity said, and disconnected.

. . .

Forty-five minutes later Trinity was seated at a small table near the back of the Starbucks. She kept her eye on the entrance while she sipped from a water bottle and nibbled on a bagel with cream cheese. She spotted Hobbs as she entered the establishment. True to her word, she wore a dark blue suit and her black hair was cropped closely to her head. Hobbs had failed to mention that she was quite tall, Trinity estimated the woman stood nearly six feet. Hobbs paused as she entered and took in the interior of the restaurant. Trinity gave a slight wave when Hobbs eyes passed over the area where she was sitting. Hobbs returned the wave, walked over, and sat down.

"You want anything?" Trinity asked.

"I'm good," said Hobbs. She extended her hand. "Madeline Hobbs."

Trinity shook the proffered hand and said, "Trinity Glass."

"You work with Doug?" asked Hobbs.

"Yes," said Trinity. "He gave me your contact information; said you might be willing to give me a hand on something."

Hobbs smiled. "I'm sure he did." She waited a moment, and when Trinity didn't speak, she added, "I'm listening."

Without revealing their names, Trinity explained about the meet between Bertrand and Williamson. If she agreed to help, Hobbs would be providing an extra team to aid in the apprehension, as well as a place for initial interrogation.

"I'm going to need more complete details," Hobbs said. "Identities would be a good place to start."

"I'm counting on your discretion," Trinity said. "If word gets out the deal will be blown. I will of course allow your office to publicly take credit. I only need credit in Caldwell's eyes."

Hobbs had intense dark blue eyes. She looked directly into Trinity's eyes, but offered no response. Trinity sighed. "Ok," she said, "I'll give you everything."

L oyal listened to the first disc of _LA Outlaws_. He was enjoying it, but kept drifting off and having to restart. He decided to save it for the drive out to Borrego which was bound to be very uncomfortable. The book would be a great distraction. He was just sitting there letting thoughts flow randomly through his mind when he heard footsteps on the stairs. His hand slid down to the gun and he readied himself. There was a short rap on the door then he heard O'Keefe say, "It's Pat, Loyal. Don't shoot."

The door opened slowly and Pat O'Keefe came in. He was carrying a bag and two cups with straws peeking out of the lids.

"I brought us some Plant Power," he said as he entered. "Have you had lunch yet?"

Loyal shook his head and smiled. "Thanks Pat."

O'Keefe handed Loyal his food, then sat on the couch with his own. The two men ate and talked about inconsequential things. O'Keefe gave updates on his family, Loyal explained about his upcoming trip to the desert for a wedding. As he was getting ready to go O'Keefe asked Loyal if he had provided the legal assistance for Van Winters. Loyal nodded.

"Good thing," said O'Keefe. "Hammond has that guy in his sights. That lawyer of yours is doing a good job of keeping him away from Winters."

Loyal slept deeply for several hours after O'Keefe departed. He woke to find that the sunlight was fading for the day. He maneuvered himself out of the recliner, flinching when his broken ribs clacked against each other. He turned on some lights against the approaching darkness, used the bathroom, and poured himself a tall glass of water. He stood at the kitchen counter, drinking the water and thinking about the next day. He went into the bedroom and picked out some clothes to take to Borrego. When he returned to the living room Trinity was sitting on the couch smiling up at him.

"Hey Loyal," she said.

"Trinity," he said, "you're back."

Trinity cradled a mug of hot coffee between her hands, savoring the heat that radiated from the ceramic cup. Loyal sat across the kitchen table from her with a steaming mug of his own. He had insisted on trying to sit in a kitchen chair at the table this morning. He had spent three days in the recliner and was still in serious pain. Trinity wondered about the wisdom of him driving himself to Borrego, but said nothing. He was determined to go.

"I need to be to Palomar Airport by 10:00," Trinity said glancing at her phone. "It's 7:45 now." She looked across the table at Loyal. "I've got about 90 minutes. Anything I can do for you?" Before Loyal could answer her phone rang.

"Doug," said Trinity as she answered the call.

"Your team is getting in early," Caldwell said. "Arrival at 8:30."

"I'll be there," Trinity said and disconnected.

"New timeline," she said to Loyal. "I've got about twenty minutes."

"I've got everything ready to go," said Loyal. "Just need a little help getting dressed and down to the car."

Trinity stood and walked around the table to his chair. "Alright then," she said. "Let's get you up."

Twenty minutes later Trinity watched as Loyal drove off in his Altima. She had helped him into his slacks and a Tommy Bahama, assisted with getting socks and shoes on his feet, and helped him down the stairs. After a lingering kiss and a gentle embrace, she eased him into the driver's seat, clicked the seatbelt into place, and closed the door. Moments later he was gone. With a sigh, Trinity went back up the stairs, gathered her things, ensured the door was locked, and drove toward the airport.

L oyal settled into the driver's seat and allowed Trinity to fasten his seatbelt and close his door. Driving did not require the use of his left arm and his rib pain was manageable. He had taken a Vicodin with his coffee. He had three pain pills remaining. To keep his mind off the pain he started *LA Outlaws* again. The tires of the Altima ate up the miles while the story unfolded. Soon Loyal was winding down Montezuma Grade into Borrego. His adventures of the previous August had brought him to the small desert town, and to the home where the wedding was taking place. Whereas the landscape in August had been harsh and barren, it now was covered with a low green carpet and tiny blossoming flowers. Loyal rolled down his window and breathed in the fresh dry air. He loved the smell of the desert.

The wedding was being held at Peter's house on the

outskirts of the small town. Peter was Maggie's godfather, Maggie was dear friends with Elsie, and Elsie was the bride to be. Loyal had met Peter briefly the previous August and found him to be honest and forthright. There were several cars parked in front of the large adobe home. Loyal parked next to Maggie's yellow Meyers Manx. His plan was to call her and ask for someone to help him out of the Altima, but he found to his dismay that his phone had no service in the area. He was able to unfasten his seatbelt with his right hand, but his ribs protested when he attempted to open the driver's door. Loyal steeled himself for the burst of pain, then opened the door in one smooth motion. He sat for a moment, breathing shallowly, and waiting for the pain to subside. Just as he was steeling himself for exiting the vehicle a familiar voice said, "Need a hand?"

Loyal turned his head and saw Peter approaching from the rear of the vehicle. He was a tall man, his skin tanned a deep brown from life in the desert sun. He wore khaki shorts, a loose button down shirt, and a wide brimmed hat.

"Maggie said you had some broken ribs," Peter said as he looked down at Loyal.

"Yeah," said Loyal. "I could definitely use a hand."

Peter helped Loyal maneuver out of the Altima and carried his duffel bag into the house for him. He pointed out a basket where each guest had deposited their cell phone. "It is a tech free event," he said. Loyal turned off then added his. Peter showed Loyal the guest room he would be using, then led him out to the pool area where a small group was seated around an outdoor table. Peter led Loyal over to the table and helped him into a seat. The conversation stilled as Loyal was seated, and Peter took the opportunity to introduce him to the group.

"This is Loyal," he said. "Loyal, I know you already know Maggie and Phil. Let me introduce everyone else." He indicated the young woman next to Phil. She had pale skin, golden hair, and amber eyes. "This is Elsie," Peter said, "the bride to be." He pointed to the other man and woman at the table. "This is Andrew and this is Kimmy, Phil's twin brother and his wife." Loyal smiled and said hello to everyone.

"Don't let my arrival interrupt your conversation," he added.

Peter excused himself then returned with a large tray of croissants and fruit. Another trip to his spacious kitchen resulted in coffee, orange juice, and sparkling water. He then settled his large frame in a chair and rejoined the conversation. Topics were varied. Andrew and Kimmy had arrived earlier in the day from their home in Idaho. He was a pilot for a major airline, as well as a private pilot, and they had flown from Idaho to Borrego in their 1967 Piper Comanche. It had been over a year since everyone was in the same place at the same time. Loyal added little to the conversation. He was content to listen and observe. After nearly a week in relative isolation he was simply enjoying the sound of animated conversation and laughter.

. . .

At noon Peter announced that lunch would be served in the living room. After that the guests were on their own for a few hours. The wedding was scheduled for 6:00 that evening and there were still a few last minute preparations that needed to be handled. Phil helped Loyal get to his feet. As he was walking toward the living room Elsie appeared by his side. She touched his elbow gently, then steered him into the dining room.

"I've not met you Detective, but I feel as if I know you," she said. "I just want to thank you for all you did last Summer."

"I'm not sure I actually did anything," said Loyal.

"You did," said Elsie with a genuine smile. "Thank you so much for coming to our wedding."

"It's my pleasure," Loyal said, and realized that he truly meant it.

The afternoon passed quickly. Loyal spent much of it with Andrew and Kimmy. Storm, Maggie's impossibly large German Shepherd, had attached himself to Loyal and lay curled up beside the detective's chair. Maggie and Elsie had disappeared to "beautify", and Phil and Peter were hard at work in the pool area with last minute adjustments and decorations. Loyal found Andrew and Kimmy to be interesting conversationalists. He told them a bit about himself, his work, and Stella. Kimmy was delighted to hear about his impending status as grandfather and informed

Loyal that she and Andrew were also expecting their first child. Andrew spoke of his and Phil's childhood and of the perks and pitfalls of twin-hood. They were fraternal, not identical, and Phil was by far the more handsome and athletic of the two.

"Junior high and high school were especially frustrating for me," he said. "Phil was better looking, so the girls flocked to him. He was more athletic, so the coaches liked him more." Andrew paused. "Sometimes I actually wished he wasn't around. Feel kind of bad about that, but it's tough always feeling less than." He laughed. "It all worked out fine. I've got Kimmy, a child on the way, a job I love. I'm grateful for Phil now."

L acey descended the curving staircase and paused in the entryway. She spun a complete circle, looking at everything. None of this would belong to her after this morning. Bertrand was still sleeping upstairs. She planned on taking a walk, clearing her head, then talking to him. Their marriage was over. He would be angry, she knew this, and he had every right to be. She wouldn't fight him on anything except her mother's care. She hoped he would at least continue to pay for that.

On impulse Lacey walked into Liane's bedroom. Her sister lay in her bed, curled up on her right side, knees to her chest, her left arm casually atop the comforter. Lacey crossed the room and looked down at her sister. She gently smoothed Liane's dark hair away from her forehead. In sleep Liane's features relaxed and looked a bit more like Lacey's.

"I've made a decision," Lacey whispered. "I'm leaving Bertrand, but it's going to be okay. Van and I will take care of you." You'll never have to worry Liane," she said, leaning down to kiss her sister's cheek. "My loyalty lies with you."

115

A t 5:30 Peter leaned into the living room and said, "Wedding is in half an hour. Time to dress up and get ready." Andrew and Kimmy excused themselves and headed to their guest room. Peter helped Loyal up, then asked if he needed help with anything.

"I think I'm okay, thanks," said Loyal. He walked to his guest room noticing that Storm followed closely behind. The large dog spun several circles then settled down on the carpet, his large brown eyes focused on Loyal. Loyal looked down at his slacks and decided they were in fine shape for the ceremony. He slowly removed his Tommy Bahama, replacing it with another one of his signature button downs. By 5:50 he had brushed his hair and teeth and was back in the living room. Andrew and Kimmy joined him soon thereafter. They walked as a group to the pool area.

. . .

The sun was slowly sinking behind the mountains to the West and leaving a crimson shadow in the sky, which was turning a deep shade of blue. Small twinkling lights had been strung around the pool area. A flower covered wooden arch had been set up on the East end of the pool area, the expansive desert providing a breathtaking background. Peter stood in front of the arch, a broad smile on his face. Maggie stood beside him, Storm silent by her side. Music began playing. Loyal managed to stand and turn as Phil and Elsie walked slowly towards the arch. Loyal was surprised to see that Peter was performing the ceremony, ordained officiant yet another aspect to the man of which Loyal had been unaware. The ceremony was short, Elsie and Phil exchanged vows, rings, and a kiss, then the party was underway.

Saturday morning found Trinity, Parker, Silva, and Hobbs drinking coffee at the Carlsbad FBI Office and fine tuning their plans. According to the audio file, the meet between Bertrand and Williamson was set for 11:30 at the Henshaw Scenic Vista Observation Site. Trinity, Hobbs, and Parker, along with Liu, Sharpe, and Chandon, three agents Hobbs had rounded up, would be in place at that location one hour before the scheduled meet. Silva, along with two more agents, Hasan and Hendrickson, also provided by Hobbs, would be keeping an eye on Ann Marie Williamson, and would apprehend her when given the go ahead by Trinity. The goal was to take each of the three players into custody and isolate them. Interrogations and possible deal making would follow the arrests. Trinity was buzzing from adrenaline and caffeine, her right leg bouncing as they spoke.

.   .   .

At 9:30 Trinity, Hobbs, and Sharpe left Carlsbad in Trinity's Denali. Parker, along with Chandon and Liu, followed them, driving in a black Suburban. Silva, driving in a black Suburban with Hasan and Hendrickson, headed to Pacific Beach. Ann Marie Williamson was a woman of habit, playing tennis at the Pacific Beach Tennis Club every Saturday morning. Trinity, Hobbs, and Sharpe said little on the drive to the back side of Palomar Mountain. The day was clear and bright. The foliage along the way green and lush thanks to all the springtime rain. Trinity pointed out the viewpoint as they passed it. She pulled to the side of the road and parked exactly as she had on her previous trip. The car was so close to the edge of a steep and dangerous slope that she had Hobbs slide over the console and exit from the driver's side. Sharpe followed suit from the back seat, then eased into the driver's seat where he would remain with the vehicle. Parker had not turned off on the road to the viewpoint. He, Chandon, and Liu had traveled a mile further on the 76, and were parked in the parking lot of the Lake Henshaw Cafe.

Trinity, her Fraser Volpe gyro-stabilized binoculars swinging from her neck, led Hobbs to the spot that offered a clear view of the viewpoint parking lot. The FBI agent wore an FBI windbreaker, Trinity wore OSI's version of the same thing. Both wore dark blue slacks, shoes they could run in, and belts with guns, encrypted radios, zip ties and handcuffs. Hobbs sat on the ground with her back against on oak tree, Trinity remained standing.

"Everyone knows the drill, right?" Trinity said. The other agent nodded.

"You record Roberts making the drop, then let him leave. Parker, Liu, and Chandon will stop him at the base of the grade. I'll alert Sharpe to bring the car down to block Williamson when we take him down," said Hobbs.

"Exactly," said Trinity. "As you know, we need to make sure to keep the two men apart. You'll radio Parker when Roberts drives away. Silva, Hasan, and Hendrickson should be detaining Williamson's ex wife momentarily." Trinity was silent for a moment, then added, "Ann Marie Williamson is the weak link. We need to get her to talk."

The intense desert sun woke Loyal early on Saturday morning. He lay in bed a moment, dreading the pain any movement was sure to bring. He let his mind drift back to last night's post-wedding party. The small group had stayed up until the wee hours of the morning laughing, drinking, and dancing. Loyal, obviously, had not been one of the dancers. He had allowed himself a few beers which, combined with the pain medication, had put him in a mellow and relaxed mood. He had especially enjoyed his time talking with Peter and Maggie. Peter had been Maggie's father's best friend. Her parents and unborn sibling had been killed in a freak mudslide and Maggie's Aunt had been granted conservatorship over Maggie and the considerable estate that accompanied the six year old. Aunt Joan had not been unkind, she simply lacked the emotional depth the young orphan required. Peter had gladly stepped in as a surrogate father, spending every available moment with Maggie.

Loyal could see the depth of their relationship written on their faces. It made him think of Stella.

Loyal blinked and brought himself back to the present. He swallowed a Vicodin, only two pills remaining, and gave it a few minutes to work its magic. He then maneuvered himself out of the bed, dressed, combed his hair, and brushed his teeth. Shoes were an impossibility. He hadn't really thought about that until he removed the pair Trinity had so kindly put on his feet Friday morning. He decided he would ask Maggie for help. Loyal exited his bedroom, smelled the tantalizing aroma of fresh coffee, and followed its scent to the kitchen. He poured a mug, then walked out to the pool area. It was empty except for Maggie. She stood at the East end of the sparkling water, her back to Loyal, the expanse of the desert in front of her. Loyal paused a moment and took in the scene. He hadn't liked Maggie when they had first met the previous August. He was surprised, but pleased, that his feelings had changed from dislike, to grudging respect, to honest friendship in the intervening months. Not wanting to startle her, Loyal gave a low cough as he approached.

"Loyal," she said as she turned to face him. "You are up early." She glanced at his bare feet but said nothing.

"Yep," said Loyal. "I've got to be getting back to the coast."

"How are the ribs?"

"Painful," said Loyal.

She glanced at his bare feet. "You need some help?"

"It's embarrassing as hell," Loyal said, "but, yes."

An hour later, shoes and socks on and thanks and good-byes said to the slowly waking wedding attendees, Loyal plucked his phone from the basket, patted Storm on his massive head, slid painfully into his car with Peter's assistance, and drove out of the desert. At the top of Montezuma Grade, as he passed through the tiny town of Ranchita, Loyal's phone regained service and began to emit a steady stream of pings, text messages and voice-mails received during the previous twenty-four hours. Loyal pulled over and looked at his phone. There were text messages from Stella and O'Keefe, both inquiring about how he was feeling and if he needed anything. He sent a brief response to each indicating that he was on the way home from Borrego and doing fine. There was a voicemail from Maynard Lily, left Friday afternoon, updating Loyal on Van Winters' situation. Hammond was pushing hard and Van's lack of a corroborated alibi was problematic. "If he finds one piece of circumstantial evidence," Lily's voice boomed out of the phones speaker, "the kid might be in some trouble." The last voicemail, left just over an hour ago, was from Gladys Kramer.

"Detective, this is Gladys Kramer." She was whispering, her voice trembling. "I need to talk to you. I discovered something that I think may be very important. Please call me back as soon as possible."

Loyal tapped call back. Gladys' phone rang six times, then switched to voicemail.

At 11:25 Bertrand Roberts pulled into the viewpoint parking lot. He remained inside the Suburban for a moment, then the door swung open and he stepped out. He was dressed casually in dark blue jeans, gray sweatshirt, and tennis shoes. A black ball cap concealed his thick dark hair. He carried a navy blue Coleman soft-sided cooler in his left hand. Roberts proceeded slowly to the far end of the viewpoint. He set the cooler on the ground, then leaned his elbows against the railing and stared out into the distance. Less than five minutes later a low slung red Corvette pulled into the parking lot and parked some distance from the Suburban. Roberts turned at the sound of the engine. He noted the Corvette then walked briskly back to his vehicle. The cooler remained on the ground.

When Roberts pulled out of the parking lot Hobbs radioed

Parker and informed him that his quarry was on the move. Trinity continued simultaneously filming and watching through the Fraser Volpes. Williamson walked casually down the viewpoint walkway, picked up the cooler and retraced his steps to his car. He opened the door, slid in, and was just about to close the door when Trinity and Hobbs approached, badges out. Simultaneously, Sharpe wheeled the Denali into the parking lot and wedged the vehicle behind the Corvette. Williamson took one look at the agents and slammed the car door. Before Trinity or Hobbs had a moment to react, the Corvette was in gear and moving forward. Williamson drove over curbs, the underside of the car scraping in protest. Trinity and Hobbs raced for the Denali, throwing themselves in from the passenger side. Sharpe wheeled the vehicle around and sped off after Williamson.

The Corvette turned right out of the parking lot and headed up the hill toward Palomar Mountain. The Denali followed suit. Trinity spoke urgently into the radio.

"Williamson is running. We are in pursuit, heading up the East Grade."

Parker responded. "Roberts in custody."

"Go to the bottom of the South Grade," Trinity said. "Williamson is in a newer model red Corvette." She gave the license plate number.

"Copy," said Parker.

The East Grade of Palomar was a windy two lane. The lane leading up bordered the steep cliff for a bit, then transitioned so that it hugged the steep mountain face. Sharpe drove smoothly, negotiating the hair pin turns expertly. Williamson remained about fifteen feet in front of them, moving fast. About a football field after they passed over a cattle grate in the road, a yellow sign warned of an upcoming series of switchbacks. The suggested speed was twenty-five miles per hour; a suggestion Williamson ignored. As he entered the second turn, Williamson applied the brakes too heavily and the Corvette began to fishtail. Sharpe slowed a bit, and all three agents watched in fascination and horror as Williamson slid into the oncoming lane, overcorrected, and headed straight for the road's edge and the steep descent that lay beyond it.

L oyal pulled back onto the road and accelerated. He was about an hour away from Shorebird Lane. He considered calling the Sheriff's Department and requesting a health and welfare check on Gladys Kramer. She had sounded nervous and concerned, but not necessarily afraid. As he was nearing Lake Henshaw he tapped her number again. It rang, as before, then went to voicemail. He left her a brief message then disconnected. Loyal pressed the accelerator. The Altima was nearing seventy miles per hour, sailing easily through the lazy curves around Lake Henshaw, when a black Suburban pulled out from East Grade right in front of Loyal. He pressed the brake pedal urgently, his ribs screaming in protest at the sudden movement and deceleration. Loyal honked his horn loudly. The driver of the Suburban made no move to even look in Loyal's direction, just sped away in front of Loyal, heading West.

· · ·

Loyal kept up with the black vehicle until it made a screaming turn onto South Grade, which led up to Palomar Mountain. Loyal sped past the turn off and began the descent into Pauma Valley. It was mid morning on a Saturday in spring and traffic was building up. Motorcycle riders were out for a day of adventure, motorhomes and trailers were heading to desert campsites, cars full of day-trippers and hikers were out looking to spend some time outdoors. Fortunately for Loyal, most of the traffic was headed in the opposite direction as he was and he was able to keep up a consistent speed. He negotiated the round-about at the junction of the 76 and Valley Center Road, opting to stay on the 76 which led straight to the coast. Just past Fallbrook he felt a strong desire to talk to Trinity. He knew she was likely in the middle of apprehending Roberts, but couldn't resist placing a call to her. The call went straight to voicemail and he left a message voicing his concerns about Gladys Kramer. He then tried Gladys one more time. Six rings, then voicemail. Loyal disconnected and increased his speed.

Trinity held her breath as the Corvette, seemingly moving in slow motion, slid toward the edge. Unbelievably, the car smashed into an oak tree that was growing straight up from the face of the cliff. The strong tree somehow managed to absorb the blow and held, keeping the vehicle from plunging over the edge and taking Williamson down to certain death. Trinity, Hobbs, and Sharpe were out of the Denali in moments and running towards the Corvette. The car was parallel to the road, the driver's side door smashed against the oak, the engine still rumbling. Looking in, Trinity could see Williamson, apparently unconscious, his body held in place by his seatbelt, and head lolling forward against the steering wheel. The oak tree was making crackling and popping noises, it's roots straining against the load.

"We don't have much time," Trinity shouted. "This tree isn't going to hold much longer." She tried the passenger door and found it locked. Hobbs appeared beside her, tire jack in hand. "Step back," she warned, then swung at the passenger window with surprising strength. The glass shattered. Hobbs threw the tire iron to the side and reached inside the vehicle to open the door. She then leaned in, unstrapped Williamson, grabbed him by the torso, and hauled the man out. Trinity leaned in to the car, grabbed the Coleman cooler, then turned and snatched up Williamson's feet. The two women hauled him across the road to the Denali. Less than a minute later, with a loud crack and a boom, the oak's roots gave way. Trinity watched in disbelief as the tree and the Corvette disappeared from view in a cloud of dust.

L oyal leaned to the right and opened his glove box as he approached the gate on Shorebird Lane. He pulled out his note pad, which was still open to the page on which he had noted the gate code. He punched it in and, as the gates moved aside, drove onto Shorebird Lane. He angled the car straight down the cul-de-sac and parked in front of Gladys' house. Getting out of the car without help was a struggle and very painful. Cursing under his breath, Loyal forced himself up and out of the Altima. His right hand unconsciously reached down, confirming that the PM9 was exactly where it should be. His phone, sitting on the passenger seat, rang. Leaning down to grab it would be painful and difficult. Ignoring the ringing, he walked as rapidly as possible to Gladys' front door, which he found slightly ajar. Loyal rapped his knuckles against the door, leaned in slightly, identified himself, and called her name. He received no response.

· · ·

Loyal pushed the door more fully open and stepped into the entry area. Again, he identified himself and called her name. Again, there was no response. Loyal stood still and listened. The house was eerily silent. Loyal took a deep, silent breath in through his nose. There was the scent of something baking in the air. Cinnamon mixed with... what? He breathed in again. It smelled like bananas too, just on the edge of burning. Loyal swiveled to the right and reached his hand out to push open the swinging door that led to the kitchen. He paused a moment, his instincts telling him to beware. Entering an unknown situation through a closed door was dangerous. At the same time, bursting into an elderly person's kitchen with a gun drawn could provoke a heart attack. Loyal opted for caution, and held the PM9 down by his side. He pushed the door slowly inward, stepped warily into the kitchen, and swiveled to his right to look beyond the door. It took him less than a second to process what he was seeing and react. Gladys Kramer's still form was crumpled on the kitchen floor, a small puddle of blood forming beneath her head. He started to bring the PM9 up, but his hand never got there. There was movement from behind the door, a figure with one arm raised. Loyal attempted to maneuver himself back behind the swinging door but his broken ribs prevented the quick motion that was necessary to accomplish that. The raised arm came down, the object in the assailants hand connected with Loyal's head, and he was down.

Trinity instructed Sharpe to accompany Williamson in the ambulance to the hospital where he would be evaluated, then placed under arrest. A towing company had been called to haul the Corvette back up to the road and then to an impound lot. Trinity left Chandon at the scene to deal with that situation. She had radioed Parker as soon as the Corvette and oak tree disappeared from view, instructing him to drop Chandon at the scene, pick up Hobbs, then to proceed with Roberts to the FBI facility in Carlsbad. She then got back into the Denali and called Caldwell with an update as she drove towards the coast.

When she had first picked up her phone to call Caldwell, she had seen the missed call and voicemail from Loyal. Caldwell was the priority, so she made that call first. After updating her boss and disconnecting, she listened to the message from Loyal. He sounded like he had everything under control. Trinity opted to wait to call him back. She had wound her way down Palomar Mountain and executed the roundabout at the base of the Grade. She was now on the 76 heading towards the Carlsbad FBI offices. Just before the on ramp to Interstate 5 she decided to call Loyal. She listened through the rings. He did not pick up. Trinity's interior warning system was beeping. Just as she had on the previous Monday evening, she felt sure something was wrong. She placed a call to Hobbs.

"Hobbs," she said. "Something has come up. I need you to take the lead on Roberts' and Ann Marie Williamson for now."

"What?" said Hobbs. "This is your bust, Glass. Caldwell's not going to like this."

"I'll explain when I get there," Trinity said. "It's important."

"So is this case," said Hobbs. "You have a responsibility here."

"I know," said Trinity. "I have a loyalty elsewhere too."

She disconnected before Hobbs could respond, threw her phone onto the passenger seat, and accelerated towards Shorebird Lane.

The crack from the heavy object hitting his skull reverberated around in Loyal's head. A painful echo bouncing back and forth between his ears. It felt to him as if he was falling in slow motion. Time and space were suspended for a brief moment. Images flashed before his eyes; Trinity, Stella, Lacey. He thought briefly of Phil's twin brother Andrew, and his comments about Phil being the alpha in their relationship. As his body spiraled towards the unforgiving kitchen tile, his eyes locked, first, on the marble rolling pin in the hand of his assailant, then, secondly, on the face of the person who had assaulted him. Recognition flashed and his last thought before he landed hard on the kitchen floor was, "I was right." Pain radiated from his head and ribs. His face was pressed hard against the kitchen tile. Out of the corner of his eye he saw black tennis shoes approaching. The assailant was standing over him. He had dropped the PM9 when he had been struck. It was about 4 feet away from him, there was no way he could reach it in time. He raised his right arm to block the impending second blow.

Thehe Denali's tires squealed as Trinity turned onto Batiquitos Drive. She stopped the Denali in front of the closed gates of Shorebird Lane and slid out, 45 in her right hand, her left hand tucking her phone into the windbreaker pocket. She climbed the gate, dropped back to the ground, and sprinted towards Loyal's car which was parked at the deepest part of the cul de sac. The Altima was empty. Trinity ran to the bright red front door of the house that Loyal had parked in front of. It was open. Holding the 45 in front of her, and keeping low, she entered the house. She paused in the entry, listening and looking. She heard a thump from behind a swinging door to her right. Without a pause, Trinity pushed through the door. Her trained eyes took everything in in one glance. Loyal, down on the floor, arm raised. An older woman, likely Gladys Kramer, down and seemingly unconscious. Liane Barnett, marble rolling pin held high in her left hand, about to bring the heavy implement down on

Loyal's head. Trinity dove over Loyal and straight into Liane, wrapping her arms around the younger woman's torso. They went down with a crash. Liane was writhing and struggling to break free, but Trinity had the advantage. She rolled Liane over so that she was face down, pulled the zip ties she hadn't used on Williamson out of her windbreaker pocket, and secured Liane's hands and ankles. Then she turned to Loyal who was struggling to get up.

He was on his hands and knees. Blood flowed freely from the right side of his head. Trinity made a move to help him, but he shook her off.

"Check on Gladys," he said.

Trinity moved to the older woman's side. She had a head wound very similar to Loyal's. A small puddle of blood had pooled beside her gray-haired head. Trinity checked for respiration and pulse. Gladys was alive, unconscious, and breathing shallowly. Trinity removed her phone from the windbreaker pocket and dialed 911.

She identified herself to the dispatcher, and explained the situation quickly and concisely. Holding the phone between her shoulder and ear, she helped Loyal to his feet and eased him onto a bright yellow barstool. She grabbed a dish towel, placed it on his head wound, and raised his right hand to his head to hold the towel in place. She retrieved the PM9 and placed it in his lap.

"Somethings burning in the oven," Loyal mumbled. Trinity turned the oven off.

"I need to move my car," she said. "It's blocking the gates. You ok?"

Loyal looked at Liane on the floor. She was wiggling around, trying with no success to free herself from the zip ties. He nodded. Still on the phone with emergency services, Trinity exited the house, scaled the gate, moved the Denali, then climbed back over the gate and returned to the house. She could hear sirens approaching as she re-entered the kitchen. The scene inside remained unchanged.

L oyal allowed the paramedics to gently place him on a gurney. As he was being wheeled toward the swinging kitchen door, Hammond burst through with a bang. Loyal kept his face neutral, silently enjoying seeing Hammond so worked up. Hammond scanned the room, his eyes landing momentarily on Loyal, then moving on. Loyal watched as Trinity approached Hammond, badge out. She explained about Liane's attacks on both Gladys Kramer and Loyal.

"I'll be accompanying Detective Truesdale and Gladys Kramer to the hospital," she told Hammond. "We'll all be available after they are examined, treated, and released to answer your questions."

Hammond started to protest, but Trinity's badge and expression silenced him. Loyal allowed a small smile to play across his face.

.   .   .

Gladys Kramer was admitted to the hospital. Loyal was treated, prescribed pain medication, and released. Trinity drove Loyal to the Sheriff's Department upon his release. Maynard Lily was waiting for them in reception. He took in Loyal's battered appearance, but made no comments about it. Instead he asked, "How do you want this to go?"

"I'll answer any questions regarding my involvement," Loyal said. "Nothing about anyone else."

"Understood," Said Maynard. He turned to Trinity. "What about you?"

"I'll answer Hammond's questions about Shorebird Lane. Everything else is classified."

"You want me to represent you?" asked Maynard.

"Yes," said Trinity, "where do I sign?"

Loyal waited alone in an interview room while Trinity and Maynard met with Hammond. When Hammond and Maynard finally entered the room and sat at the table with Loyal, he could tell by Hammond's expression that things with Trinity had not gone as Hammond had hoped. A small smile played across Loyal's lips at that thought. Hammond glanced back to make sure the red light was glowing. Maynard placed his own recording device on the table. Hammond stated the date, time, and people present for the record. Before he could ask the first question Maynard interrupted saying, "We request Captain Williams be present at this interview." Hammond pushed back from the table, walked to the door and leaned out. He spoke briefly to someone out of sight in the hallway. He then rejoined Loyal and Maynard at the table. Five silent minutes passed, the door re-opened, and Captain Williams entered the room. His expression was grim.

The Captain looked at Hammond and Maynard. "I'd like a minute alone with Detective Truesdale," he said. Hammond started to speak. Captain Williams silenced him with a look.

"I don't recommend this," Maynard said to Loyal.

"It's ok Maynard," Loyal said. "Give us five minutes."

The Captain walked Hammond and Maynard to the door. He leaned out and depressed the button that turned off the recording device. Loyal saw the red light blink off. Williams returned to the table and sat opposite Loyal.

"You have a lot to answer to," Williams said.

Loyal opened his mouth to speak, but Williams held up his hand to silence him. "First," the Captain said, "you should not have been investigating this case. Second, anything you discovered should have been reported to this department, Hammond specifically. Third, we have a seriously injured civilian." He paused. "None of this should have happened Loyal. I can't protect you on this one." Loyal nodded, but said nothing.

"I want to hear everything, and I mean everything," Williams said. "Understand?"

Loyal nodded again. The Captain stood, walked to the door, motioned for Hammond and Maynard to come back into the room, and pushed the button to resume recording.

Trinity found three missed calls and two voicemails from Douglass Caldwell when she turned her phone back on following her conversation with Len Hammond. She called back without listening to the voicemails, she was fairly sure of the content. Caldwell answered on the second ring.

"What the hell is going on out there Glass?" His voice was rough with anger.

"I can explain Doug," Trinity said. "I'm ten minutes away from everything."

"I give you a pretty long leash Glass." Trinity winced at his phrasing. "Do I have to reel you in?"

"No Doug," Trinity said. "Let me sort this out. I'll fill you in completely."

Caldwell disconnected without a response. Trinity threw her phone on the passenger seat with a quite "Dammit," just under her breath.

·   ·   ·

When Trinity arrived to the FBI office she found that Hobbs had done as she had requested and taken control of the situation. Roberts had lawyered up immediately and was sequestered with his attorney in an interview room. Ann Marie Williamson was in an interview room with a female agent. She had not requested representation yet, just kept asking to call her ex-husband. He was, unfortunately for her, unavailable at the moment. The hospital had admitted him and Sharpe was by his side. Trinity and Hobbs exchanged some terse words, tensions eased slightly, and they agreed to start with Ann Marie Williamson.

Trinity and Hobbs entered the interrogation room, excused the female agent, and sat opposite Ann Marie Williamson. Trinity introduced herself and Hobbs, recited the time, date, and occupants of the room, and indicated to Mrs. Williamson that the conversation was being recorded.

"I'm told you have been asking for your ex husband," Trinity said.

Mrs. Williamson nodded. She had been crying. Her face was flushed, her eyes swollen. "I need to speak with him," she said.

"I'm afraid that's impossible," Trinity said. "Your ex husband has been taken into custody."

Mrs. Williamson's eyes widened. "Why?" she asked. "Can't you tell me what's happening?"

"We have evidence that you have been laundering money for him," Trinity said. "You are looking at a lengthy prison sentence." She paused, then said, "We can help you avoid some of that prison time if you cooperate with us."

The room was silent for a moment. Anne Marie Williamson's face had fallen into her hands. Her shoulders shook slightly as she silently cried. Hobbs broke the silence. "Look Ann Marie," she said, "we can help you, but you have to help us. We have definitive proof. Someone's going down hard." Mrs. Williamson raised her face and looked at the two agents. Hobbs continued. "It doesn't have to be you."

L oyal answered Hammond's questions as honestly as he could. There were gaps in his explanation. He left out any mention of O'Keefe. Hammond pressed hard. Maynard deflected questions Loyal didn't want to answer. When asked how he made the jump to the conclusion that Liane was the perpetrator, Loyal recounted his conversation with Andrew, Phil's twin brother. That, coupled with the call from Gladys Kramer, had put her at the top of his suspect list. When asked about a possible motive Liane might have, Loyal simply shook his head.

"Mrs. Kramer was suspicious about something," he said. "Hopefully she will be well enough to fill you in." He paused, then asked, "Do you have any information about her condition?"

"She's conscious," the Captain said. "We'll be going to the hospital after this to speak with her."

. . .

Two hours had passed by the time Loyal and Maynard exited the Sheriff's Department. Loyal was exhausted, hungry, and wracked with pain. Maynard drove him to his Altima on Shorebird Lane. The cul de sac was a hive of police activity. It took another forty-five minutes for Loyal to get his car. When he was finally cleared to drive away, he thanked Maynard, slid awkwardly into the vehicle, and headed to Oceanside. He parked in front of his garage, painfully maneuvered himself out of the car, and hobbled up his stairs. Once inside his apartment, he sank into his recliner and fell asleep.

It didn't take much pressure to get Ann Marie Williamson to flip on her ex husband. She was terrified of serving prison time and told them everything she knew. Jack Williamson had not told her where he was getting the money, but she was able to provide approximate dates and dollar amounts. Apparently Jack Williamson had been accepting bribes for contracts for several years. Trinity explained that, for Ann Marie's own safety, they would be keeping her in custody. The sobbing woman was handed off to another female agent, and Trinity and Hobbs went to an interrogation room two doors down to talk to Bertrand Roberts. He, of course, said nothing. His lawyer did all the talking. Trinity and Hobbs left the room, frustrated, after 30 minutes.

Trinity stepped outside the offices and placed a call to Loyal. He answered on the fifth ring.

"I woke you," Trinity said.

"Just dozing," said Loyal.

"I've got piles of paperwork," Trinity said. "I'll come over when I'm done."

"Door's unlocked," said Loyal. "Announce yourself."

"Will do," said Trinity with a smile.

Loyal ended the call with Trinity and placed his phone on the end table. As soon as he set it down it rang again. Loyal checked caller ID; O'Keefe. He accepted the call.

"Hey Pat."

"Hi Loyal. You home?"

"Yep," said Loyal.

"I'm coming by," said O'Keefe. "I'll be there in twenty."

"Door is unlocked," said Loyal. "Announce yourself."

Twenty five minutes later Pat O'Keefe was sitting on Loyal's couch, Loyal remained in the recliner.

"The Captain knows you had help from inside the department," O'Keefe said.

"I know," said Loyal. "I never said your name, Pat."

"There are rumors that your feet are going to be held to the fire on this one."

Loyal sighed. "I wouldn't be surprised. I promise I won't involve you."

O'Keefe had an uncomfortable look on his face. "I'm sorry to bring it up."

"Listen Pat," Loyal said, "you risked a lot to help me. I won't let this touch you."

"Captain Williams and Hammond spoke with Gladys Kramer," O'Keefe said after a brief silence. "She doesn't have proof, but she thinks Liane used her car on Sunday night. She has a tennis ball hanging in her garage and always lines the car up a certain way. It was slightly off on Monday."

"Does Liane even know how to drive?" Loyal asked.

"I guess Gladys has been giving her lessons."

Loyal was silent for a moment. "Liane will never be convicted."

"Probably not," said O'Keefe.

"None of it makes any sense," said Loyal.

"No," said O'Keefe, "it definitely does not."

T rinity parked her car beside Loyal's Altima. She turned off the ignition and sat still, eyes closed, breathing slowly. She had handed the case off to the prosecutor who would be seeking indictments from the Grand Jury. Eventually she would be called on to testify, but until that time her job in California was complete. Douglass Caldwell had informed her that she would be flying out of Palomar McClellan the following day at 12:30 pm. She would return to Washington DC and sit through an exhaustive debriefing. Originally Caldwell had wanted her on a flight at 9:00 this evening. To say she had asked for more time was too light a word, to say she had pleaded was too strong. Trinity thought for a moment. Perhaps pushed was the right word. She had "pushed" for 12 more hours. This had been difficult to do without revealing to Caldwell the reason she wanted to stay, which was Loyal. Twelve hours wasn't much, but it was something. She would embrace these hours. Despite only knowing him a week, Loyal meant so much to her. She wondered if love was too strong a word. Leaving him would be painful. Trinity opened her eyes, slid out of her car, and mounted the stairs to Loyal's apartment. She knocked, announced herself, then opened the door and went inside. Loyal, to her surprise, was standing in the kitchen. Despite his obvious discomfort, he smiled when she walked in the door.

Trinity crossed the room. Loyal opened his right arm and she leaned carefully into him. She was careful to lean toward his right side, avoiding the broken ribs on the left. She rested her head against his chest and felt the tension flow out of her body. Trinity knew herself well. She was not a reckless person. Still, in this moment, she considered throwing everything to the wind and staying here with Loyal. She felt him wrap his right arm around her slender frame and draw her as close as his broken body would allow. She took a long breath, then slowly let it out. Neither spoke for a long moment. Eventually Trinity pulled herself away and looked up at him.

"I'm on a plane tomorrow at 12:30." She said.

Loyal sighed. "That fast?"

"Yep." Said Trinity. "My boss doesn't waste any time." She paused. "I was hoping for more time with you."

"So was I." Said Loyal.

Sunday morning found Loyal standing with his back against the kitchen counter and coffee cup in his hands. He watched as Trinity nosed around in the refrigerator. She was looking in the fruit and vegetable bin, which was located in the lower part of the fridge. Loyal couldn't help but smile as he watched her.

"Showing off?" he said.

Trinity straightened and turned to look at him, an apple in her left hand. She smiled. "Maybe," she said as she walked over to him and leaned into his right side. Loyal tilted his head down and breathed in the scent of her cinnamon-ginger hair. He had known her only a week, but felt that this was where he belonged. He wondered if love was too strong a word. The emotional side of him wanted to ask her to stay. The logical side of him knew it would do no good. All the aspects of Trinity Glass that he found himself so drawn to, her strength, intelligence, bravery, curiosity, and loyalty, were the same aspects that made her an exceptional agent. She would go where her boss directed her to.

Loyal straightened. "I don't suppose you need a ride to the airport?" he asked.

Trinity tilted her face up at him. "I think it's better if we say goodbye here." She held his eyes for a long moment. "We will be together again, Loyal."

Loyal briefly tightened his right arm around her, then relaxed his hold on her.

"I'm counting on it," he said. Twenty minutes later he stood at the top of his stairs and watched as Trinity descended the eleven steps. The fog was thick and gray, by step seven she was no longer visible.

Monday morning was bright and sunny. Loyal woke early. Despite the pain radiating from his ribs, he showered, shaved, and dressed in slacks and a Tommy Bahama. He had no plans for the day, yet felt that getting up and dressed would be good for his state of mind. After Trinity had descended into the fog the previous morning, Loyal had spent the day in a listless haze. The depth of his feelings for Trinity surprised him and left him feeling adrift. He held on to the sliver of hope that they would see each other again. So, Monday was to be a fresh start for him; sunny day, shower and shave, pressed clothes, a new attitude. He was just pouring his second cup of coffee when his phone rang.

Loyal picked up the device, hoping it was Trinity, and saw the number for the Carlsbad Sheriff's Department. He accepted the call.

"Hello," he said.

"Truesdale, it's Captain Williams. We need to meet."

"Okay," said Loyal. "You want me to come by the station?"

"Yes," said Captain Williams. "Can you be here at 11:30?"

Loyal answered in the affirmative and disconnected. He ran his hand through his nearly dry hair. Something was up. The Captain had sounded tense. Loyal remembered O'Keefe's belief that Captain Williams thought that Loyal had had help from inside the department. O'Keefe had mentioned Loyal's feet being held to the fire. Perhaps this was the moment.

Loyal arrived to the Sheriff's Department at 11:15. He spent a few moments chatting with Fatima, accepted a visitor's badge from her, then made his way up to the Captain's office. Williams was standing in front of his desk with his back to the door. He turned when Loyal entered. This movement revealed the Under Sheriff, Jerome Bastille, standing just to the left edge of Captain William's desk. Loyal groaned inwardly. The Under Sheriff was the second highest position in the chain of command. There were only two reasons for Bastille to attend this meeting. Either Loyal was going to be congratulated for his work on the Barnett-Roberts' case, or he was about to be disciplined. Judging by the two men's grim expressions, Loyal did not think congratulations were in order.

· · ·

Bastille motioned for Loyal to sit, then took a seat behind the desk. Captain Williams sat across from Loyal. Bastille folded his hands together, placed his elbows on the desk and leaned forward. His gaze never left Loyal's face.

"You pushed too far this time Truesdale," he said. "I can't ignore your actions." He paused for a moment. "But, you have had an exemplary career and I can't ignore that fact either. So here are your choices. You retire today, with full benefits, or I fire you." Bastille leaned back in the chair. "Either way, your time with the Carlsbad Sheriff's Department is coming to an end."

Loyal took a beat before answering. He studied Bastille's dark brown eyes, looking for any sign that there was wiggle room for him. He saw none. Bastille could have simply fired him, the offer to retire immediately was a lifeline thrown out of respect for his years of service.

"I'll retire," Loyal said.

Bastille nodded. "I have the paperwork prepared and ready. Before you sign I have one question. Who is your insider in the department."

Loyal's eyes met Bastille's and held for a long moment.

"I have no insider," he said. The room was silent for a long moment. Bastille's eyes never left Loyal's. Finally the Under Sheriff looked away. He slid the paperwork across the desk to Loyal and said, "Then let's get this signed."

On the way out of the station Loyal stopped by Hammond's office. The detective was behind his desk, head bowed low over paperwork. Loyal cleared his throat, Hammond raised his head. Their eyes held for a moment.

"You'll be glad to know I've officially retired," said Loyal. Hammond remained silent.

"I have a retirement gift from me to you," said Loyal. He reached in his pocket and brought out a red USB drive which he dropped on Hammond's desk.

"You didn't count on my security cameras," said Loyal. "This is just a copy. I have the original, and my lawyer has a copy as well. Stay the hell away from me and my family or everything goes to the Captain."

Without another word, Loyal turned and walked away.

L oyal and Stella stood on the sand of Ponto Beach and stared out across the blue Pacific. The sun was sinking rapidly into the ocean waves, painting the sky with orange and pink brush strokes. Seagulls and Pelicans flew across the horizon, their black forms silhouettes against the brightly colored sky. A cool breeze ruffled Loyal and Stella's hair.

"So you are really retired?" Stella asked.

"Yep," said Loyal, "it is official."

"I know you don't like it Dad," Said Stella. "But, I think it is a good thing. You can use this time to do anything that you want to. Plus, your future grandchild can always use Grandpa time."

Loyal allowed a small smile to play across his face. "You are right about that," he said. "It is just hard, Stella. Being a detective was a huge part of my identity."

Stella reached out and clasped her father's hand. Her

grip was warm and firm. "There is so much more to you than your career Dad. You will find your new path." Loyal squeezed her hand.

"I hope so Stella," he said, "I really hope so."

I learned a long time ago that people are easy to fool. Few look beyond what is right in front of them. My mother, Lacey, the doctors, the teachers, they all accepted that I was never going to progress beyond a certain point. Fooling them was simple; sucking my thumb, tugging my ear, never demonstrating understanding about what was going on around me. Some might question why I chose that path. I ask them, why not?

Recovery after my accident was slow and painful. Mommy loved taking care of me, and I discovered I loved being taking care of. She devoted her life to me. And Lacey, perfect angelic Lacey, was forced to as well. Lacey was always more loved than I was. I never understood why my parents preferred her. It made no sense. We were essentially the same. Why was I always considered to be "less than"? After the accident I realized I could become more important than Lacey, more beloved, if I remained damaged. It worked with Mommy, but then she went away and I was back to living in Lacey's shadow.

With Bertrand, I was simply invisible. He never knew that I sat outside his home office door and listened to his conversations with Donald Blomgren. He assumed, like everyone else, that I was incapable of complex thought or action. That's why Donald had to die. He made a comment about me during one of the radio conversations. He thought he had seen me on the trail. Bertrand didn't believe him, but I couldn't take the chance, could I?

And then there was Gladys. Poor Gladys. I actually liked her. She thought she knew me better than anyone. In a way, perhaps she did. I suppose helping me made her feel useful. I was so used to people thinking I couldn't do anything that she surprised me by encouraging me to try new things. She believed in me. She taught me my passion; painting. But when she contacted the detective about her suspicions that I had driven her car, she had to go.

None of that matters now anyways. Everything has worked out fine for me. The police, lawyers, doctors, and judges all believe what they want to believe, that I am incapable of making judgements, that I am mentally incapacitated. I'm happy where I am, in this low security mental institution. I have meals and am free to pursue my passion. Gladys actually visits me. She brings me canvases, brushes, paints, and books on wildlife. She still wants to believe in the good in me. So did Lacey. What was it she whispered in my ear on her final morning? "Don't worry Liane, my loyalty lies with you." I guess she found out a bit too late that mine does too. My loyalty lies with me.

ACKNOWLEDGMENTS

Sincere thanks to all the readers of A.I. Smith. Your enthusiasm, love of the characters, and kind words encouraged me to continue writing.

Many thanks to Detective Terry Coker, LASD (ret.) who spent hours discussing guns and crime scenes with me. Any errors are mine alone.

Thank you to my cold readers: Sarah Binau, Terry Coker, Madison and Edith Cooper, Hayley Helms, and Mark Palmerton. Your input made all the difference.

Sincere thanks to Marta Palmerton for editing the proof, and gratitude to Kym McNabb for taking the basic idea and transforming it into another winning cover.

Deepest thanks to Brett, who walked in the door nearly

two years ago and said "You need a detective." His idea brought Loyal to life. Thank you Brett, I love you.

62242688R00257